The Half-Breed

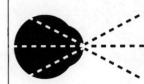

This Large Print Book carries the
Seal of Approval of N.A.V.H.

Secret Fires #2

The Half-Breed

Bobbi Smith

Thorndike Press • Waterville, Maine

Published in 2001 by arrangement with Leisure Books,
a division of Dorchester Publishing Co., Inc.

Thorndike Press Large Print Romance Series.

The tree indicium is a trademark of Thorndike Press.

The text of this Large Print edition is unabridged.
Other aspects of the book may vary from the original edition.

Set in 16 pt. Plantin by PerfecType.

Printed in the Unites States on permanent paper.

Library of Congress Cataloging-in-Publication Data

Smith, Bobbi.
    The half-breed / Bobbi Smith.
        p.   cm. — (Secret fires ; #2)
    ISBN 0-7862-3584-5 (lg. print : hc : alk. paper)
        1. Inheritance and succession — Fiction. 2. Racially
mixed people — Fiction. 3. Illegitimate children — Fiction.
4. Fathers and sons — Fiction. 5. Texas Rangers — Fiction.
6. Ranch life — Fiction. 7. Texas — Fiction. 8. Large type
books. I. Title.
PS3569.M5116 H3 2001
813′.54—dc21   2001045056

*This one is for Wendy, who was wise enough
to marry my David.
May you live happily ever after.
Love, Mom*

Acknowledgments

My thanks to Anderson News Reps Marti Anderson, Becky Maycumber and Charlotte Lawrenz for their help with my signings at the bases near Kansas City. You're terrific!

Thanks, too, to a perfect Wal-Mart Manager Steve Cawood and Anderson Merchandiser Rep. Chuck Maddox. You are true heroes!

Prologue

Circle M Ranch
Sidewinder, Texas
1874

Sixteen-year-old Chase McBride was tense as he stood in the study of the Circle M ranch house looking out the window. The ride to the ranch had been long and tiring, but it didn't matter. What mattered was that he was there and he was going to speak with Tom McBride. The message he brought was urgent. There was little time left. He heard footsteps coming into the room and turned just as a deep, accusing voice rang out.

"Who the hell are you, and what are you doing here?"

Tom McBride was angry as he strode into his study to find a tall, dark-haired young man standing across the room. He didn't know who this stranger was, and he was irritated at being called away from his work. Whatever it was this boy wanted, it couldn't be that important.

"My name's Chase — Chase McBride," Chase answered, facing for the first time in his life the man who was his father.

Tom went silent at his words. He had never seen this youth before, but recognition shot through him as their identical gazes met. The boy was of obvious Indian heritage, but there was no mistaking the blue eyes that stared proudly back at Tom. The McBride blue eyes were a distinguishing characteristic, and all of his offspring had them. Tom muttered a vile curse and slammed the study door shut behind him to guarantee privacy. He didn't want anyone in the family to hear what he was about to say.

"Why are you here? I made it plain to your mother when she told me she was pregnant that I wanted nothing to do with you," he snarled, furious that the boy had sought him out.

Chase stiffened and glared back at the older man. He could see the family resemblance in him and regretted it. Though he knew by birth he was a bastard, it seemed to him there was more than one bastard in the McBride family.

"I know," Chase answered tightly.

"I gave money to that priest from the mission so she'd leave me the hell alone. I couldn't have her coming after me all the time, demanding I pay for some child I couldn't even be sure was mine."

Chase's hands balled into fists at the insult to his mother. For all that she had made a mistake as a young girl becoming pregnant by a married man, he knew that she had loved Tom McBride deeply — and still did. That thought infuriated him even more. Tom McBride didn't deserve anyone's love or devotion.

"I didn't come here for any money," Chase said, barely controlling the fury that filled him. A deep, abiding hatred was growing within him for this man, and he found he couldn't wait to be away from the Circle M.

"Then why the hell are you here? Did you think this would be some kind of sweet family reunion?" Tom sneered.

"I'm here because my mother asked me to come to you. She's . . ." He stopped, finding it hard to say the next word.

"She's what?" Tom demanded, wanting to finish this interview and get the boy off the Circle M. "Pregnant again?" Tom smiled with vicious delight.

Chase took a threatening step toward him, even though Tom McBride was a big man —

a good four inches taller than Chase was and at least forty pounds heavier. Then he stopped. He had come for his mother's sake. Fighting with this man would not accomplish what he needed to do.

"She's dying," Chase told him. "There isn't much time left, and she begged me to come and find you. She still loves you, and she wants to see you one more time."

"I was done with your mother when I walked away from her all those years ago." Tom looked at him, his expression unfeeling and indifferent. "What we had was enjoyable while it lasted — what I can remember of it — but she never meant anything to me. It's her problem if she made more out of it than it was."

Tom recalled that Morning Sun had been a pretty enough maid seventeen years ago. He'd met her at a neighbor's ranch where she lived with her brother, who worked there taming horses. The Comanche were always good with horses, and her brother had been no exception. The thought of bedding an Indian girl had excited Tom then, especially since his wife, Emily, had been pregnant with his first son, Stone, and no longer responsive to him. He'd taken full advantage of the innocent Morning Sun's bed and had enjoyed it for a while until she'd told him she was pregnant. He'd walked away then without a second thought; he wasn't about to worry about some half-breed bastard he couldn't even be sure was his own.

"Please." Chase hated to beg. It wasn't in his nature. He'd learned long ago that you had to fight for what you wanted.

"Don't you understand English? I said no." Tom was curt and cold. "Now get out of here. I got work to do."

"But she's dying." Chase ignored McBride's insults as he tried to fulfill his mother's last desperate wish. "There isn't a lot of time left."

Tom shrugged and his piercing blue-eyed gaze met Chase's. "I don't care."

"But you're my father — "

"Don't ever call me that again. I've got a wife and a real family — two sons and a daughter. You're nothing to me. You might have cut your hair and put on white man's clothes today, but there ain't nothing going to hide the fact that you're a breed. Now get the hell out of here and don't come back to the Circle M — unless you're looking for trouble!"

Chase's rigid self-control snapped. This man had caused his mother endless suffering through the years, and he'd had all he could take of his arrogance. Without thought, he launched himself at the bigger man, wanting only to strike out at him and hurt him as he had hurt his mother.

His action caught Tom by surprise. Chase managed to land several fierce hits before the older, bigger man took control and sent him sprawling with one powerful blow to the jaw. Several of Tom's ranch hands came running at the sounds of the fight and found Tom bodily throwing Chase from the house.

"Get off my property and stay off!" Tom ordered as he shoved Chase out onto the dirt.

"You all right?" Jeb Riggs, the ranch foreman, asked as he came to see what all the trouble was about.

"I'm just fine," Tom answered tersely.

Jeb looked down at the stranger, who was barely more than a boy. The youth glanced up at him as he got to his feet, wiping blood from his mouth. Their gazes met. In that instant, Jeb knew the truth, but he said nothing.

Tom stood unmoving on the porch with Jeb, watching until Chase had mounted up and ridden away. Only when Chase had disappeared out of sight did Tom and Jeb head back toward the stables.

"Who was that, Pa?" asked Tanner, Tom's youngest son, as he ran up to join them.

He'd seen his father fighting with the stranger and wondered what had happened between them. "Why'd you get so mad at him?"

"He was nobody important, Tanner. Don't worry about it. I sent him packing. He won't be back."

Jeb shot him a quick look, but Tom didn't notice. Tom was just glad that his wife had been in town and missed it all. He didn't need any more aggravation.

Tanner didn't ask any more. He glanced off in the distance, hoping to get a last look at the stranger who'd so enraged his father, but the youth was out of sight. Tanner didn't know what had caused his father's fury, but he did know it had to be important. It wasn't often that his father got physically violent with anyone.

Chase did not look back as he rode away from the Circle M. He held himself stiffly in the saddle. His left eye was swelling shut and his lip was cut and bleeding, but he didn't care. There was only one thing on his mind, and that was getting back to his mother as quickly as he could. The news he was bringing would sadden her, but at least he would be by her side.

A fierce hatred for the man who had

fathered him burned inside Chase. He had grown up at the mission where his mother had worked as a cook to support him. During those years, he had longed to know his father and to have him there with them so they could be a family. The good priest had tried to help him, but it hadn't been the same as having his real father. Now, though, having met the man who'd sired him, Chase realized it had been better this way. Any childish fantasies he'd had about Tom McBride had been banished forever.

He had asked the man for help —

He had been refused.

He had begged him to visit his mother —

He had been refused.

Chase was glad now that Tom McBride hadn't been part of his life. If he never saw Tom McBride again, it would be fine with him.

It took Chase almost four days of hard riding to reach the mission. When he rode up to the small house he shared with his mother, the priest came to meet him.

Morning Sun had died three days before of a high fever.

Chapter One

Benton, Texas
1886

"You wanted to see me, Captain Hale?" Texas Ranger Chase McBride asked as he reported to his commander.

"Yes." Rod Hale looked up from where he'd been working at his desk. "I understand you brought in the Lawson gang. Good work. They've been terrorizing West Texas long enough."

"Thanks." Chase appreciated the captain's praise, but knew that wasn't the reason he'd been summoned.

"Here — this is for you. I've been keeping it for you." The captain held out an unopened letter to him. "It arrived some time ago."

Chase frowned as he took the missive. He couldn't imagine who'd written to him.

Then he glanced down at the sender's address, and his expression darkened. He crumpled the letter in his hand as he looked back up at his commander. "Is there anything else, Captain?"

"You know someone in Sidewinder?" Hale asked easily, surprised by Chase's reaction. Chase was one of the best Rangers under his command, but he knew very little about him, other than that his mother had been Comanche. Chase was a loner, a man who kept to himself, and he'd made it known that he liked it that way.

"No." His answer was terse as he denied the existence of the man who had denied him.

"All right, well, get the hell outta here," Hale ordered, relaxing back in his chair with a grin. "Go take it easy for a while. You've earned it. You'll be hearing from me."

Chase nodded and strode from the room. As he left the building, he was tempted to drop the letter in the dirt and walk away. There was a lawyer's name on it, but the fact that it came from the Texas town of Sidewinder told him all he needed to know: Tom McBride was trying to get in touch with him. But why?

Chase headed straight to the Golden Slipper Saloon. It wasn't crowded, and he was glad. He ordered a whiskey at the bar, then took the drink to a deserted table in the back. He needed time alone to think. Tossing the envelope on the table, he stared down at it in disgust. Memories threatened, but he denied them.

"So," cooed the red-haired, voluptuous bar girl known as Missy as she came to stand before him. "You're finally back in town, Ranger."

Though she was just eighteen, Missy knew her own mind, and she'd had her heart set on bedding Chase McBride from the first time she'd seen him. He was a tall, lean man who was darkly handsome in a powerful, dangerous way. He wore his black hair longer than most men and had piercing blue eyes that at times seemed almost silver in their intensity. Some of the girls wondered why she was so attracted to a breed, but that just made Chase more appealing to her. Danger excited Missy, and she could tell that this man was dangerous.

"Got in this morning," he answered, giving her only a cursory glance as he took a drink of his liquor. The last thing he wanted was female companionship right now. He had only one thing on his mind.

"And you came here just to see me." She flashed him a wickedly inviting smile as she allowed herself to believe for a moment that he really had come for her. A tingle of excitement pulsed through her. "Can I get you anything? Anything at all?" She said the last in a husky voice, her meaning explicit as she leaned toward him a little, giving him a better view of her burgeoning breasts above the low-cut bodice of her gown.

"No." Chase's dismissal was curt, his gaze never leaving the letter that lay before him on the table.

Missy tried not to let her disappointment show. She prided herself on making sure her customers had a good time, and hoped that one day Chase would let her prove that to him. "You just let me know if you change your mind."

When she'd gone, Chase set his glass aside, then picked up the missive and opened it. He supposed it was curiosity that drove him, for he truly didn't care what Tom McBride might want. In fact, Chase was surprised the man had known where to find him, since they'd had no contact in years.

Dear Mr. McBride:
In accordance with instructions contained in the last will and testament of Thomas J. McBride, dictated to me and dutifully signed and witnessed on this

date, the fifth of March, this year of our Lord, 1886, I am forwarding this letter to all potential heirs to his estate so they may be informed of the conditions for inheritance prescribed in the above legal document.

It is the intention of your father, Thomas J. McBride, to bequeath equal shares of the Circle M Ranch and all his remaining assets to each of his progeny, and to his wife, Clare Brown McBride. Mr. McBride has stipulated, however, that in order to be eligible for this bequest, his progeny must present themselves at the Circle M Ranch no later than nine months from the date of this letter, to remain there pending the arrival of the other heirs, at which time the details of the inheritance will be specified. Those of his progeny who do not appear within that period will forfeit their shares of the estate. The forfeited shares will then be added to the award of Clare Brown McBride.

Thomas McBride has made it clear that no exceptions will be made to the conditions he has outlined.

The official business of this letter concluded, I feel it is my duty as solicitor to the estate and longstanding friend of the McBride family, to include the information that Thomas McBride is gravely ill, that his condition has been pronounced terminal, and that he is not expected to live out the year.

Hoping to see this matter drawn to a conclusion that is satisfactory to all, I remain,

Yours most sincerely,
William Benton Hanes, Esq.

So the bastard was dying and he wanted his family gathered around. A sneer curved Chase's mouth as he reread the letter just to be sure. The look of hatred on his face changed into an almost wry smile as he lifted his glass and drained it in one swallow. Thomas McBride might want his "progeny" gathered round his deathbed, but Chase knew it would be a cold day in hell before he showed up. There was definitely going to be one son missing from this tender family gathering. McBride had told him long ago on his one and only visit to the Circle M never to come back, and Chase had no intention of going now. He had no interest in any of the man's possessions and wanted nothing to do with him. If Tom McBride really was dying, well then, good riddance.

Chase folded the letter and put it back in

the envelope, then stuffed it in his pocket. He would have another drink, then get himself a room at the hotel and call it a night. He could never be sure how long it would be until Captain Hale had another assignment for him, so he wanted to get all the rest he could. It was going to feel good to sleep in a real bed for a change. He got up and headed to the bar to get a refill.

"Good news?" Missy asked as Chase reached the bar. "You're smiling."

"Yeah, real good news," he said. Chase knew it was cold to feel this way, but he had to admit this was the best news he'd had in a long time. He couldn't think of anyone more deserving of facing his maker than Tom McBride.

"Feel like celebrating?" she offered again, moving closer, hoping against hope that her determination would pay off. She did so want to get her hands on this Ranger.

Chase eyed Missy. She was pretty enough and certainly desirable. Heat stirred within him. He did feel like celebrating, but not the way she had in mind. He denied his baser urges, having vowed to himself long ago never to chance fathering a child without the benefit of marriage. He had seen how being used and abandoned had tortured his mother, and he had known the rejection and

21

pain of being branded a bastard. No child of his would ever suffer that way.

"I sure do. Let me buy you a drink." He paid for her liquor and got himself a refill.

Missy saw the heat in his gaze, and a shiver of excitement ran through her. She took up her glass and casually leaned into him as he turned to face her.

"I've got a room upstairs all ready and waiting for a big celebration." Her voice was low and her smile slow and knowing as she trailed one hand down his chest. She let it linger at his belt buckle.

Chase covered her hand with his and drew it away from him. "I haven't got time for that kind of celebrating, darling, but you enjoy your drink." He lifted his whiskey.

Missy had been almost certain that he was hers for the taking. "I could make this a day *and* night to remember for you."

"It already is," he answered, draining his glass and setting it down on the counter. He ignored the meaning of her words and left her standing there.

Missy looked on in frustration as he strode from the saloon — so tall and lean and downright sexy. She silently cursed his iron-willed self-control. Most men of her acquaintance would have practically dragged her upstairs to get what she had so

22

blatantly been offering, but not this Ranger. She wondered if she would ever be able to get him alone.

It was a cold day in hell.

Chase had never dreamed this day would come, but with the news his captain had just given him, it had.

"I'll go to Sidewinder, Captain," Chase volunteered as he sat across from Rod Hale in the Ranger office two days later. Anger and determination were burning fiercely within him. He'd just learned that Terry Malone, the leader of the outlaw gang that had murdered Ranger Frank Anderson a short while before, had been killed in a shoot-out near Sidewinder and that Blackie Sherwood, the last surviving member of the deadly gang, was suspected to be hiding out in the area. Frank had been a friend of Chase's, and he wanted to see the killers brought to justice.

"You're familiar with Sidewinder?" Rod asked astutely, remembering the letter.

"I was there once," Chase answered. "And I've got the perfect cover."

"What cover?"

"That letter I got the other day was from my father's lawyer. The old man's dying and wants his 'family' back with him."

"I didn't know you had family." He heard the sneer in Chase's voice and wondered at it.

"I don't. I hadn't planned on going back. That relationship was severed long ago," Chase said coldly. "But if I can track down the last of Frank's killers by showing up in Sidewinder, I'll do it. Frank was a good man."

Rod nodded and smiled grimly. Chase was his best tracker. If anybody could hunt down Blackie Sherwood, it would be Chase. He pulled out the Wanted poster on Sherwood and handed it to him.

Chase studied the picture. Sherwood was dark-haired and, according to the description on the poster, a big man. A jagged scar ran down his left cheek.

"Let me fill you in on everything I know about him," Rod began. "The most distinguishing feature is that scar." He gave Chase the rest of the information he had on the outlaw.

Chase listened intently. "I'll be ready to ride in less than an hour."

Chapter Two

"She is a pretty one," Black Hawk said in his native tongue as he stared down at the golden-haired captive lying on the ground before him. She was wide-eyed with terror, and he liked her fear. It made him feel powerful. His raiding party had attacked a white man's ranch two days before and taken this woman captive. She was to be a present to his chief when they returned to the village.

"Running Dog will like her. He will be pleased with your gift," Howling Coyote agreed as he took a long drink from the whiskey bottle they were sharing. "Too bad you are giving her to him. She would give us great pleasure tonight."

"We will take our pleasure from this fire water," the warrior replied, grabbing the bottle from his friend and drinking deeply. "But there is no reason we cannot look at this prize I will give him."

In one quick movement, Black Hawk grasped the woman by her bound wrists and hauled her up to stand before them. Though she was visibly trembling, she met his gaze straight on, her chin tilted defiantly. He smiled, aroused by her show of bravery.

"She is a bold one," he said. "Perhaps, too bold."

He reached out and grabbed the neck of her blouse. She tried to free herself from his hold, but brute force won out. He tore the material downward in one quick, savage motion, revealing the swell of her breasts shielded from them now only by her thin chemise. The men leered at her, their lust evident in their expressions.

The woman gasped, startled by his assault. She wanted to cower, to hide herself from them, but instead she stood her ground. She refused to give them that victory over her.

Both renegades drunkenly ogled her bared flesh; behind them the rest of the raiding party watched. When Black Hawk reached out again to openly paw the woman, Howling Coyote grabbed his arm.

"You said yourself that she is meant for Running Dog. You said we would only look," he cautioned. The heat was burning within him, too, but he knew how fierce Chief

Running Dog could be. He did not want to anger him.

Black Hawk glared at his friend as he tilted the bottle to his mouth again. He knew Howling Coyote was right, and it frustrated him. He wanted a woman right now. "Then let us see more of this prize."

He grasped the chemise strap and tore it from her shoulder. His rough treatment left scratches upon her tender flesh, but he managed to completely expose one full, rounded breast for all of the raiding party to see.

"She is a fine one!" the others shouted from where they were drinking by the campfire.

Black Hawk and Howling Coyote stared at the golden woman and each took another deep swallow from the bottle. The urge to take her then and there and forget Running Dog altogether was strong within them, but they knew there would be a price to pay. In disgust, Black Hawk roughly shoved the captive back to the ground and turned away from the sight of her sprawled before him. The two renegades stumbled back to the campfire. All in the raiding party continued to drink until the power of the liquor rendered them senseless.

Faith Bryant remained where she had fallen. She was too frightened to move, too frightened to do anything but pray. Prayer seemed her only hope. She had been living in endless terror since she had been kidnapped when the renegade band attacked her family's ranch. She had tried to fight off the warrior who'd grabbed her as she'd made a run for the house from the stable where she'd been hiding when the raid had begun, but his strength had been overpowering. He had subdued her with bruising force and ridden off holding her in a brutal grip. The raiding party had raced from the ranch at top speed and for two days had ridden almost nonstop before finally making this camp.

From the stories that she'd heard of what happened to Indian captives, Faith had no delusions about what was to become of her. She had been bound and manhandled, and she realized with painful clarity that she was helpless. Short of being miraculously rescued or somehow escaping on her own, there was little hope she would ever see her loved ones again.

A tormented sob threatened, but Faith bit it back. She didn't want to do anything that would draw the drunken warriors' attention back to her. Silently, she offered up a plea for strength to see her through the ordeal. She loved her family. She had to get back home to her parents and to her fiancé, John. Surely John had learned of her capture by now and was on her trail. They were to be married in just three months, and she was certain that he would do everything in his power to save her. She clung to that belief, refusing to give up hope. It was all she had.

Faith slowly became aware that the camp had grown quiet. Covering her exposed flesh as best she could with the tatters of her torn chemise and blouse, she shifted her position slightly to see what had happened. She was startled to find that all but one of the raiding party were slumped around the fire, seemingly oblivious to the world.

All her life, Faith had heard her mother preach the evils of demon liquor, but right now she was glad that her father had had the bottles of whiskey in the house. The one renegade who remained conscious was drinking so heavily that she believed he would soon join the others in their drunken stupor, and when he did . . .

Faith began to work at the rope that bound her wrists. She had been afraid to try to free herself, knowing that her captors were watching her closely, but now she knew she could try. If her prayers were answered and the last renegade passed out, she would find a way to make her escape. She knew the chances of reaching safety were slim, but she couldn't just remain there, a helpless victim. She had never been one to give up without a fight. She had to try to save herself. There was no one else to do it right now. It was up to her.

Each minute seemed an eternity as Faith anticipated the warrior's move. Nearly an hour passed before he finally closed his eyes and surrendered to the whiskey's power. It had taken Faith that long to loosen the rope enough to slip one hand out, but at last she was able to free herself.

Terror and caution drove her as she inched backward into the shadows of the night. She could make no quick moves, fearing she might disturb the raiding party or the horses. Her breathing was strangled, her hands shaking as she crawled away. She was glad that she'd been wearing her split riding skirt when she'd been taken captive. Trying to make this escape in skirts and petticoats would have been impossible. She did not begin her headlong flight until she had gotten a good distance from the camp. Only then did she get up and break into a run.

Faith expected at any minute to hear the bloodcurdling screams of the renegades as they came after her, but all she heard was the eerie silence of the night. Onward she ran over the rocky, uneven terrain. She stumbled and fell, scraping her knees and hands, but that little pain didn't matter. She knew what fate awaited her at the hands of her captors, and she preferred death trying to flee than being forced to submit to their savage domination. Nothing mattered but escape. She had to get home to her family. She had to get home to John.

As the hours passed, Faith willed her weary limbs to keep moving. She wasn't sure where she was going, but she didn't care as long as it was away from the raiding party. She had to put as many miles as she could between herself and her captors before daylight.

A shudder of pure horror wracked Faith as memories of the last few days haunted her. Again and again, in her mind's eye she saw the fierceness of the surprise attack. She saw the ranch buildings in flames and heard the raiding party's soul-chilling screams as they wreaked their bloody havoc on the homestead. Visions of the endless miles riding double with the warrior tormented her; her flesh was still tender, bruised as it was by the steely grip he'd used to hold her prisoner against him. Tears traced down her cheeks, but she didn't bother to wipe them away.

Gasping for breath, Faith staggered on as

the hours and miles passed. She needed to rest, but there would be no rest until she found help — until she was safe. As she thought about it, Faith realized that she would never feel safe again. Her days of innocence and trust were gone — destroyed forever. Now there was only desperation and unholy terror; they drove her, forcing her to move.

The only thing that kept her from complete despair was the belief that if her escape wasn't discovered until dawn, she might have a chance to elude them, to find a place to hide before they began tracking her. Another shudder wracked her as she imagined what they would do to her if they did catch her, how they would torture her. The thought quickened her already desperate pace and evoked a strangled cry from her. She would find a haven. She had to. She wouldn't give up her hope for freedom.

It seemed she'd been running for hours when Faith finally saw what looked like the faint glow of a campfire in the distance. For an instant, her spirits soared. She had found help! Ahead, there was someone who would protect her and take her to safety. Ahead, there was salvation.

Then reality returned.

Caution overtook Faith. She slowed her

pace, moving stealthily onward, fearful of just who might be in the camp. Many of the men who rode the range were just as dangerous as the renegades in their own way.

Faith edged as close as she could to get a look at the campsite. She hoped it was a company of cavalrymen or some ranch hands. They would help her. They would defend her. She was certain of it.

Her hopes were dashed as she positioned herself to survey the scene below.

Sitting before a small, low-burning campfire was a bare-chested, fierce-looking warrior. Faith did not recognize him as one of the raiding party, but there was no mistaking the aura of danger about him. As she was watching, he looked up in her direction. His gaze was narrowed, his expression sharp and suspicious. She remained completely still, barely allowing herself to breathe, not daring to do anything that might draw his attention. Unarmed as she was, she stood no chance against him in a direct confrontation. The moment seemed to last an eternity, but finally the warrior looked away.

Faith drew a ragged breath as her soul screamed in silent frustration.

Was there to be no salvation for her?

Was this to be her fate — to die, lost and alone, at the hands of a renegade?

In that instant, Faith's fear turned to fury. She was not going to give up — not without a fight. She had made it this far. She was going to survive, one way or another. Soundlessly, she slipped back out of view of the campsite to make her plan. There had to be a way to save herself.

Chase knew someone was nearby. He hadn't survived this long by ignoring his instincts when they screamed a warning, and they were screaming one right now. He lowered his gaze and pretended to relax. He rested his hand on his sidearm, his every muscle tense, anticipating an attack at any moment.

But none came.

Chase grew puzzled. If someone was out to kill him, he certainly would have taken a shot by now. He continued to act naturally as he tossed what was left of his coffee into the fire, then set his mug aside and stretched out on his bedroll. He drew his hat down low, shielding his eyes, and pretended to fall asleep, but all the while his gun was in hand and his nerves were stretched taut. He waited.

Faith was certain that the warrior by the campfire hadn't seen her, so she knew she could disappear back into the darkness on foot and continue on as she had; or she could wait until she was sure he was asleep, then sneak into the encampment, steal his horse and make a desperate ride to safety. She was an expert horsewoman and believed herself capable of handling the renegade's mount, but both plans were fraught with danger. Still, Faith knew she had little choice. Only on horseback did she have a chance to really escape the danger that threatened her. As soon as the sun rose in the morning, the raiding party would come searching for her, and she had to be as far away as she could get.

Her decision made, Faith crept up to study the campsite again. For a moment, she was frightened, for the warrior wasn't sitting before the fire anymore. She feared that he had somehow seen her and was coming after her, but as quickly as the terror gripped her, she spotted him bedded down nearby.

Relief flooded through Faith, and for the first time, she felt a small flicker of hope. She could do this. All she had to do was wait a little longer to make sure that he really was asleep and then make her move. The only difficulty she could imagine was that the Indian's horse might prove a bit wild, but she had to chance it. She'd always prided herself on her ability to handle horses, and she prayed that this mount wouldn't prove to be the exception.

Each minute seemed an hour as Faith concentrated on what was to come. Any recklessness on her part could prove fatal, so she had to be careful. When at last she thought enough time had elapsed, she began to crawl slowly and silently toward the encampment and the magnificent stallion that would take her to a safe haven — to her family — and to John.

John. Faith's heart ached at the thought of her handsome fiancé. She longed to be in his arms. Only when he was holding her again would she believe that this nightmare was over. Only when she had been reunited with her loved ones would she be convinced that everything was all right.

Faith crawled onward toward the horse, staying low, making certain that her every move was silent. When she reached the place where the stallion was tied, she got to her feet. The mount shifted nervously as she began to untie him, and she knew there was no time to waste. She had to make her escape and fast! She had just started to swing up on the horse's back when powerful arms grabbed her.

Chapter Three

In the darkness of the night, Chase didn't know who the intruder was and he didn't care. He'd been ready for trouble, and trouble was exactly what he got as he snared the would-be horse thief around the waist. The thief put up a fierce struggle. Only when Chase heard the scream did he realize his thief was no man. He was dealing with a woman! His surprise was so great that he almost released her.

"Hold still!" he commanded.

Faith was fighting with all her strength against the warrior's hold, kicking at him and twisting wildly against him. She was frantic to free herself from his iron restraint, desperate to take the horse and flee. She was so caught up in her struggle that it took a moment for her to realize he'd spoken to her in English. Only when she was slammed back against the solid, hard-muscled width of his chest and held pinned there with her arms at her sides, did she become aware that this was no ordinary renegade.

"Damn it, woman! I said hold still!" Chase ground out, furious at her resistance and wondering how this golden-haired wildcat of a woman had ended up in his camp trying to steal his horse in the middle of the night.

He looked down at her as he held her tight against him. Only now as she finally stilled in his arms did he notice that her blouse and chemise were torn and her pale flesh was bared to his gaze. She was filthy, and there were scratches and bruises evident upon her flesh. They were a silent testimony to abuse she'd suffered, but not at his hands. He wondered who she was and what had happened to bring her to him.

"What are you doing here?" he demanded harshly, still not releasing her even though she had quieted. He wasn't sure he could trust her if he freed her. He was surprised, though, by how small she seemed — and how delicate. But she'd proven that her looks were deceptive.

"Let me go," Faith said tightly. She held herself rigidly against him, waiting fearfully for what might come next. It was obvious now that he was no warrior — he wore pants and boots and spoke English — but she had seen his face. This man had Indian blood running in his veins, and that alone was enough to terrify her.

As abruptly as he'd snared her, Chase released the woman and stepped away. He stared down at her as she turned to face him, clutching her torn blouse to her breast, awkwardly trying to cover herself.

"My name's Faith — Faith Bryant," she said, keeping her expression guarded, hiding her fear from him. He was tall and dark and fierce-looking, and when her gaze met his and she saw for the first time the silver-blue of his eyes, a shiver slid down her spine. He might try to appear white, but to her, he was an Indian all the same. "I was kidnapped from my family's ranch near Dry Gulch by a raiding party two days ago. I got lucky and managed to escape tonight when the renegades got drunk on my father's whiskey."

A muscle worked in Chase's jaw. He could well imagine what she'd suffered at their hands. He understood her bruises and desperation now. He recognized, too, that she was a remarkably brave woman. He lifted his gaze to stare out into the darkness. "How far away are they?"

"I don't know . . ." She stopped, looking away as she swallowed tightly. Then she looked up at him again. "I've been running for hours just trying to get as far away from them as I could before sunrise."

He nodded, his gaze sweeping over her once more, taking in her ruined blouse. He didn't say anything, but turned to go to his saddlebags. When he came back to her, he was carrying a shirt.

"Here. Put this on."

In the flickering light of the campfire, Faith stared down at his darkly tanned hand as he held the garment out to her. A shudder of revulsion wracked her. She realized her reaction to him was illogical — he was trying to help her — but she recoiled, a part of her still terrified and believing that he was just like the renegades.

The horror of the last few days returned full force, and Faith balked. In mindless terror, she started to run blindly into the darkness. She wanted to disappear into the night, to lose herself in the wilds of West Texas. But he was there before she could escape, his hand clamping down firmly on her upper arm, stopping her when she would have fled into the night.

"I'm not going to hurt you. My name's Chase McBride. I'm a Texas Ranger." Her reaction to him didn't surprise Chase in the least. He'd been shunned for most of his life because of his Indian blood. Right now, though, it angered him, for he was only trying to help her.

"You're a Ranger?" she repeated in disbelief.

"Yes. Now cover yourself," he said flatly, offering her the shirt again. "You're safe with me. I give you my word, no harm will come to you while you're under my protection."

She was trembling so violently that he had to help her, holding the shirt so she could slip her arms into it.

"Rest for a while." He directed her to sit by the fire.

Realizing his own state of undress, Chase picked up his shirt and put it on. He wanted her to be as comfortable as possible in his presence. When he'd made camp, it had been a hot night with no breeze to speak of, so he'd shed the shirt seeking what relief he could. Considering how upset Faith was, he knew it would be best if he kept as much distance between them as possible. He knew, too, that the danger she'd just escaped was not over yet.

Faith glanced up at Chase as she huddled before the campfire. She saw the badge on his shirt shining in the fire's glow and willed herself to put aside her panic. He truly was a Ranger.

"How long until sunup?" Faith asked as she huddled before him, trying to regain her courage and determination.

"We've got an hour or so yet, but we have to be ready."

"Ready for what?"

"They're going to be coming after you, and we'll be waiting for them."

"No!" The thought of running into the raiding party again unnerved her. "Can't we just ride for town? Can't we just get away from here now?" Her panic was real.

"How many were there in the raiding party?" he asked, ignoring her questions.

"Six."

Chase nodded thoughtfully. "Can you fire a gun?"

"Yes," she answered.

"Good. They'll be tracking you, looking for you. They don't know about me. We'll have the upper hand."

"I just want to get back home!"

"If we try to make a run for Dry Gulch, we'll be riding double, and they might be able to catch up with us. Don't you want revenge? This is our best chance."

"But you're only one man," she protested.

At her statement, Chase turned a proud, cold-eyed look on her. "I'm a Ranger, and it's only one raiding party."

Faith studied him closely and knew he would be more than a worthy adversary.

"It's my job to keep things safe," Chase went on, "and that's what I'm going to do. Are you up to it, or do you want to wait here for me?"

"I'm going with you," she declared.

"All right. We'll ride out at first light, so get all the rest you can. Are you hungry? Do you want anything to eat?"

"No."

Faith sat in silence and watched Chase pack up his few belongings and saddle his horse.

"Here." Chase came to stand before her, his sidearm in hand. "You said you knew how to shoot. How good are you?"

"Good enough. My father taught me." She took the weapon from him and tested its weight in her hand.

He watched her handling the gun and was satisfied that she knew what she was doing. "We'll ride out in about half an hour — as soon as I can follow the trail you made."

Faith nodded. Actually having a gun in hand suddenly made her feel as if she was no longer a victim, but in control. A grim smile curved her lips as she stared down at the sidearm. "I'm ready."

Chase saw the change in her expression

and understood. He sat down a short distance away to await the dawn. It was going to be a long day and a dangerous one, but there was no alternative. He preferred to be the hunter — not the hunted.

The sun was the enemy this morning, Black Hawk decided as he shielded his eyes against its glare. He was trying to follow the golden woman's tracks on the hard ground, but the pounding in his head and the brightness of the sun made it hard for him. Behind him, the others grumbled their discontent as they followed along. Several of them had wanted to ride on and let her go, certain she could not survive on foot alone in the wilds.

"Do you think she lived through the night, Black Hawk?" Howling Coyote asked, his mood as foul as his friend's. He had enjoyed the firewater the night before, but now wondered at the wisdom of drinking so much of it.

"She was not a stupid woman. We will find her," he vowed. He was angry — angry that every step his horse took sent pain shafting through his head, and angry that the golden one had managed to escape him. She was only a female. He was a feared warrior. Still, he had to respect her courage. However, her efforts would be for nothing. No captive had ever escaped Black Hawk and lived to tell about it.

They continued on, tracking the fleeing woman, watching the land for signs of her passing as the sun rose higher in the sky.

"They're coming!" Chase told Faith in a whisper as he quickly made his way back to her. He had left her hiding behind a rocky outcropping on a hillside while he had ridden out to scout the area ahead. He'd caught sight of the renegades heading toward them and knew their position was the best they could find for the showdown to come.

"How close are they?" Faith asked, keeping a tight grip on the revolver he'd given her.

"Less than half a mile out," he reported, "and they're tracking you."

He'd been right, Faith realized. If she had convinced him to ride straight for Dry Gulch, the raiding party would have hunted them down before they could reach town.

She cast a sidelong glance at the Ranger as he hunkered down beside her, rifle in hand, ready for the fight to come. For all that he had proven himself so far to be a civilized man, right now he appeared the savage. His profile was strong — harsh and unyielding

— as he focused on the trail below. The length of his black hair added to his untamed look. His concentration was complete. Nothing was going to distract him from his duty.

Drawing a deep breath, Faith steadied herself for the confrontation to come. She had had no chance to defend the ranch against the renegades' attack. She'd been in the stable tending to her horse when they'd ridden in. She had been taken captive as she'd tried to reach the house to get a gun. She didn't know what had happened to her family and only prayed that they had survived.

Black Hawk and Howling Coyote led the way as they continued to track their missing captive. They believed she had to be close by somewhere, and they were determined to find her as quickly as they could.

Chase waited, rifle in hand, ready for what was to come. When the first two warriors of the raiding party came into view, he took careful aim, but did not shoot. He wanted to make sure they were all within range before he fired.

Chase heard Faith gasp and thought it was fear at seeing the renegades again. Only when she whispered his name did he glance over to see a rattlesnake making its way steadily across the rocky terrain straight toward her. He tossed a fistful of dirt at the menacing snake, hoping it would veer away, but the snake was not diverted. It was almost within striking distance, and Chase knew what he had to do. He took aim.

Black Hawk was shocked by the gunfire and signaled his warriors to attack. He didn't know who was shooting at them, and he didn't care. They charged ahead, screaming and firing wildly.

Chase shot the snake and then turned to take aim at the raiding party as the warriors rode at full speed toward them, their weapons blazing.

"Now!" he shouted to Faith.

Faith needed no encouragement. Just the sight of the renegades enraged her. They were just as they had been at her ranch, a deadly menace bent on slaughter, and the chilling memory filled her with grim determination. She joined Chase in firing.

Their murderous volley rang out as the renegades closed on them. Three of the renegades fell in the first onslaught. Chase and Faith gave them no reprieve. Pausing only long enough to reload, they continued their barrage and were satisfied when another of the warriors tumbled from his horse and lay unmoving in the dirt.

"You all right?" Chase called to Faith as he jumped up and prepared to go after the renegades.

"Yes," she responded, taking aim and firing off another round at one of the two surviving warriors who were wheeling their horses around to take flight.

He nodded and ran to where he'd tied his own horse, ready to race after the fleeing Indians.

Faith watched Chase gallop off, uncertainty gnawing at her. She reloaded her gun again and waited. The sounds of more gunfire in the distance came to her and increased her vigilance. Still she waited. Time passed. It seemed an eternity before she finally heard someone riding her way. It sounded like more than one horse, and Faith's every nerve was stretched taut. She had Chase's gun and enough ammunition to protect herself for a while, but if both renegades had survived and come back after her, she didn't know how long she would be able to hold out against them. Faith crouched low and said a silent prayer that Chase had prevailed.

The sound of the horses grew louder. She swallowed tightly, her finger on the trigger.

Waiting — Ready —

Chapter Four

Chase's solitary figure came into view, and Faith gasped at the sight of him. He was riding slightly slumped, his left arm bloody. Behind him, he led one of the Indians' ponies.

Faith hurried down to meet him.

"It's over," he said as he reined in before her.

"What happened to your arm?" she asked worriedly.

"It's nothing, just a flesh wound." He dismissed her concern as he dismounted and tied up the horses. "Are you all right?"

"I'm fine, thanks to you. But let me have a look at your arm."

"I can take care of it."

"It'll be easier if I do," she countered. "Take off your shirt and sit down for a minute."

Chase hesitated. He wasn't used to anyone offering him help. Then he realized she was right. Ignoring the pain that stabbed at him, he unbuttoned his shirt and shrugged out of it, while Faith went to get his canteen.

Faith turned back to find Chase standing before her, his shirt off. Once again he looked the warrior, his broad shoulders and powerful chest bared to her view. She paused as she realized she would have to touch him. It had been difficult enough riding double with him, but now to put her hands upon him while he was half naked . . .

The sight of the blood on his arm jarred Faith back to the reality of her situation and forced her to action.

Chase had been wounded because of her. He could have been killed.

Faith had to help him. She could do no less. He had risked his life for her.

"I need your knife," she said, coming to his side.

"What for?" he asked with a frown.

"To make a bandage."

"What are you planning on using?"

"The bottom of this shirt, if you don't mind." She gestured toward the shirt he'd given her.

Chase handed her the knife he wore on his belt and then sat down to watch. Faith realized she'd have to take the shirt off to cut the strips, and she modestly turned her back to him to do it. Chase looked away as she shed the garment and began to cut the strips of material, but not before he'd caught another glimpse of her bruises. The injuries inflicted upon her still angered him, and he felt grimly satisfied with the outcome of his showdown with the raiding party. He thought about how deftly she was wielding the knife as she cut the strips of cloth from the garment, and he couldn't suppress a half smile.

"You're smiling?" Faith asked, turning back to him when she'd finished the task and donned the shirt once more.

"I wondered how good you'd be with a knife, but I shouldn't have worried — especially after seeing how well you handled that gun."

"My father made sure that I knew how to defend myself."

"He did a good job."

Faith shrugged slightly. "I just wish I'd been armed when the raiding party attacked our ranch."

He understood her feelings of frustration and helplessness. "If you had been, you would have been killed instead of taken captive. You can't change what happened, but hopefully we'll find out that your family is all right."

"You'll take me to Dry Gulch?"

"Yes. It's three days' ride from here, isn't it?" He wanted to get to Sidewinder as soon as he could but he felt responsible for seeing her home safely.

"Yes, but my family's ranch is even closer." Faith brightened at the thought of being united with her loved ones. "We can head there, but I'm sure we'll find my father and John coming after me on our ride in."

"Is John the lawman from Dry Gulch?"

"No. John's my fiancé. He's the banker in town," Faith said happily as she directed her attention to his wound.

Chase was surprised to learn she was engaged, for she wore no ring, then realized the raiding party must have taken it. He wondered how her fiancé was going to react when he found out what had happened to her. He hoped this John truly loved her.

Chase looked at Faith as she tended his arm, her touch gentle. He studied her silently and was disturbed by the feelings that stirred within him. She was beautiful with her golden hair and pale loveliness, and he grew angry with himself for even thinking of her in that way. He looked away. She'd suffered greatly at the hands of the renegades, and she deserved better from him. He would respect her and keep her safe until he could return her to her family.

Faith was unaware of Chase's thoughts as she bent to her task. She concentrated on washing his injury and tried not to notice how hard-muscled his arm was or how warm his flesh felt to her touch. She cast a quick glance at him and found his expression stoic as he stared straight ahead. He didn't even flinch as she finished cleansing the wound, and she was amazed at his self-control. Once she was sure the bleeding had stopped, she wrapped a strip of cloth around it.

"How does that feel?" Faith asked.

"It's fine." Chase flexed his arm as he got up and deliberately moved away from her. The wound hurt, but he was glad to find that his motion wasn't restricted. He put his shirt back on. "Thanks."

"No — thank you." Faith looked up at him, her gaze meeting his, her expression heartfelt. "I know what would have happened to me today if I hadn't been with you. I owe you — "

"You don't owe me anything. It's my job." He kept his tone cold. He didn't want her gratitude, and he didn't want to think about what might have happened to her if she hadn't stumbled onto his campsite last night. He told himself that he would see her home and then be on his way as quickly as possible.

Chase's coldness had its desired effect on Faith. She stiffened almost imperceptibly.

"Get ready to ride." Chase turned away from her and went to see to the horses. "You can take my horse. I'll ride the other one."

"Good."

Faith sounded relieved that they wouldn't be riding double again, and Chase frowned as he gathered up his gear. He caught sight of the dead snake that had ruined their chance of surprising the raiding party and realized in disgust that it had been a sidewinder. His scowl darkened even more, and he wondered if the snake was an omen of things to come.

Thoughts of the upcoming "family reunion" in Sidewinder returned, troubling him. He figured Tom McBride and his "real" family were every bit as vicious as that snake had been. Then he reminded himself that he had wanted this assignment so he could bring the man who had killed Frank to justice. He owed Frank that much. Frank had been his friend.

"Do you need any help?" he asked.

"No." Faith adjusted the stirrups and mounted the horse.

Chase swung up onto the Indian pony's back in one smooth motion and took up the reins. Faith watched him, and a shiver of awareness went though her. He looked the warrior again, mounting with such a fluid movement. She quickly turned away from him, thinking only of her family and of John eagerly awaiting her return. She concentrated on the reunion to come, anxiously hoping that they would meet on the trail. The less time she spent alone with Chase McBride, the better.

Chase led the way back toward Dry Gulch and Faith's family's ranch. The miles and the hours passed. Chase kept a careful watch just in case there might be more trouble, but the rest of the day was uneventful.

Faith was glad. She wanted only to hurry home. She couldn't wait to see John. Thoughts of her handsome betrothed kept her spirits up as they traversed the countryside. John was tall with blond hair and blue eyes. He'd come to Dry Gulch about four years earlier from back East and had begun courting her last year. Their wedding date was set, and she could hardly wait.

As her thoughts lingered on John, her gaze fell upon Chase. He was riding a short distance ahead of her, moving as one with the

Indian pony. She wondered how his arm was doing. He wasn't favoring it at all, and she admired his ability to withstand pain. It must hurt. He was definitely a strong man, and a brave one, too.

Faith tried to imagine what John would have done if he'd been the one she'd found last night. She couldn't imagine John going after the renegades and setting a trap for them as Chase had. He would have ridden for town without a second thought, preferring the safety of civilization to taking on the raiding party alone. She dragged her thoughts back to reality as Chase reined in.

"It's almost sundown. We'll stop here for the night," he told her.

Faith realized for the first time just how hungry she was as they made camp. It was dark by the time Chase had tended to the horses and brought what bedding he had to spread out by their small campfire.

"I've got some dried meat in my saddlebag," he offered.

Faith went to get the provisions and brought the wrapped meat back to him.

"Take what you want and I'll eat what's left," Chase told her as he arranged his one blanket on the ground. "You sleep here." It was an order, not a suggestion.

"Where are you going to sleep?" Faith was

a little nervous about the night to come. She found she wanted him near. She'd feel safer knowing he was close at hand.

"Don't worry. I'll give you your privacy." His answer was terse. He assumed that she wanted him away from her.

"No — I — "

"I understand. You won't be bothered. I'll be keeping watch."

"When will you be able to get some sleep?"

"I'll be fine." He cut her off as he took his portion of the meat from her. He started to stride off out of the light of the campfire.

"Chase — ?"

He looked back questioningly.

"Your arm — is it all right? Do you want me to change the bandage tonight?" she offered, wanting to make sure the wound was kept clean.

Chase stared at Faith across the campfire. A heat that had nothing to do with the burning fire seared his consciousness and made him aware with every fiber of his being just how beautiful she was. He frowned, scowling at his own reaction to her. "It's fine. Good night."

He turned his back on her and disappeared into the darkness.

Faith stared after him, completely surprised by his actions. She had thought he would stay close. She had thought he would be nearby.

But he had gone.

She was alone.

Feeling suddenly bereft, she sat down on the blanket he'd provided and ate the dried meat. It wasn't the most tasty fare, but she didn't care. She drank deeply from the canteen, then bedded down for the night. She almost wished she still had Chase's sidearm, but she told herself he was nearby to protect her, even if she couldn't see him.

Chase sat just beyond the range of the campfire, his rifle close at hand in case of trouble, though he doubted there would be any tonight. It hadn't taken him long to eat the dried meat, and he had already promised himself that he'd hunt down something suitable for dinner the following night. He kept careful watch over the countryside, making sure that no one was sneaking up on them. He wanted to make sure Faith got some rest. She'd been through a lot and needed all her strength for what she was about to face. He hoped her reunion with her family would go as she expected, but he couldn't help wondering what had happened at the ranch after she'd been taken captive. A Comanche raiding party didn't attack and ride off with just one captive. He had said nothing of his fears so far, and he would not say anything. He would take her home and hope for the best.

Chase watched over Faith as she bedded down in his blanket before the fire. He kept his vigil long into the night, allowing himself to sleep only in the early morning hours when he was sure nothing was going to happen.

Faith stirred and came awake as the eastern sky began to brighten. She was surprised by how soundly she'd slept through the night. She'd expected to be restless and nervous, but somehow knowing that Chase was keeping watch had allowed her to relax. She sat up and found Chase across the campfire from her.

"Good morning," Faith greeted him, unsure whether to be relieved that he was there or nervous before him. Though she was fully clothed, she hugged the blanket protectively to her breast as she met his gaze. Except for the awful mornings with the renegades, she'd never awakened with a strange man nearby before.

"Morning," he answered. "We need to head out as soon as we can. It's a hard ride, and the sooner we get started, the better."

Faith realized that any modesty on her part was pointless. She hurried to rise and folded the blanket for him.

While Faith tended to her private business, Chase took a piece of cheese from his saddlebag and waited for her return.

"It isn't much, but it's all I've got," he said, offering her the chunk of cheese.

"It looks like manna from heaven to me," she answered. She was grateful for any sustenance. Cheese was good, although eggs and a fried steak would have tasted much better this morning.

They were on their way shortly thereafter, breaking only to rest and water the horses. Late in the afternoon, dark, threatening storm clouds gathered in the sky to the north and west.

"Looks like we're in for some bad weather," Chase remarked studying the sky as the wind picked up. "We'd better find some kind of shelter."

"Where? There aren't any ranches for miles."

"We'll find something."

Chase urged his mount onward. His keen gaze scoured the countryside for anything that would offer them protection from the elements. The coming storm would be a strong one.

Lightning rent the sky and thunder rumbled violently across the land. Both horses shied, but Chase and Faith kept tight rein on them. The rain began in a furious downpour, and Chase was glad when he finally spotted a rocky outcropping that would offer them at least some protection from the onslaught.

"Faith! Come on!"

They reached the rocks and rushed to dismount and tie up the horses. They raced toward the overhang, seeking shelter from the storm's fury.

Chapter Five

The protected area was cramped, barely able to hold them both. Faith found herself huddled against Chase, her back to him, his chest and thighs hard against her. His nearness so disconcerted her that she was tempted to throw herself back out into the wrath of the storm. Only the violent lightning strikes kept her there.

When Chase shifted position, seeking some bit of comfort, Faith was so nervous that she actually jumped away from him just as a bolt of lightning struck nearby.

Chase reacted instantly, grabbing her and hauling her back into the sheltered area.

"Don't be a fool! I'm not going to hurt you, and it's dangerous out there." His blue eyes were ablaze with anger as he glared down at her. He was certain she was acting this way because of his Indian blood. He didn't have to like it, but he understood. "I told you I'd see you safely home, and I will."

Faith was trembling. She didn't know if it was from the chill of her wet clothing, the shock of the close lightning strike, or Chase's disturbing nearness. "I'm sorry."

He growled something unintelligible as he dropped his hands away from her and looked out across the storm-ravaged land. He tried to keep a distance between them, but no matter how they stood, they were touching.

Irritation filled Chase as he noticed how sleek her pale hair was when it was wet, and how his drenched shirt clung to her like a second skin. He was tempted to step out into the cold rain himself to take his mind off how Faith felt pressed against him this way.

Chase scowled as he stared out into the storm. This assignment had been complicated enough before Faith, and now he had the added burden of making sure she got home safely.

Glancing down at her again, Chase immediately regretted having thought of her as a burden. She was a woman who had already accomplished the extraordinary — she had survived being kidnapped by a Comanche raiding party and had somehow managed to escape. There weren't many females who were smart enough, strong enough or brave enough to do what she had done — even if she was as skittish as a newborn foal around him.

Faith stood with her arms wrapped around herself for warmth. It looked like the rain was letting up a little bit, and she guessed Chase would be as glad as she was. Judging from the tone of his voice before, he was as impatient to deliver her to her home as she was to get there.

"It's clearing up," Chase observed as the sky lightened. "We should be able to get another hour's ride in before sundown."

"The faster we get back to the ranch, the better," she agreed. "I'm worried about my family."

"And I'm sure they're worried about you, too."

"You never did say what you were doing out here in the middle of nowhere," she ventured.

"I was heading for Sidewinder. I've got business there."

Faith knew Ranger business was serious. "I hope it goes well for you."

"So do I." Thinking about Tom McBride turned Chase's mood grim. He didn't want anything to do with that family — not the father, not the mother, and certainly not the children. It was only to bring Frank's murderer to justice that he was going. "I think it's let up enough that we can ride now."

Chase moved from the shelter of the rocks to scan the sky. Only a light drizzle was falling, and to the north and west it was clear.

Faith followed him to where they'd tied the horses, and they were on their way again. Each mile they covered brought her closer to home and to John.

That night they made camp in an area where it hadn't stormed. It was dry, and Faith was glad. Chase built a fire and then went to hunt, returning with a rabbit for her to fix for the evening meal. After they'd eaten, Chase again left her alone by the fireside and disappeared into the darkness to keep watch over the campsite.

Faith was miserable as she lay in her still-damp clothes beneath the damp blanket before the fire. She hoped that the fire would eventually dry things out, but it wasn't going to happen any time soon. She tossed and turned fitfully, seeking comfort and sleep. When at last she did fall asleep, it was a troubled slumber filled with tormented, disjointed dreams of the Comanche raid on her home.

"No!" Her cry split the stillness of the night.

Chase had been keeping careful watch and could see no reason for Faith to scream, but he charged down to her side, his gun drawn and ready. Kneeling beside her, he could see the look of horror on her face as she sat up.

Confused by the power of her nightmare, Faith struggled to understand where she was and what had really happened. She stared up at Chase, her eyes wide as it took her a moment to realize that he was not one of the renegades.

"It's all right, Faith," Chase reassured her, sliding his gun back in its holster. "There's nothing to be afraid of. I'm here."

She looked so distraught that he was tempted to take her in his arms to comfort her, but he didn't. He deliberately kept a distance between them and waited for a look of reason to appear in her eyes.

The sound of his deep, even voice soothed her terror.

"What happened?" she asked in a whisper.

"You were dreaming."

Faith nodded, disjointed images of the nightmare slipping into her thoughts and taunting her. "It was the attack. They were chasing me down and — ”

"You're safe now. There's nothing to fear."

She blinked and drew a ragged breath as she stared at his Ranger badge. "I know. You're here."

Exhausted but reassured, she lay back.

Chase stood and moved away. He paused to watch over her for a moment and make sure all was well, then returned to his vigil.

The rest of the night passed uneventfully, and they were once again on the move just after first light. They set a steady pace and rode until the horses were weary late in the day.

Faith allowed herself to be excited as they made camp that night. Tomorrow, she would be home. Tomorrow, she would be back with her family. It surprised her that she slept soundly that night, as anxious as she was about the day to come. But she did. When she awoke she was rested and eager to cross the final miles to the ranch. They were almost there!

With every passing mile, the landscape looked more and more familiar to Faith. She quickened her pace. She wanted to be home. She wanted to see her mother and father. She kept a lookout, too, for John and the search party she was certain he was leading to find her. It had surprised her that they hadn't run into them by now, but that didn't matter. All that mattered was that she was safe and back home at long last.

Chase kept up with Faith, silently understanding her growing excitement — and her desperate need. He mentally readied himself for what he knew they might find when they reached the ranch. Comanche raiders were deadly. He hoped his concern was misplaced, but logically he knew what to expect. He had said nothing to her about his suspicions. Her emotions were already in a fragile state, and he hadn't wanted to destroy her belief that her life would return to normal. He wanted that for her. He hoped it was possible.

But he wasn't counting on it.

"We'll make it today!" Faith called out to him. "It won't be long!"

She was smiling, and it was the first time Chase had seen her look so happy. *She was beautiful.* She was an innocent, fresh and almost untouched by the ugliness of life.

Chase had thought of Faith as smart and brave, but the recognition of her innocence hit him hard. As he envisioned the pain she might soon have to face, an unexpected need to protect her stirred within him. He had never felt this way before about a woman, and he girded himself against it. His only responsibility was to see her safely home to her family and fiancé. That was all. She wanted nothing more from him. She needed nothing more from him.

They rode on.

It was near noon when Chase reined in, forcing Faith to stop, too.

"We should rest the horses for a while," he told her.

"Oh, Chase, no! Please! We're so close. It's less than an hour's ride from here. Please, Chase," she begged him. "Take me home."

There was no denying her, and he knew it.

"All right, let's ride."

She graced him with another brilliant smile and started off at a trot. He joined her and stayed close by her side as they covered the final miles.

"It's just over the next hill!" Faith told him in delight. "I'm home, Chase — I'm really home!" She started to gallop over the rise, then reined in to turn back and look at him. "Thank you."

He nodded, but didn't say anything. For all her excitement, they still didn't know what they were riding into — what they would find. When she kneed her horse ahead again, he followed her.

Faith's excitement knew no ends. She was home! At last, she was home! There had been moments during the last trying, dangerous days when she'd thought she might never see the ranch or her family again, but thanks to Chase, she was here. She wanted to ride in at a gallop. She wanted to yell and shout and let her parents know she was back. Instead, she cried. Her tears fell freely as she made her way over the last short distance that separated her from her loved ones.

At the top of the hill, Faith told herself, she would see the house, and everything would be as it had been. Horses would be in the corral. The hands would be working the stock. Her mother would be fixing the noon meal, and her father would be heading in from the stable to eat. Faith's heart was soaring with happiness.

And then she reached the top of the hill.

Below there were only the ruins of a fiery destruction.

"No! Chase — ?"

Faith glanced his way, her expression desperate as she tried to deny the truth of what she saw below. Putting her heels to her horse's sides, she raced down the trail that led to the house. She denied the reality of what had happened until she reined in before the burned-out ranch house and threw herself from the horse's back.

"Mama! Papa!" she cried as she ran toward the steps that led to the porch.

The nauseating stench of burned wood nearly overwhelmed Faith. She stopped and stared at the ruin of her family's home. It was a blackened skeleton against the sky.

Faith headed toward the stable to see if anything was left there, if anything had survived, but all had been destroyed. There was no sign of her parents.

"Where is everybody?" she demanded of Chase as she ran back to the front of the house where he had dismounted and was waiting for her.

"I'm sorry, Faith," he said in a low voice.

"No, no, you don't understand," she said frantically, still not believing what had happened. "They're in town. I'm sure of it. Let's ride there right now."

Faith didn't wait to hear Chase's answer. She rode out, away from the ruins of what used to be her home, away from the truth she could not yet accept.

Chapter Six

Faith concentrated only on reaching Dry Gulch. She could not, would not allow herself to think about the horror she'd just discovered at the ranch. She was going into town, and she was certain she would find her parents and the ranch hands there — safe and unharmed.

Each mile seemed endless as Faith charged forward with Chase riding at her side. He had said nothing, and she was glad. There was no way she could talk right then — not until she'd seen her parents again and been reassured that they were all right.

When at last Dry Gulch came into view, Faith began to tremble. Fear ate at her. She willed herself to be outwardly calm, but deep within her heart terror reigned. She considered going to John's house or the bank where he worked, but she didn't; she was certain he would be gone — out riding with a posse, tracking her. She headed for the sheriff's office instead, ignoring the shocked stares of the people on the streets as she rode through with a half-breed alongside.

Faith reined in before Sheriff Kelly's office and dismounted, quickly tying up her mount. She drew a deep breath. Surely the sheriff knew about the attack and could tell her where her parents were staying in town.

Faith started toward the door with Chase beside her. She looked up at him to find his gaze intent upon her. She didn't say anything, but hurried ahead, desperately needing answers to the questions that were haunting her.

"Sheriff Kelly?" Faith called as she burst inside.

"Faith? Faith Bryant? Oh, my God!" Sheriff Melvin Kelly leaped to his feet, the papers he'd been reading dropping from his hands as he stared at her in shock. He'd thought she was dead. He'd thought the Comanche had her and they would never see her again. Yet here she was. "You're alive!"

"I escaped, and Ranger McBride here brought me home," she explained quickly, not wanting to go into detail now. All that

73

was important was finding her parents. "But where are my parents?"

Sheriff Kelly's shocked expression changed. He looked stricken, and didn't answer her immediately.

Faith rushed on. "Are they staying at the hotel? Or did John put them up? We went to the ranch first and I saw what happened but — "

The lawman didn't know what to say. He could only stare at Faith, thinking of all that she must have suffered at the hands of the renegades, and knowing that she was going to suffer even more when he told her the horrible truth of what had happened to her parents.

"Tell me, Sheriff," Faith finally finished, staring at him in desperation, wanting affirmation that her parents were in town, alive and well.

Chase could tell what was about to happen from the look on the Sheriff's face. He stepped up to Faith's side.

"Well, Miss Faith . . ." The sheriff swallowed nervously, then cleared his throat. He glanced away for a moment as he tried to gather his thoughts.

"What's happened to them, Sheriff?" Faith insisted, growing a little hysterical at his continued hesitation. "Where are they? I

need to see them. Everything's been so horrible — "

Sheriff Kelly came out from behind his
desk. "Miss Faith — I'm sorry. There's no
easy way to tell you this, but . . ."

Even though he didn't finish the sentence,
Faith's knees started to buckle. Chase saw
the weakness in her and slipped an arm
around her waist to help her sit down in a
chair. They both looked up at the sheriff and
waited for him to go on.

"What — ?" Faith whispered, her lips
barely moving, her gaze unwavering.

"They were killed during the raid, Miss
Faith. I'm sorry. They were dead when we
found them — all of them," he finished
grimly, thoughts of the gruesome scene he
had ridden into playing in his mind. He
could never tell her the truth of how terrible
it had been.

All color drained from Faith's face.

They were dead —

Her beloved parents were dead —

She could no longer control the emotions
that roiled within her. A sob of pure misery
erupted from her as she wept. Chase was
there, slipping an arm around her to hold her
as she gave vent to the torment in her soul.

"I'll go get John for you," Sheriff Kelly offered.

Faith lifted her head to look at him, her expression even more confused. "John's here? He's in town?"

"He should be at the bank right now. I'll get him."

"Thank you." A great shudder wracked Faith as her tears continued. Vaguely, she wondered why John was in town. He should have been out searching for her.

The sheriff left the office and hurried off toward the bank, leaving Chase and Faith alone.

The one thing that had kept Faith going during her ordeal was the belief that if she stayed alive and somehow managed to escape, she would be able to go home to her parents — that they were at the ranch waiting for her to return, worrying about her safety, praying for her.

The truth was brutal and savage and final.

Faith could only imagine how horrible it must have been on the ranch after she'd been taken captive. The warrior who'd taken her had ridden away with her immediately, so she'd had no idea that others in the raiding party had remained behind to murder everyone and burn the buildings.

"They're dead, Chase," Faith repeated weakly, somehow wanting him to deny it, to tell her she was wrong. "The raiding party killed my parents. . . ."

"I'm sorry." It was all he could say. He knew there was nothing he could do except offer what little comfort he could. Before they'd ridden into the ruins of the ranch, he'd feared that this would be what she'd discover, and he'd been right. Chase wished there was something he could do to make it better. But there wasn't.

Faith began to cry again, leaning against Chase, clinging to his strength. She gave herself over into Chase's keeping, finding some solace in his powerful yet gentle embrace.

Chase held Faith. If there had been some way he could have borne the misery and heartbreak for her, he would have. He knew exactly what she was feeling.

Chase knew the horror of returning home to discover that your loved ones had died while you were gone.

Sheriff Kelly raced across town toward the bank where John Blair worked. He was thrilled to be able to tell John that his fiancée had returned as if from the dead. He hurriedly let himself in. The two tellers looked up at him worriedly as did the customers.

"Is there trouble, Sheriff?" Max Wilkins,

the head teller, asked.

"No. No trouble. I just need to talk to John. Is he in his office?"

"Yes, sir."

The lawman hurried through the swinging half-gate to the door that was closed against intrusion. He knocked and waited.

"Sheriff Kelly?" John stared at him as he opened the door. He was at a loss as to why the lawman would be paying him a visit.

"John, I need to talk to you — privately."

"Of course, come in." John could see the urgency in his expression and stood aside to let him pass.

Sheriff Kelly glanced around, impressed, as always, as he entered the office. John was a very successful citizen of Dry Gulch, and his office reflected that success.

"What's wrong, Sheriff?"

He cleared his throat. "It's Faith, John — "

"You've found her — " John said without much emotion.

"Yes, and — "

"Have a seat," John interrupted him. He gestured the sheriff to the chair that faced his desk while he sat down behind the desk.

John had been expecting this moment since Faith had been abducted in the raid, and he'd been dreading it. It was never pretty what the Comanche did to their captives before they killed them, but he was glad that, at least, someone had finally found her body. He would take care of her funeral arrangements just as he had her parents' and the ranch hands'. It was a gruesome task, but there was no one closer to the family who could do it.

"Where was she found?"

"A Texas Ranger brought her in."

"A Ranger?" He frowned, wondering how a Ranger would have known where to bring her remains. "How did he — ?"

"John," Sheriff Kelly said with some force to get his attention and shut him up for a minute. "John, you have to understand. She's alive. Faith is alive!"

John stared at him, his expression turning to one of complete and utter disbelief. "No — she can't be — "

"She's down at my office now. I just gave her the news about her parents, and it hit her hard. I told her I was coming to get you for her."

"Dear God," John choked as wild, conflicting emotions tore through him. *Alive? Faith was alive? She should be dead!*

"I know this is a shock for you, but she needs you, John, in a bad way. Come with me now?" Sheriff Kelly stood. He was a little confused by the banker's reaction to the news that the woman he loved was alive. He had thought John would be racing from the bank to his office to see her. Instead he was sitting, unmoving, his expression dark and troubled. "John? Is something wrong? I thought you'd be — "

"No, nothing's wrong. Let's go. Faith is alive — I have to see her!"

As he hurried out of his office, the tellers looked at him expectantly.

"Mr. Blair?" Max inquired, curious as to why the lawman was there.

"They've found Faith. She's been brought back in alive," John explained quickly as he crossed to the door.

"That's wonderful news!" both tellers proclaimed.

"Yes, yes, it is." John gave them a pained smile as he left the building.

"What do you want to do now?" Chase asked Faith when she'd quieted. "Is there anything I can do to help you? Anything you need?"

"Just my parents back alive and well," she said sadly, slowly coming to grips with the reality of her situation.

"If I could do that for you, I would," he told her.

"Chase — thank you." She looked at him

with heartfelt emotion. "You've been wonderful, and I appreciate everything. John will be here in a minute, and then you'll be rid of me for good and you can head on to Sidewinder."

He was silent. He found himself wondering how she was going to manage once he'd gone. It had become a natural thing these last days to protect her and watch over her. "You'll be all right with him?"

"Oh, yes. John's wonderful."

Chase had his own opinion about that, but kept it to himself. He just knew that if the woman he loved had been kidnapped as Faith had been, he would have gone after her and wouldn't have rested until he'd found her. He could only wonder why her fiancé hadn't.

The door to the office opened then, and a tall, blond-haired man rushed in.

Chase saw Sheriff Kelly coming behind him and knew this must be Faith's fiancé.

"Faith?" John cast only a cursory glance at Chase as he came inside.

"John! Oh, John!" Faith cried as she stood and rushed to him. Her tears began again as she went into his arms.

Chase felt a twinge of some unfamiliar emotion as he watched the other man enfold Faith in his embrace. He looked on for a moment longer, then quietly left the office. He nodded to the sheriff as he went. There was nothing more for him to do there. He had done his job. He had helped to save a young woman and had brought her safely home. Faith was with the man she loved, and, as difficult as it was going to be for her to accept the loss of her parents, Chase knew her fiancé would take care of her now.

Stepping out onto the sidewalk, Chase stared up at the clear blue sky and took a deep breath. Sometimes being a Ranger was hard, dirty work, but then there were times like this when things did work out. He headed toward the one and only hotel in town.

It took Faith a long moment to finally get some control over her turbulent emotions. *She was with John — Everything would be better now.* Slowly her crying ceased, and she drew slightly away to look up at him. John was looking down at her, his expression serious and troubled.

"Faith — are you all right?" His concern was real. She was filthy and bruised, and her clothing was in disarray. She was even wearing what looked like a man's shirt.

"Now that I'm with you I am," she answered, believing it.

"Sheriff? Could you get Dr. Rogers and have him meet us at my house?"

"Right away."

"Thank you for your help, Sheriff," John told him. "And thanks — " He looked around for the man who'd brought Faith back and discovered the Ranger had gone. "Oh, he's gone already."

Faith was sorry that she hadn't had a chance to tell Chase good-bye. As John led her from the sheriff's office, she wondered if she would ever see the Ranger again.

Chapter Seven

John paced the floor of his parlor as the doctor tended to Faith privately in the second-floor bedroom. His mood was black as he faced the truth he was dealing with: Faith was alive and had been returned to him after having been a captive of the Comanche for God knows how many days and nights. He swore a vile curse and stalked to his small liquor cabinet to pour himself a shot of whiskey. This situation deserved at least that much.

What the hell was he going to do?

Snarling to himself, John considered his options. None of them were pleasant. True, he and Faith were engaged. But he had proposed to her before. The situation now was different.

John knew Faith had suffered greatly in the attack, and God only knows what had happened to her while she was a captive, although he had a vivid imagination and could very well guess. It made his flesh crawl to think about what had been done to her. He realized, then, that she could already be pregnant by one of the Comanches, and he knew that there was no way he could take her as his wife, no way he could take her to his bed to be the mother of his children.

John realized his decision was harsh, but he couldn't help it. It was the way he felt. Everyone would know that the wife of John Blair had once been a Comanche captive, and he could just imagine all the talk that would result. Hell, it had probably already started. The tellers at the bank knew — and the doctor. He had worked hard to attain his position in life. As much as he cared for Faith, and he did care for her, he realized she would be much better off living somewhere else where no one knew of her past.

John wasn't sure how he was going to handle everything, but he would wait to talk with the doctor and then tell Faith of his decision. He would give her enough money to help her start a new life away from Dry Gulch. Certainly that offer would bolster her spirits. John believed she probably would be as glad to get out of Dry Gulch as he would be to see her go.

Dr. Rogers finished examining and treating the wounds to her breasts and shoulders.

"I think you'll be fine in a week or so," he counseled her. "There's nothing serious and there should be no scarring."

"Thank you, Dr. Rogers," Faith said quietly.

He was quiet for a moment, considering her seriously as he attempted to broach the horror of what he feared she'd suffered. The marks on her breasts had been proof to him that she had been manhandled, and he could well imagine what other horrible things had been done to her when she'd been helpless and in the power of the Comanches.

"Faith, I know this is a delicate subject, but were you injured in any other way?" he asked solicitously. He admired her greatly for having survived her ordeal and only wanted to help her in any way he could.

"No!" Faith answered quickly. His question shocked her, but she knew it shouldn't have. She was well aware of the terrible things that were generally done to captives, and she considered herself blessed that she had escaped that degradation.

"Are you sure?" he pressed.

"Nothing happened!" Faith protested, angered by his insinuation.

Dr. Rogers believed she was deluding herself. "My dear, everyone knows the way captives are treated by renegades."

"No one touched me that way!"

He was condescending as he continued to ignore her protests. "We realize this is not your fault, but if you've been violated — "

"I said no one touched me that way!" Again she denied what he was implying. She clutched the robe John had provided for her more tightly around her to shield herself from this verbal assault.

The doctor saw her movement as one of self-defense against the truth. It saddened him to see her upset this way, and he knew he had to speak with John about her situation.

"Well, I believe we're done for now. I'll leave you alone to rest for a moment while I speak with John."

Faith watched him leave the room, her gaze cold upon him.

He glanced her way, his gaze sympathetic but pitying as he closed the door behind him to give her privacy.

The doctor sought out John where he waited in the parlor below, and he noticed immediately the empty glass next to the bottle of whiskey. He understood why the man was upset and wished there was some way for him to put his worries to rest.

"How is she?" John demanded as he came into the room.

"She is a very fortunate woman," he replied. "There were some minor injuries, but over all, her health is good."

"That's good news." He was relieved that she had suffered no crippling injuries. "So you believe she'll recover fully?"

"Physically, yes. Mentally . . ." He hesitated, giving extra emphasis to his words.

"Doctor — you mean — ?"

They shared a look of male understanding.

"I'm sorry, but I'm afraid so — in my opinion, at least."

"I don't understand."

"She refuses to admit that anything happened in that way," the physician explained. "I tended to her cuts and bruises, but Faith insisted that she was untouched in an, um, intimate manner."

"How could that be? We all know what those murdering renegades do to their captives! How could she think we'd believe she was still an innocent? Her reputation is ruined."

"I agree, but when I spoke with her about it, she denied that anything had happened.

88

Her blouse was torn and so was her chemise, and she did have marks on her breasts that would indicate she had been abused in some way."

John tensed, thinking of what she had suffered and knowing that she had been ruined by the attack. "Thank you, Dr. Rogers. Is there anything more I can do for her?"

"I don't think so. Faith has been through a terrible time, John. She's just lost her whole family and her home. You're all she has left in the world, you know," he advised him.

John listened to his words and muttered some response as he showed the doctor from the house. Once he'd shut the door, he stood alone in the hallway. He was lost deep in thought as he glanced up the stairs at the closed bedroom door where Faith rested. He had proposed to Faith because she was beautiful, and the daughter of a successful rancher. They got along passably well, and he had been sure she would do him proud as his wife. Now, though, all that had changed. He couldn't marry a woman who'd been an Indian captive, no matter how pretty she was.

Just thinking of touching Faith left him feeling disgusted. No matter what she said, he knew what had happened to her while she was with the raiding party, and so did everyone else in town. It was a stigma that would never be forgotten.

That she denied being violated only proved to him that she had probably lost her mind during the ordeal. The last thing he needed was an insane wife. For all that she had seemed coherent enough when he'd spoken with her earlier, he would certainly be the one who was stuck with her if she lost her mind after they married. Her parents were dead; he would be completely and solely responsible for Faith, and that was one burden he did not want.

John girded himself to face her as he started up the stairs with the clothes and personal items the doctor had thoughtfully brought for Faith. It wasn't going to be easy having this talk with her right now, knowing how delicate her condition was, but he would be doing her no favors if he let her go on believing that nothing had changed between them.

Everything had changed.

John mounted the stairs and knocked softly on the closed bedroom door.

"Come in," Faith called out. She was feeling uneasy since the doctor's visit and needed John's loving reassurance. Once she was in his arms, she was certain she would feel whole again — and safe.

"I wanted to check on you and see how you were doing," John said as he entered the room to find her sitting in the bedside chair, clad in the robe. "Dr. Rogers said you were going to be all right."

"I will be now that I'm here with you," she told him. "John — tell me what happened at the ranch. I need to know. And I need to see my parents. Are they buried here in town?"

"Yes, Faith. They were buried together in the church cemetery."

She nodded, but didn't speak.

"The raiding party killed everyone who was there. You're the only survivor. It was the next day before we even found out about the raid. I took care of all the funeral arrangements, then rode out with several of the deputies trying to find you. But we couldn't find a trace of the raiding party's trail anywhere."

Faith was encouraged to learn that John had tried to look for her. A part of her had harbored the fear that he hadn't tried at all. It surprised her, though, that they couldn't find the trail. There had been so many men in the raiding party; it should have been a simple thing to track them.

"Oh, John — " She stood up to go to him and was surprised when he took an evasive step back. She wondered at his reaction to her. "What's wrong?"

"I think it would be best if you got dressed. Here are some clothes and personal items the doctor brought over. Once you've changed, we can arrange for you to stay at the hotel for now. I want to make sure we do nothing to further damage your reputation."

Her reputation? He was worried about damaging her reputation? And what did he mean by "further damage"?

Faith frowned. She needed John's warmth and strength. She needed him to hold her close and tell her that he loved her. She needed the reassurance that everything would get better eventually. After all, they still had each other.

Faith realized then that she was still clad in only the robe, and the situation could be considered compromising by some. She told herself that John was concerned about her and was protecting her — in a way.

"Everything has been so terrible," she sighed wearily. "Thinking of you was the only thing that kept me going. It was the only thing that got me through it all."

Her sentiments made him uneasy.

"I'm glad, dear." He kept his tone deliberately distant. "It would be best now if you got dressed, so I can take you over to the hotel before it gets any later. We can see about buying you new clothes tomorrow."

Faith felt John was her only hope to regain the happiness that had been so violently stolen from her. Suddenly, the courage that had sustained her in the face of torture and possible death was gone. She felt fragile and helpless and very much a woman in need of a strong man. Lifting her tear-filled gaze to his, she moved toward him. She wanted more than anything to be wrapped in the warmth and strength of his embrace. She wanted to know that he would shield her and protect her. Faith had always prided herself on being a strong woman, but right now she needed John to be strong for her.

"Oh, John — just hold me," she managed in a choked voice as she went to him.

Faith's whole world had been destroyed. She needed unconditional love and acceptance. She looked up at him adoringly. He was so handsome. A sudden hope bloomed within her that, maybe, he would marry her now, tonight. They could go to the justice of the peace right there in town and then she would never have to be separated from him again. The prospect was heavenly.

John couldn't very well reject her as she came to him, but he held himself stiffly as he grasped her upper arms. He hated to admit it, but he was repulsed by her now. No trace of the tender emotion he used to feel for her existed. He only wanted to get away from her.

"John, we could elope tonight. Then we could be together. We'd never have to be apart again." Her hopes were soaring at the possibility, and she lifted her lips to his, wanting affirmation of his love for her.

John stiffened even more at her outrageous suggestion.

Marry her now? Tonight?

He immediately believed the only reason she wanted to get him to the altar so quickly was to give a name to whatever bastard child she might be carrying. He was completely repelled by the idea. His grip tightened on her upper arms, and he held her slightly away from him, refusing her kiss. It was all he could do not to thrust her out of the room.

"What's wrong?" Faith was shocked and devastated by his rejection.

"We need to go slowly right now, Faith. There's no reason for us to rush to get married. A lot has happened to you, and you need time to learn how to deal with it. Things aren't the same as they were."

"What do you mean, 'things aren't the same as they were'?" she demanded, an icy chill running through her.

"You know what I mean, Faith," John said. "We both need time to come to terms with all that's happened."

"I told Dr. Rogers the truth, John — no matter what the two of you believe, I was not raped by the Indians!" She was growing furious, and the anger strengthened her.

"I know, I know," he said patronizingly. He had imagined this moment would be ugly, and it was.

"I thought you loved me," she challenged, devastated now as she recognized the truth of his feelings. She shrugged his hands off her arms as anger seared her. "I thought you cared about me. I guess my first suspicion was right when it was painfully obvious that you didn't search very hard for me."

"I told you we tried to track — "

"If you cared, John, you never would have given up trying to save me! If you loved me, you would have kept searching until you found me!"

"You're overreacting. Calm yourself, Faith."

She stood tall and proud before him. Her pride was all she had left. "Please leave and allow me some privacy."

"Faith — "

"Get out!" she ordered.

John was more than glad to leave her. "I'll take you to the hotel when you're dressed."

His answer was the door slamming in his face as he backed out into the hall.

Chapter Eight

Righteous fury sustained Faith as she threw off the robe and started to dress. It irked her to have to wear clothing that Dr. Rogers had provided, but her own things were in terrible condition. Her riding skirt was filthy and her blouse was in tatters and beyond repair. She picked up Chase's shirt and just held it for a moment, staring down at the ragged bottom where she'd cut off the strips of cloth she'd used to bandage his arm.

Chase had defended her and wrought vengeance upon the raiding party. He had stood beside her and protected her. He had stayed with her until he'd thought she was safe. For all that she'd been wary of him at first for his Indian blood, she knew now that Chase McBride was more of a man than John could ever hope to be.

Faith carefully folded the shirt. She would return it to him. It would give her the chance she needed to thank him.

Quickly shedding the robe, she donned the dress. She wanted to get out of John's house and out of his life as fast as she could. She had survived being kidnapped by Comanches. She would easily survive ending her engagement to John.

It seemed to Faith that the latter was the better escape. She had thought she loved John and he loved her. She'd been wrong. Just because he was good-looking and educated and had promised her a wonderful future didn't mean he really loved her. She'd been taken in by his smooth manners and promises. Faith vowed then and there that she would never allow herself to be fooled by a man again.

Her hands were trembling as she finished fastening the buttons on the borrowed day gown, but her convictions had never been more firm. She didn't know what she was going to do, but she would do it without any help from John Blair! He was lower than the most vile renegade! She was glad to get away from him, and glad to have found all this out about him before they were married.

Faith had washed up before the doctor's visit, but she wanted desperately to bathe again. She felt soiled inside and out from her conversation with John. There was no time now. She would bathe and wash her hair once she'd taken a room at the hotel.

Finally dressed, Faith accidentally glanced in the mirror. She stared at her own reflection for a moment. Outwardly, she looked the same; now that she had clothes on, no one could see her injuries. She didn't appear to have changed at all. Only she knew the changes that had taken place within her.

With her head held high, Faith gathered up her few belongings and left the room. She descended the stairs. As she reached the hall, John came out of the parlor.

"I'll escort you to the hotel," he said, moving to open the front door for her.

"Don't bother," Faith bit out coldly. "I'm sure I can make it to the hotel by myself. I don't need your help."

"Faith, my dear, you're not thinking clearly," he said in a condescending tone.

She smiled tightly at him. "That's where you're wrong, John. I am thinking very clearly. You may consider our engagement at an end. There will be no wedding, so you won't have to worry about my reputation any longer. Any concerns about my reputation from now on will be mine and mine alone. I am perfectly capable of taking care of myself, and I'm going to do just that."

Faith walked past John and let herself out of the house. John was her last connection to her old life, and it was over.

Fear of the unknown ate at her and sorrow tempered her every thought and action, but she refused to surrender to them. She would worry about what she was going to do with the rest of her life later. Right now, she just wanted to get away from John. Leaving him felt more liberating than freeing herself from the raiding party had.

She didn't say another word. She simply walked away.

Faith's emotions were in turmoil as she made her way through town to the small hotel. After the way John and Dr. Rogers had treated her, she wasn't sure how the rest of the townsfolk were going to act around her. She found out quickly.

"Faith! It is you! We heard talk that you were back, but we weren't sure." Mildred Hawkins came up to her. "How are you, my dear?"

"I'm fine, Mrs. Hawkins," she replied. The older woman was a pillar of what little society there was in Dry Gulch.

"Oh, my, you're such a strong young woman — I doubt if I would have been able to show my face in town, let alone walk about as if nothing had happened. Why, after all you've been through, I would have thought you would just want to — "

"Thank you for your concern, Mrs. Hawkins," Faith broke in.

"And your parents — I'm so sorry."

"Thank you." Faith didn't wait for her to say any more. She started walking on again.

She sensed rather than saw a bit of a disturbance across the street a minute or two later and glanced up to see three young girls watching her closely and whispering behind their hands to one another. Looking away, Faith went on. She would not rush. She would not give them that power over her.

Faith thought of Chase then. Chase had never treated her as if she were soiled or ruined. He had been concerned for her and had helped her in every way he could. For all that he was a half-breed, he had proven to be more honorable than John or the people in town would ever be.

She entered the hotel and approached the desk. "I need a room, please."

The desk clerk knew her. "Yes, Miss Bryant. I'm sorry about your family, but it's good that you're back."

Faith only nodded, not sure whether it

was good that she was back or not. She took the key he offered.

"Please have a bath sent up to my room right away."

"Yes, ma'am."

She hurried up the stairs and let herself into the room. She didn't feel any peace until the door was locked behind her.

A short time later she heard the maids in the hallway and started toward the door to let them in. She was reaching for the doorknob when she overheard a part of their conversation.

"She's the one," one maid was whispering. "The one everybody thought was dead."

"From what I've just heard around town, she'd be better off if she was dead," the other returned.

"I know. I wonder how she can even think about showing her face anywhere."

"The poor thing — "

Faith was frozen in place, listening to them. It took all her considerable self-control to open the door once they'd knocked and admit them as if nothing was wrong. *What did they know about her situation? How could they judge anything about her? Her family had been killed! She'd been kidnapped! Her home had been destroyed! She hadn't done anything wrong. She hadn't done anything to deserve this!* Faith controlled herself and smiled politely at them, but she was very glad when they left.

After stripping off her clothes, she sank gratefully into the tub of hot water. She grabbed the washcloth and soap and began to scrub herself. It almost seemed she would never feel clean again. Sinking down beneath the water for a moment, she soaked and washed her hair. She rinsed it repeatedly to make sure all the soap was out and then rose from the tub and toweled herself dry. Weary though she was, she knew she should think about getting something to eat, but right then the bed looked very inviting. She wrapped the towel around her and decided to rest for just a little while before venturing out again.

Chase was at the stable when he heard the first of it. He'd gone there after checking into the hotel to take care of the horses and overheard a conversation between the stable owner and one of his hands as he worked at unsaddling his mount.

"You ain't heard the news yet, Fred?" Al Dexter asked.

"What news?"

"The Bryant girl. She's alive!"

"Damn!"

"I know. Who woulda thought it, but Mary Ellen overheard talk that she was over at John Blair's and the doc was taking a look at her."

"Wonder what kinda shape she's in. Can't be good, considering."

"That's for sure. We all know what them bloodthirsty Comanche are like and what they do to women — "

"How'd she get back to town? I woulda thought we'd never see her again."

"Don't know how she managed it, but the poor gal, she might have been better off not making it back."

Chase finished what he was doing and left the stable without speaking to either man. He was angry at the attitude of the people in Dry Gulch and wondered if they had any idea of the hardships Faith had suffered just to come home again — or if they even cared. He hoped her fiancé would take care of her. She deserved better than the way these folks were acting.

It was late afternoon as Chase started back to the hotel to clean up before going to get some dinner. He planned to be riding out of Dry Gulch first thing in the morning. Blackie Sherwood was still out there somewhere —

"McBride!"

He stopped and looked back to see the sheriff coming up behind him on the sidewalk.

"Sheriff Kelly." Chase nodded and waited for him to catch up.

"How are you doing?"

"I'm fine. How did everything go with Faith?"

"John took her on home with him, so I guess everything will work out."

"I hope so. She's an incredibly brave woman to have lived through what she did. She deserves some peace and happiness now."

"How did you find her?" the sheriff asked.

"I didn't find her," Chase told him with a slight smile. "She found me."

"What?"

They started walking toward the hotel as Chase told him what had happened.

"She escaped on her own?"

"That's right. There aren't many women who are brave enough or smart enough to do that."

"I'll say." The sheriff's estimation of her rose, although he still felt sorry for her.

"I decided to go after the raiding party rather than risk their tracking us down, so we doubled back and were ready for them the next day."

"You fought the raiding party?" He was amazed.

"Yes. They won't be attacking any other ranches."

"Damn!"

"Did you know Faith is a good shot?" Chase again smiled slightly.

"That doesn't surprise me, knowing her father. Richard taught her to take care of herself."

"He did a good job, but I hope she'll be all right with what everybody's saying."

"What do you mean?"

"Down at the stable I heard them talking about her. It wasn't pretty." His gaze hardened as he looked at the lawman.

Sheriff Kelly shrugged a little bit guiltily, for he could imagine what folks would say about Faith; he'd had the same thoughts himself. "There's no controlling talk."

"She deserves better from the people she thought were her friends."

"John will take care of things. He's a good man."

"I hope you're right."

They stopped in front of the hotel, and Sheriff Kelly held out his hand to Chase.

"Thanks for all you did, McBride."

"I was glad to do it."

They parted company and Chase went

into the hotel. As he was passing the front desk, he heard the clerk speaking to another man.

"She's here?"

"Yes, she registered just a little while ago."

"Why didn't she stay with Blair?"

When the men realized Chase had heard them, they stopped talking.

Chase walked straight up to the desk clerk.

"Is Faith Bryant staying here at the hotel?"

"Yes, she is, Mr. McBride. Is it true what we've heard?" the clerk asked.

"That depends on what you've heard," Chase said, his gaze icy as he regarded the two men. He well understood what Faith was facing now in this community.

"Why, that you saved her! Is it true? Did you rescue her from the renegades?"

"I did bring Miss Bryant back home, but she escaped from the raiding party on her own. She's a very brave woman — a smart one, too. Which room is she in?"

"She's in 212."

Chase nodded to the two and strode away. He didn't know why Faith was at the hotel, but he intended to find out. He had thought she would be staying in her fiancé's home. He climbed the steps and hurried down the hall to Faith's room, then knocked on the door. If nothing else, he could at least say good-bye.

Faith was in the process of slowly getting dressed. She was realizing just how hungry she was and how long it had been since she'd had a good meal.

As she buttoned the bodice of her dress, Faith let her mind race. The first thing she had to do, she knew, was go to the bank the next morning and see if there was any money in her father's account. They had never been rich, but they had always managed to live comfortably. The prospect of dealing with John again left her feeling sickened, but she had to do it. Her father's money was in John's bank. There was no way to avoid it, so she stiffened her resolve, determined to get it over with as quickly as possible. Once she knew how much money there was, she could figure out what her future held. One thing was for certain, though, she had to buy at least a few other clothes. Right now her wardrobe was nonexistent. The one dress, a nightgown, her skirt, riding boots and Chase's shirt would not go very far. She was at that moment penniless and homeless. Logically, she knew she had to start a whole new life, but she also knew that she was not going to start that life in Dry Gulch. Not after what she'd been through already.

Faith wished she had family to turn to, someone she could go to for help, but the last of her father's sisters had died the year before back East, and she had no one on her mother's side. She truly was alone in the world. She shivered at the thought and braced herself for the challenges to come. It was not going to be easy. She just hoped there was enough money to help her start a new life somewhere else.

Faith gazed out the hotel room window, staring out at the slowly darkening sky. She was overwhelmed by memories of how just a few days before she had been helping her mother fix dinner for her father and the hands. It was almost impossible to believe that they would never be together again. She bit back a poignant sob and forced her thoughts away from all that she'd lost. She'd think about her mother and father later. Right now she had to focus on surviving.

The knock at her bedroom door startled her. She hoped it wasn't John.

"Who is it?" she called out guardedly.

"It's Chase."

Chapter Nine

Faith could not explain the sudden excitement that filled her when she heard Chase's voice. She was relieved that it wasn't John. Seeing him would only have caused a fight, but seeing Chase again — that was different. She hurried to open the door and found him standing before her, his darkly handsome, manly presence seeming to fill the entire doorway.

"Chase?"

"Hello, Faith." His voice was deep as his gaze went over her appreciatively. She was a beautiful woman, and she looked every bit the lady as she stood before him. She had washed her hair and was wearing it loose around her shoulders in a softly curling, golden cascade that begged to be touched. Chase forced his thoughts away from how lovely she looked.

"Why are you here?" Faith was surprised

to find that her voice was a bit breathless.

"I heard the clerk mention that you had checked in, and I wanted to come and see how you were."

"Come in," she invited, wanting to speak with him privately for a moment.

"No, I'd better not." He wanted to talk to her, but he was concerned about the gossip that would start if anyone found out he was in her room.

"Please — " Her gaze met his pleadingly.

"All right." He started forward. "But leave the door open."

She understood and appreciated his concern, but knew it was a little late. "It really doesn't matter, Chase. I'm already ruined."

He frowned, his expression darkening. "What do you mean? Why are you here? I thought you would be staying at your fiancé's home."

"No. The engagement is off, and it's better this way — much better."

"Why? You loved him." He was shocked.

Faith laughed wearily, "I thought I did, but I was wrong. John Blair is not the kind of man I want to marry, and I am glad I found out now, before there was a wedding."

"What happened?"

She lifted her gaze to his, and he could see the turmoil within her. "John and the doctor didn't believe me when I told them what happened to me. They thought the renegades had — "

"I'm sorry." He spoke up, stopping her, not wanting to humiliate her further than she already had been.

"I'm not." Her answer was firm.

"You're not?"

"No."

"What are you going to do? Do you have any other family or friends to help you?"

"I don't have any family left at all."

"And friends?" Chase thought she would surely have some friends in town to come to her aid now that she was in such dire circumstances.

For just an instant, he saw a flash of pain in her eyes, but as quickly as it had come, she masked it.

"No. There's no one here."

"What are you going to do?"

"I don't know yet."

He could see the fear in her, even though she was doing her best to deny it. "I was going to have dinner. Have you eaten yet?"

"No. I haven't."

"Join me?" he offered.

"Thank you. I'd love to. Are we going to have cheese or will you get us a rabbit?"

"I was hoping there was a decent restaurant in town."

For the first time, she laughed. "There is."

Chase escorted her from the room, and together they left the hotel.

The restaurant was only slightly busy as they entered. They sat at a quiet table at the back, and the waitress took their orders. They ignored the sidelong glances from the other customers as they waited for their food to be served.

"What are you planning to do?" Chase asked.

"I thought about staying and trying to rebuild the ranch, but I can't — not after everything that happened today."

"I'm sorry."

"There's nothing for you to be sorry about. You're the only one who's helped me."

Chase didn't say anything, but he understood.

"I have to go to the bank in the morning and see how much money my father had. He never talked about money, so I'm not sure what's left. I hope it's at least enough to start a new life somewhere."

"Where are you planning to go?"

"I hadn't really thought about it yet." She was frowning. "What's Sidewinder like? I know it's bigger than Dry Gulch, but that doesn't take a whole lot."

"You don't want to go there," he said flatly. "It's not a particularly friendly place."

"So you've been there before?"

"About ten years ago, and I never planned to go back."

"It could have changed. It could have gotten better. No matter what, it's got to be better than Dry Gulch."

Chase shrugged. He had no love for either place.

Faith suddenly wondered if Chase would consider taking her with him when he rode out the next day. It wouldn't take her long to finish up her business in town. She was sure she could be ready to ride before noon.

"Chase — could I ride with you tomorrow? I promise I won't hold you back or get in your way. I just want to get out of Dry Gulch as fast as I can."

He was surprised by her request, and his first reaction was to refuse. "You'd be better off taking the stage."

"It only comes through town twice a week. It was here yesterday, and there won't be another one for three more days. I don't think I can stand to stay here that long. If you take me with you, I promise I won't cause you any trouble."

"It wouldn't be wise, Faith." Chase tried to be gentle, but he knew riding cross-country with him would not help her reputation any.

Faith did not allow her disappointment to show. "I'll pay you to take me," she offered.

"This isn't about money. I'm on Ranger business, Faith. You'll be safer if you wait for the stage," Chase explained.

"I know I'd be safe with you." Her trust in him was complete. She knew what kind of man he was.

"Riding with a Ranger is no place for you. You're a lady."

A small, tremulous smile touched her lips and was the only hint of what his words meant to her. *At least Chase still thought she was a lady.* "My mother did try to make me into one."

"She did a fine job, and by the way, you look lovely."

"Thank you." Color came to her cheeks at his words. She realized that seeing her this way was quite a change for him.

Chase thought her fiancé was an absolute fool to let her go. If he'd been in the same situation, he would have stood proudly by Faith's side and protected her from everything and everybody.

But, Chase reminded himself, he wasn't

her fiancé. He had already lost precious days bringing her back to Dry Gulch. Not that he wouldn't do it again. It had been a matter of life and death, saving her from the raiding party, but she was safe in town now, and he was a Ranger on a mission. He had a job to do, and he had to do it. Frank was dead, and he was going to see to the capture of the man responsible.

Faith wanted to try to argue her point with him, but their food came and she had no chance. As much as she wanted to, she made up her mind that she wouldn't beg Chase to let her ride with him. She was going to get out of Dry Gulch, one way or another, but if worst came to worst, she would make the trip alone. She could do it. She had escaped from the raiding party. She could handle anything. Certainly, there was no one who would try to stop her. That last thought was grim, and she pushed it away as she allowed herself to enjoy the meal.

Chase found he was troubled by the realization that after tonight, he would never see Faith again. He glanced up at her, mentally comparing the lady she was tonight to the wildcat who'd tried to steal his horse from the campsite. They were like two distinctly different women, yet he knew they were the same. Faith was that complicated

116

and that simple. She was a survivor. It bothered him to leave her in Dry Gulch alone, but he could delay his mission no longer.

Chase concentrated on his food, glad to have a hot, regular meal for a change.

When at last they were done eating, Chase paid for the meals and escorted her from the restaurant. It had grown dark outside, and the evening was cool and pleasant.

"I didn't get a chance to thank you properly at the sheriff's office, but I do appreciate everything you've done for me," she told him as they strolled back to the hotel.

"I'm just glad you were able to find me when you did." The thought of what might have happened to her still troubled him.

"So am I." She paused, then asked, "Would you mind going to the cemetery with me? I haven't gone yet and I need to see where my parents were buried."

"Of course not. Where is it?"

Faith led him toward the small church and was glad of his company. She had to face the horror of all that had happened, and Chase's presence would strengthen her. They sought out the small cemetery behind the church and located the fresh graves that marked her parents' resting place.

In the pale moonlight, she could make out the names on the markers — Richard

Bryant and Elizabeth Bryant. Her throat tightened and tears burned in her eyes.

They really were dead. There had been no escape for them. It was over.

Chase stood quietly by while she knelt before the graves and gave vent to her sorrow. Her keening touched him deeply and stirred his long-suppressed memories of his own mother's passing.

Faith didn't want to cry, but she found she couldn't stop the powerful emotions that were tearing at her. It had barely been a week since the attack, yet it felt as if an eternity had passed. So much had changed, and it was final now — her life would never be the same again.

Faith touched each grave marker tenderly, then stood. She gazed down lingeringly one last time at the names carved there, and then turned away to find Chase waiting for her.

"Are you ready to go?" he asked quietly.

"Yes." She nodded.

He opened his arms to her and she went to him. He held her tenderly as she slowly pulled herself together. Neither spoke. When at last Faith drew away, he kept a supportive arm around her shoulders as they walked from the cemetery.

"Hey, girlie!"

A drunken shout from across the street assailed them as they emerged onto the sidewalk and started back to the hotel.

"What ya been doin' back there in the dark with that half-breed?"

Chase stiffened at the verbal assault.

"It's all right, Chase," Faith said quietly. "It's just a couple of drunks. Let's go to the hotel."

"Hell, that's the Bryant girl, Les! Maybe she's really taken a likin' to them Indians, you know what I mean?" the other drunk slurred knowingly as the two men started to cross the street to follow them.

Chase and Faith kept walking.

"He's got an arm around her, Sid," Les said. "He must be enjoyin' her a lot and wantin' to keep her with him. She must be givin' it to him real good."

"How come we let his kind walk around our town? He's a breed and they're just as bad as Indians!"

"Maybe we should teach him a lesson."

"Hey! Breed!"

Chapter Ten

Chase heard the two men shout, then the sound of running steps behind him. He dropped his arm from around Faith and turned, ready to face them down.

"You've got the name wrong, boys," he said in a slow and deadly voice. "It's not 'breed.' It's McBride. Chase McBride."

The two drunks stopped short and stood staring stupidly at the glint of the Ranger badge on his chest.

"You have anything you want to say to me or Miss Bryant?"

Les was known for getting stupid drunk and this night was no exception. He didn't know danger when it looked him in the face. " 'Miss Bryant'? Hell, she's nothin' but a slut now that them renegades done had their way with her. That's prob'ly why she's taken such a likin' to you!"

Les never saw the blow that knocked him

flat on his back in the dirt. He lay there stunned and moaning from Chase's powerful attack.

Chase turned on Sid, his expression cold and menacing. "Get him out of here!"

Sid rushed to help his friend.

Chase watched, his hand resting on his sidearm, until Sid had gotten Les to his feet and all but dragged him off. Chase had known a number of good men who'd been shot in the back walking away from trouble, and he wasn't about to turn his back on these two until he was sure it was safe. Only when they'd gone did he relax his guard and turn back to Faith.

Chase was shocked to find that she was standing there in the moonlight beside him, a single tear tracing a path down her cheek.

Deep within Chase, the hardness that had sustained him for so many years shattered. He was used to people treating him as the drunks had, so it did not surprise him anymore and it had lost the power to hurt him. He had learned how to fight and he had learned how to ignore a lot of it. But with Faith it was different. She was an innocent in all this. His harsh expression softened. He did not want her to suffer as his mother had. He would protect her.

Chase spoke quietly. "You'll be riding to

Sidewinder with me tomorrow. I'm getting you out of this town."

"Are you sure?" Her voice was barely a whisper. She couldn't believe that he really meant it after being so determined not to take her before.

"Yes, I'm sure," he answered with no hesitation. "You take care of your business in the morning, and as soon as you're done, we'll ride out."

"Thank you."

Chase just nodded tightly in response. "I'll have to find a horse for you. I sold the Indian pony to the stable owner when we got here, but there are several other saddle horses at the livery that I'm sure would be all right for you. For the right price, the owner could probably be convinced to part with one."

"I won't know how much money I've got until I speak with John at the bank."

"Don't worry. I've got money enough to cover it."

"I'll pay you back."

"I'm not worried. I don't think you're going to get away from me anytime soon."

"No, you're stuck with me now," Faith said, smiling openly at Chase.

"We'll be fine once we're out of Dry Gulch."

They shared a look of understanding and said no more as they started toward the hotel again. This time, Chase did not put his arm around her.

Chase saw Faith to her room, wanting to make sure nothing else happened to her. They made arrangements to meet for breakfast before he left her. He stood in the hall listening until he heard her lock the door. Only then did he go to his own room.

The night was hot, and there was little relief to be found in the close room as Chase undressed and stretched out on the bed. It was hard to believe that it had been just that morning when they'd discovered Faith's ranch had been burned. A lot had happened in a very short time, and his thoughts grew troubled as he thought about the days to come.

Chase wanted to protect Faith. He wanted to shield her from any further pain and sorrow. He knew what it was like to be an outcast, and he'd watched his mother suffer because of the way Tom McBride had treated her. He wouldn't allow that to happen to Faith. As long as she was with him, no harm would come to her.

His thoughts drifted to what he was going to face once he reached Sidewinder. There was no guarantee that Blackie Sherwood was in the area, so he would have to deal with the McBrides while trying to get a lead on Blackie. He wasn't looking forward to it.

The prospect of seeing his \father again aroused the same emotion in Chase that facing down those drunks had — disgust. He hadn't seen Tom McBride in ten years, and he hadn't wanted to.

Chase had left the mission after burying his mother and had gone to live with her people for a while. But he hadn't wanted to become too close to anybody, to need anybody. When he'd left them, he drifted around for a while, until he ultimately made contact with Frank Anderson. Frank had already been a Texas Ranger, and he'd been impressed with Chase's tracking ability. It was because of Frank's influence that he decided to become a Ranger.

Chase had never regretted his decision. Becoming a Ranger hadn't gained him acceptance — he'd come to realize he would never have that — but it had earned him respect — sometimes reluctantly, but respect all the same. He enjoyed his work. He knew life wasn't fair or easy, but if he could bring some outlaws to justice, it would be worth it.

And now he was going to get Blackie Sherwood.

Even as Chase concentrated on Blackie

and the best way to try to locate him once he got to Sidewinder, Faith eased into his thoughts. A vision of her softly haunted him, distracting him. She was innocence and beauty, two things that were missing in his life. Innocence he'd never had, having been branded a bastard from the day of his birth. Beauty he had known only in the circle of his mother's love. It had been lost to him ten years before. He'd hardened himself against beauty since then. He'd convinced himself that he didn't need it. But, he asked himself now, if he didn't need it, why was he so drawn to Faith?

Chase didn't want to know the answer.

Feeling restless, he got up and went to stand at the window. He stared out at the moonlit sky. It was a peaceful night, a quiet night. He couldn't understand why he felt so unsettled. He lay back down and closed his eyes, courting sleep, but images of Faith remained in his mind's eye and kept him awake long into the night.

As she pulled on her nightgown, Faith was still thinking about how frightened she'd been when the drunks had accosted them in the street. When Chase had handled them so quickly, she'd realized how silly her fears had been. Chase had taken on a whole raiding party. There had been nothing to fear from the drunks. Even so, she had been worried that he would be hurt, and the power of her concern had surprised her.

When she'd first laid eyes on Chase, she'd been terrified of him. Her terror had eased when she'd learned he was a Ranger, and now she was seeing him in a whole new way — she was seeing him as a man. Thinking of the horror of the drunks' taunting, she realized that he had endured for his whole life what she'd only suffered for one day. She wondered how he'd survived it all to become the strong man he was.

Faith expected sleep to be long in coming as she lay down, but once her head was on the pillow, she was asleep almost immediately. It was a deep, restful sleep, and morning came far too soon.

Faith kept a tight grip on her emotions as she sat facing John across his desk in his office at the bank the following morning.

"Are you certain that's right?" she asked quietly. "There wasn't anything else?"

"No, Faith, I'm sorry. I wish there was more, I truly do, but that's all that's left," John explained. "I've gone over all the facts and figures twice now, and that's it. There's only a total of one hundred and seventeen dollars in your father's account."

"Very well, then, I'll take that in cash, please," she requested.

"In cash? Are you sure?"

"I'm quite sure." Her eyes were sparkling in anger over his condescending attitude.

"I'll be right back." He stood and left the small office.

Faith had dreaded this meeting, but it had been unavoidable. After breakfasting with Chase and agreeing to meet him by the hotel desk before noon, she'd prepared herself for her meeting with John. The fact that it was the last time she would ever have to see him had helped sustain her through the interview. The news was terrible, and she was devastated, but she would never give John the satisfaction of seeing her despair. She had hoped to have an ample amount of money to live on for a while once she'd left Dry Gulch, but the meager $117 would not last long. According to John, her father had invested everything back in the ranch, and it had all been lost in the raid — the horses, the cattle, the buildings. The ranch was mortgaged, so the bank would take the land to pay off the loan.

The $117 was her full inheritance. It was everything she had in the world.

"Oh, Papa," she said to herself in a soft, strangled voice as she faced the complete reality of what her future was to become. Chase had told her how brave he thought she was, but she didn't feel very brave. Still, she wasn't about to reveal any of her fears to John.

"Here you are, Faith," John announced as he returned with her money. He started to count it out.

"There's no need," Faith said coldly. If he wanted to steal from her, he was welcome to it. She had already lost everything that was important in her life; these last few dollars meant nothing.

John was taken aback by her words. He handed her the small stack of bills. "Is there anything else I can do for you?"

Her gaze was riveting as she looked up at him. "No, John. You've already done quite enough, thank you."

With grace, Faith rose. She put her inheritance in her purse and walked out of his office, never once looking back. Clutching her purse tightly, she left the bank, her head high as she ignored the stares of the bank employees.

Desperate for clothing suitable for the ride to Sidewinder, Faith went to the mercantile next. There wasn't a lot to choose from, but that was fine for she didn't have a lot of money. She found two blouses, another riding skirt, a nightgown, personal items and a hat. She returned to the hotel and changed. She bundled up her few belongings, leaving out the items that Dr. Rogers had given her. It was almost noon, and Faith left the room and started downstairs to meet Chase.

"I need to check out," she told the clerk as she approached the front desk.

"Your bill's already been paid, Miss Bryant."

"It was? Who paid it?"

"Why, Mr. McBride did," he informed her. He'd been wondering ever since about her relationship with the half-breed Ranger. After all, the man had spent long hours with her the night before, and they had met again that morning for breakfast.

Faith was surprised by the news, but immediately planned to repay Chase when she saw him. "Could you please see that this dress is returned to Dr. Rogers? I won't be needing it any longer."

"Oh — of course." The clerk took the folded day gown from her and set it aside. His expression didn't betray his thoughts, but he couldn't help wondering if the good doctor would even want the garment back after she'd worn it.

"Thanks." She turned away, prepared to wait for Chase, but he was already there, just entering the hotel.

"Are you ready?" Chase asked.

"More than ready. Let's go."

She followed him from the hotel, not caring what the clerk or anyone else in Dry Gulch thought anymore. She was truly escaping to freedom this time.

"This is your horse," he said, handing her the reins of a sturdy roan mare.

"She's beautiful." Faith could just imagine how much the horse had cost him. "How much do I owe you?"

"Nothing."

"But I want to pay you. I have money, and there's no reason why you should have paid for my room and now my horse."

"We can settle up later."

Faith didn't like owing him money, but decided not to argue further just then. She would give him the money when they reached Sidewinder. Putting her meager possessions in the saddlebags, she swung up into the saddle. Chase was already mounted and ready to ride.

"How did it go at the bank?" he asked and saw her frown. "That bad?"

"Worse."

"John didn't — " Anger flashed through him.

"No, nothing like that. He was civil, I suppose. It's just that the news was not good. My father only had a little over a hundred dollars in the bank. That's all."

Chase had feared something like this. "Then it's a good thing we're getting out of here."

That got a smile out of her, and he was glad.

"You're right."

They put their heels to their horses' sides and rode away from Dry Gulch.

As they passed the church and graveyard, Faith bid her parents good-bye in her heart. She doubted she would return to their graves again, but she knew they were with her in spirit, and that was all that mattered now.

Faith turned her gaze to the horizon. She was going to Sidewinder to start a new life.

Chapter Eleven

"So why are you going to Sidewinder?" Faith asked as they sat around their campfire that night. "I know you said it was Ranger business, but can you talk about it?"

Chase was thoughtful for a moment, then explained. "I'm after a gunman named Blackie Sherwood. He killed a Ranger, and I'm going to bring him in."

"Was the Ranger a friend of yours?"

He glanced at her. "Yes."

She nodded in understanding. "You'll find him."

Chase found he was pleased by her confidence in him. It surprised him, for he never cared much what anyone thought about him. "I intend to."

"How long have you been a Ranger?"

"About five years now."

"That's a long time."

"Sometimes it seems like it," he agreed,

thinking of all the places he'd been and all the things he'd seen during those years. Then he changed the topic, not wanting to talk about himself. "What do you plan to do once we get to Sidewinder?"

"I don't know yet. The money I've got will keep me going for a little while, but I'm going to have to find some way to support myself."

Chase knew how difficult that would be. There just weren't many jobs available for women, and most of those that were were not for Faith. "What can you do?"

"My mother taught me how to sew, and I'm a reasonably decent cook, I guess." Faith had never worried about how to make a living before. She'd always assumed that she would be on a ranch.

"You did a fine job with the dried beef tonight," he told her, smiling in spite of himself.

Faith actually gave a small laugh. "No, I think you should take the credit for dinner. You were in charge of supplies."

He liked the sound of her laugh. "Yes, I was, and I made sure we have more to eat than the last time."

The weight of her worries returned, and Faith suddenly felt weary. "It's been a long day. I think I'll bed down now. Good night, Chase — and thanks."

"Good night."

Chase didn't say anything more as he got up and moved a respectable distance away. As he settled down across the campfire, he found he was worrying about what was going to happen to Faith once they parted company in Sidewinder. He frowned, lost deep in thought.

Chase sat in silence and watched Faith as she stretched out in her bedroll and closed her eyes. She had suffered greatly these last days. He had seen the pain mirrored in her gaze, yet her innocence remained. The need within Chase to protect her from all harm grew even stronger. He wanted to keep her by his side where he could be sure she was safe.

Thoughts of his mother came to him then. He remembered how sad her life had been, cut off from the man she loved and trying to raise his child. The priests at the mission had done their best to help her, but she had never known happiness. She had been abandoned and destitute and alone in the world. He would not let that happen to Faith. He would not leave her alone in a strange town to suffer the way his mother had. Not that he thought she was with child. Faith had told him that she had not been raped, and he believed her.

As Chase watched Faith, her expression

134

serene now as she slept, a glimmer of an idea came to him. He knew what he had to do to help her. There was a risk that she might not go along with him, but it was a chance he had to take.

Satisfied with his plan, Chase lay back to get some sleep, too. They had a long trip in front of them — especially with the slight detour he had in mind. He glanced Faith's way one last time, and, reassured that all was well, he closed his eyes. It would be morning all too soon.

"Where are we heading?" Faith asked late the next morning.

Chase had been riding to the south instead of due west for the last few hours, and she was wondering why. She feared that he might have heard there was trouble the other way.

"I've got one stop to make on the way to Sidewinder."

"You do? Where?" She was surprised, for he hadn't said a word about it before. She was relieved, too, to learn that there was nothing to fear.

"San Raphael Mission. It's only half a day's ride out of our way."

"But I thought you were in a hurry to get to town."

"I am, but this is important."

Faith didn't know what he needed to do at the mission and was hesitant to ask, even though she was curious. Not that she minded the detour. Dry Gulch was behind her, and that was all that mattered. She wasn't worried, for she was with Chase, and as long as they were on the trail, she could pretend that the ugly realities of her life didn't exist.

The miles passed quickly as they rode steadily onward. It was late afternoon when they topped a low rise and saw a stream flowing before them and the mission in the distance.

"I've heard of this mission, but I've never been here before. It's beautiful."

"It's where I was raised. My mother and I lived here," he explained.

Chase led the way down to the bank of the stream. He dismounted under the pretense that he wanted to water his horse, but he had an ulterior motive. He needed to talk to Faith before they rode in.

Chase girded himself for what was to come. He had never done anything like this before, and he had to admit he had more doubts about his chances of success now than he had when he went after the raiding party. Faith might not be as easily dealt with as renegades.

The thought amused him, but he did not smile. He couldn't allow himself to relax that much. He was very conscious of the fact that she was a white woman and he was a half-breed. There was no denying his heritage, and he didn't want to. Turning, Chase watched as Faith dismounted and led her horse forward to drink with his.

"This is a lovely place," Faith told him, appreciating the shade from the few trees that grew beside the stream. "Did you come here because the priests might know something about the outlaw you're after?"

"No." He paused.

Faith met his gaze and saw how serious he was. She was puzzled. "Then I don't understand why we're here."

"I came here because there is something important that needs to be done." He was ready. "There's one condition to my agreement to take you to Sidewinder that I didn't mention before."

She was shocked by his statement and couldn't imagine what he was leading up to. "What do you mean?" she asked cautiously.

"When we ride into Sidewinder, I want you riding with me as my wife. I want you to marry me, Faith." Chase spoke slowly, watching her expression, trying to read her reaction to his proposal. "Here. Now."

"You want us to get married?" Of all the things she'd imagined he might say, this was not one of them. "Are you serious?"

"Yes. Padre Rodriguez is my friend. He runs the mission, and I'm sure he'll perform the ceremony if I ask him."

"But you don't even know me," Faith said quickly, stunned and confused by his offer. "And I don't know anything about you except that you're a Ranger."

Chase didn't realize it until she finished speaking, but he'd been expecting her to say that he was a half-breed. Instead, she'd said he was a Ranger. He gazed down at her, an unusual feeling of tenderness welling up within him, surprising him. It was a foreign emotion for him.

"You're right," he said gently. "We don't know each other right now, but we've got time on our side."

"But you don't love me. Why would you want to marry me?"

"I want to marry you to protect you."

Anger flared in her eyes at what she thought he was insinuating. "I thought you believed me! But you don't! You're just like all the others."

"No, I'm not." He wasn't intimidated by her fury. "I do believe you, but I saw how you were treated in Dry Gulch and I want to make sure that never happens again."

"It will. My reputation is ruined."

"Not if you start a whole new life — as my wife. No one would ever need to know what happened."

"It doesn't matter."

"It does matter. I know what my own mother lived through, and I don't want that to happen to you."

"What happened to your mother?"

He saw the change in her expression and went on. "My mother wasn't married to my father. He used her and left her when he found out she was pregnant. She was ruined — alone and destitute until Padre Rodriguez took her in."

"It must have been terrible for her."

"It was. The padre was kind to us, but she never got over my father's betrayal. She was young, and she really believed that he loved her."

"Why didn't he marry her?"

"He was already married."

"Oh. It must have been hard for you, too."

Chase shrugged, not wanting to talk about what he'd endured. "It was difficult for both of us. There's no reason why you should have to live that way. Marry me, Faith."

"You're only feeling sorry for me." She

was not sure what to make of his proposal. "You don't really want to marry me."

"I wouldn't have ridden here to the mission if I didn't."

Faith fell silent as she considered her own situation and his offer. She was almost destitute and she was alone. There was no denying it. She had no idea how she was going to take care of herself, and Chase was, once again, offering to help her. She wondered why he cared. When she was a child, her mother had read her a story about a knight in shining armor rescuing a fair maiden. Faith didn't feel much like a fair maiden, but that badge on Chase's chest sure looked like armor to her right now.

Faith looked up at him, her gaze going over his strong features. His dark coloring was compelling and his blue eyes provided a vivid contrast. He met her gaze without fear, for he had nothing to hide.

Faith realized she knew little about him, but what little she did know, she admired. Chase McBride was a good man. He had saved her life. He had gotten her out of Dry Gulch, and he was offering to help her even more right now. In her desperate circumstances, she had little choice. She knew she'd be a fool to refuse his proposal.

"All right, Chase. I'll marry you, but . . ."

He waited to see what she was going to add.

"But I need some time before . . ." She wasn't quite sure how to broach the subject, afraid that he might grow angry at what she was about to suggest.

"Do you want it to be a marriage in name only for now?" He could see how nervous she was and guessed what was troubling her.

"Yes." She was relieved that he understood.

"We'll take our time and move slowly. That's the way it will stay until you decide you want it to be otherwise." His voice was warm.

"Thank you." She was a bit embarrassed.

"No one will have to know about your past and what you were forced to survive. You'll be my wife, under my protection. You'll be starting a whole new life — we'll be starting a whole new life — together."

Chapter Twelve

"Padre Rodriguez! Chase is here!"

The cry from the children went out as Chase and Faith rode through the gates of the mission grounds and reined in before the small house that served as the rectory. Inside, the tall, white-haired priest heard all the excitement and hurried out.

"Chase! What a blessing that you have come!" Padre Rodriguez said as he came to greet them.

Chase smiled and quickly dismounted to be embraced warmly by the older man. "It's good to see you, Padre."

"It's good to see you, too," Padre Rodriguez told him. "You are well?"

"Yes."

"Good, good." He glanced toward Faith, who had dismounted as well. He smiled in welcome. "You've brought company with you this time."

"Yes, this is Faith Bryant."

"It is wonderful to meet you."

"You, too, Padre." Faith loved him immediately. He was a man who personified loving acceptance, and his warmth was a nurturing balm to her spirit.

"We're here for a reason," Chase began quickly.

"There's no trouble, is there?" Padre Rodriguez was instantly worried. He knew how diligent Chase was in his job and hoped there was nothing serious going on in the area.

"No, there's no trouble. We just wanted to ask you a favor."

At the priest's questioning look, Chase finished.

"We would like you to marry us, Padre. I've asked Faith to be my wife and she's accepted. I wanted you to perform the ceremony."

"A wedding?" His eyes lit up at the news and his smile broadened. He had known Chase his whole life. He had watched him grow from a troubled youth into the proud, honorable man he was now. He was delighted that Chase had at last found happiness with this lovely young woman. "I would be honored to marry you," he told them.

"Thank you."

"You are getting yourself a fine man, young lady."

"I know," she answered, and it startled her to find that she meant it.

"Come, let's go inside and discuss what we must do," he invited.

They turned to go into the rectory just as a call rang out.

"Chase! Wait!"

A small, dark-haired boy not more than eight years old came charging through those gathered around, and headed straight toward Chase.

Chase saw him coming and, to Faith's surprise, knelt down and opened his arms to embrace him. "Luke! I've missed you. How are you?"

"Now that you're back, I'm fine, Chase," the youth told him. He drew back to look up at him, his eyes dancing with excitement. "I was hoping you'd come home soon."

"I had to come see you, didn't I?" Chase asked with real affection as he hugged the small boy.

"Want to see something? I got a pony now and — "

"Well, Luke, I — "

Faith spoke up quickly, seeing how much the boy wanted Chase's attention. "You go ahead. I'll be fine with Padre Rodriguez."

Chase was surprised, but he let Luke lead him away.

"You are a wise woman, my dear," the priest told her quietly as they watched Chase go.

She glanced at him in surprise.

"Luke is an orphan who lives here at the mission. He reminds me very much of Chase at that age. Chase spent a lot of time alone as a child. It is good that they found each other. Luke needs him and looks forward to his visits."

"Does Chase come to see you very often?" For some reason, the discovery surprised and pleased her.

"He is a busy man, but he comes to the mission whenever he can. He says it's because he misses me, but I think Luke is the real reason he visits so regularly."

Faith was intrigued by this side of Chase. She remembered the first time she'd seen him and how she'd thought he was a renegade. She saw no trace of that man now as she watched him disappear with Luke. There was nothing threatening about Chase.

"Come inside, my dear. We have much to talk about. How did you meet Chase?" he asked.

Faith followed Padre Rodriguez indoors,

wondering how much to tell him. She realized she would tell him the truth — up to a point.

He led her into the small room that served as his office. She seated herself in the chair before his desk as he sat down to face her.

"He saved me from a raiding party," she began, telling him all that had happened at the ranch, how she'd escaped and how Chase had brought her safely back to town. The ending, however, she romanticized a bit, for she didn't want the priest to know everything about their wedding "arrangement." "Chase didn't tell me until we were close to the mission that he wanted you to marry us. It was a surprise for me, too, but a wonderful one."

"I'm so sorry about your family. Is there anything I can do to help you?"

"Just pray, Padre. Chase has helped me through the most difficult times. I don't know where I would be without him."

"Chase is a good man — a strong man. Do you know where you're going from here? Does he plan to settle down in the area?"

"He has business in Sidewinder." She was surprised at the priest's change in expression at her mention of Sidewinder.

"Chase is going back to Sidewinder?" Padre Rodriguez asked, frowning darkly.

She wondered what he meant by "back."

"Yes. He said it was Ranger business."

"Oh."

"Why does that surprise you?"

"Has he spoken to you about his father?"

Faith told him about their conversation. "That's all he told me."

"I see. Well, I am surprised he's going anywhere near Sidewinder. Tom McBride's ranch, the Circle M, is near there."

"Chase never said a word about it."

"It could be that he has no plans to see his father and it really is Ranger business taking him there. McBride is a cold man, and I don't blame Chase for not wanting to have anything to do with him."

"Is he really that bad?"

"I met him only once during all the years Chase and his mother lived here."

"Chase never got to spend any time at all with his father?"

"No. McBride wanted nothing to do with either one of them. Only after I went to him at his ranch and spoke to him face-to-face did he agree to send money to help support Chase."

"Did Chase ever get to meet him?"

"The one and only time Chase ever sought him out was when he was sixteen and his mother was seriously ill. She was begging for Tom. She desperately wanted to see him one more time before she died. Chase didn't want to go. He didn't want to have to beg the man for anything, but because it was what his mother wanted, he rode to the Circle M by himself to ask his father to come and visit her."

"What happened?"

"Tom McBride refused and bodily threw Chase off the ranch. He told him never to come back again — that he had a 'real' family and didn't want him anywhere around."

Faith gasped at the cruelty of the story. "Poor Chase."

"It gets worse."

"What happened?"

"By the time Chase got back from the trip, his mother had passed away."

Faith paled visibly at his words. "He was so young."

"It was difficult for him, but he's grown into a fine man. He's doing a good job as a Ranger, and I'm most proud of him."

"I can see why," she agreed. "I was very blessed to have found Chase that night I escaped from the raiding party."

"Perhaps angels were guiding you to him," the priest suggested with a warm, knowing smile.

He encouraged her to talk about her family then. Only Chase's return interrupted their conversation.

"Has Luke been behaving himself for you, Padre?" Chase asked as he joined them.

"He's a fine boy. I'm proud of him, and I'm proud of you, too, for choosing such a wonderful woman to be your wife," he said. "I understand Faith found you — you didn't find her."

Chase laughed. "I see she told you how we met."

"It's a miracle that you were there that night, don't you think?" the priest remarked with great insight.

Chase had never thought of it that way before, but he realized now how fortunate they had been to find each other in the darkness of the wild Texas countryside. "Yes. Yes, it was, and that's the reason why we're here. Will you be able to marry us? Tonight? I know banns should be posted, but — "

"We can perform the ceremony as soon as you're ready," the priest told them, smiling at Chase's eagerness. "We won't worry about the banns. There are times when circumstances prevent the normal course of things. What's important is that you are married."

"Thanks."

"You will be staying the night here, won't you?"

"Yes. It'll be easier that way. Then we can head out first thing in the morning." Chase knew this wouldn't be a real wedding night for them, but it would be infinitely better spent in a real, comfortable bed rather than by the campfire in their bedrolls.

The priest was tempted to ask him about Sidewinder, but decided to wait until they had a moment alone.

"Would you like time to freshen up before the wedding?" he asked Faith.

"Please."

"Why don't I show you to a room so you can have some privacy? Shall we plan for the ceremony to begin in an hour?"

They agreed.

Padre Rodriguez showed them to a small but clean bedroom and left them alone. Years before, the workers who'd tended the fields and livestock had lived in these accommodations, but the quarters were mostly empty now, used only for travelers passing through in need of a haven.

Chase and Faith, suddenly very aware of each other, tried to ignore the bed that seemed to dominate the small room.

"Is there anything you need?" Chase asked, realizing Faith probably would like some time by herself to get ready.

"I would like to change into my clean blouse for the ceremony."

"I'll go get the saddlebags and be back in a few minutes."

Chase went to where they'd tied the horses, then took the saddlebags to Faith before leaving to walk around the grounds. The old building where he and his mother had lived now housed the orphans. It appeared to be in good repair and he was glad. He moved on to visit his mother's grave and was surprised to find Padre Rodriguez there.

"Were you waiting for me?" Chase asked, curious.

"I knew you would come," he answered easily.

"Is there something more we need to talk about?"

"When Faith and I were talking, she mentioned that you are going to Sidewinder when you leave here," the priest remarked, watching him closely to see his reaction. "I didn't bring it up earlier because I wanted to speak with you privately. She told me you were on Ranger business, but are you planning to see your father while you're there?"

Chase wasn't surprised that Faith had confided in the good priest. He had that effect on people. Everyone trusted him, and

151

everyone loved him. "I'm afraid I'm going to have to, but I haven't told Faith about it yet."

He quickly explained about the letter he'd received.

"I had no intention of going at first. I don't want anything to do with Tom McBride or his money, but when I learned the man who killed my friend was rumored to be hiding out around Sidewinder, I knew I had to go."

"It won't be easy for you, seeing your father again," Padre Rodriguez counseled.

Chase smiled, but it was a cold, cynical smile. "Yes it will, because this time I don't care."

Padre Rodriguez nodded thoughtfully. "I pray everything works out for you, and you find the man you're looking for. It will be difficult for Faith, being thrust into this situation so soon after your wedding. Will you be honest with her and explain what you're doing?"

"I'll have to. I don't want to deceive her in any way about what's going on."

"Good. Deception is never good in a marriage. The sooner you explain everything to her, the better. Openness and honesty are always best. You will make Faith a good husband, but I think you'll make your children

152

an even better father."

Guilt descended on Chase at the priest's words. Since theirs was to be a marriage in name only, there would be no children. Their marriage was nothing but a deception, but only he and Faith knew that.

To the world, they would be man and wife.

Chapter Thirteen

There was a small mirror hanging on the wall over the washstand, and Faith stood before it studying her reflection as best she could. Her hair looked as nice as it was going to, she supposed. She had brushed it out and was wearing it loose around her shoulders. There was no time to pin it up in a fancy style, and she wouldn't have wanted to — not dressed as she was.

Faith smiled at her mirror image, but it was a sad smile as she contemplated her "wedding dress" — a clean white blouse, a split leather riding skirt and boots. This wasn't quite what she'd dreamed of wearing for her wedding. She'd fancied herself coming down the aisle on her father's arm in a white bridal gown and veil, holding a beautiful bouquet, surrounded by friends and family. John was to have been waiting at the end of the aisle for her with the priest. They were going to be married and live happily ever after. She had talked with her mother often about the wedding plans, and they had both been excited about the upcoming nuptials.

"Oh, Mama," she whispered in a tear-choked voice as, once again, reality tore at her.

Memories of her parents besieged her. Her heart ached to have them with her, supporting her, loving her, but it wasn't to be.

This was her wedding day, but her family would not be there.

There would be no gown, no flowers.

Faith wondered if she would live happily ever after.

She thought of Chase then. He was the man who, at first sight, had terrified her, then rescued her from almost certain death. He had stayed with her and protected her. He was a man who knew what it was like to be alone in the world, and so could understand her loss. He was the man who was about to become her husband.

An image of Chase as she'd first seen him appeared in her mind — sitting before the campfire, his shirt off, looking untamed and savage and powerful. A shiver went through her at the memory of her first impression of him. In truth, Faith knew she hadn't been wrong. Chase was all those things, for he had fought off and defeated the raiding party, and he had saved her. She remembered the priest's words that maybe angels had guided her to him that night, and she thought now that perhaps they had.

A sense of peace settled over Faith as she suddenly realized she would much rather be marrying someone like Chase, dressed as she was in these clothes, than to have a big fancy wedding like she'd been planning and end up married to John.

Faith told herself that she was as ready as she would ever be. She was going to do what she had to do and pray that everything turned out all right.

Offering up a silent prayer, Faith left the room. She hadn't gone far when she met an elderly woman coming her way.

"I'm Cara," the old woman told her. "Padre Rodriguez sent me to bring you to the church. I see you're all ready to marry our Chase."

"Yes, I am," Faith told her with a smile. "Let's just hope Chase hasn't changed his mind."

"Chase would not do that," Cara said seriously. "He is a man of his word."

"Have you known him a long time?"

"Oh, yes. Since he was a boy. You are getting yourself a good man. He will make you proud," she said confidently.

"He already has," Faith found herself answering.

"He loves you very much." Cara looked up at her and smiled. "I hope you will be happy together."

"Thank you," she replied, surprised by the woman's observation. She wondered if the woman really knew him at all, for she was certain Chase didn't love her. She knew why Chase was marrying her. He was only marrying her because he felt sorry for her.

They made their way to the church and started to go in.

"Miss Faith?"

Faith turned to see the little boy, Luke, coming toward her. His hair had been wetted down and combed and parted, and he had changed into what she was sure were his church clothes. In his hand, he carried a small bouquet of wildflowers.

"These are for you," he said, handing them to her. "I picked them myself."

Faith looked down at the flowers, then lifted her gaze to Luke and saw the uncertainty in his eyes. "They're beautiful. That was very thoughtful of you. Thank you."

"You're welcome," he said quickly, smiling shyly up at her.

He opened the door to the church and held it as Faith and Cara went in, then followed them.

Faith stopped to look around at the beauty of San Raphael. It was cool inside, and darkly shadowed. Statues of several saints and the Blessed Mother adorned small alcoves along the walls, and incense perfumed the air. There was a feeling of peace, joy and serenity in the church. It felt heavenly to her.

At the front of the church before the altar, Faith could see Padre Rodriguez waiting for her with Chase by his side. There were people already seated in the pews, and she guessed they were friends of Chase from his youth. Cara and Luke quietly slipped into a pew near the back as she started forward, proudly carrying her wedding bouquet.

Faith fought back tears as she silently wished her father was beside her. She hoped her parents were there in spirit.

Forcing herself to concentrate on Chase, Faith studied him as he stood so tall and proud next to the priest. She thought he had never looked more handsome. He was watching her come up the aisle, his blue-eyed gaze intent upon her, his expression very serious. A shiver of awareness and sensual recognition went through her as she finally acknowledged that this man would soon be her husband.

Faith had only gone halfway up the aisle when Chase left the altar and walked toward her. He came to her side and took her arm to escort her the rest of the way to the front of the church. He cast her a sidelong glance, giving her a warm smile. She returned his smile, and together they faced the priest.

Padre Rodriguez smiled down at them both and welcomed them. Then he began to intone the ceremony. A short time later, he was concluding the final vows.

"Do you, Faith Bryant, take this man to be your lawful wedded husband, to have and to hold, in sickness and in health, for better or worse, richer or poorer, until death do you part?" He looked straight at Faith as he awaited her answer.

"I do," she responded in a soft voice.

"Do you, Chase McBride, take this woman to be your lawful wedded wife, to have and to hold, in sickness and in health, for better or worse, richer or poorer, until death do you part?" Padre Rodriguez asked Chase.

"I do." Chase did not hesitate and his answer was strong.

"I now pronounce you man and wife. What God has joined together, let no man put asunder." He looked from Chase to Faith. "You may kiss your bride."

Chase turned to Faith. After only a second's hesitation, he took her into his arms and kissed her, his mouth claiming hers with unerring accuracy.

Faith found she'd been holding her breath at the thought of kissing him. As his lips moved warmly over hers, she was stunned by the sensations that ignited within her. She was suddenly and completely aware of him as a man.

When Chase ended the kiss and moved slightly away from her, Faith found herself still staring up at him.

They were married.

Chase was her husband.

Chase was gazing down at Faith with equal intensity. He was just as surprised as she was by the feelings her kiss had aroused in him. He hadn't expected to feel anything, but the touch of her lips on his had brought a startling response deep within him. He'd deliberately moved away from her, needing to put some distance between them. She had just proven tempting to him — too tempting, and it shocked him.

Chase realized he should have avoided the kiss completely, but it was too late now. He had found out how wonderful it was to hold

Faith in his arms and taste the sweetness of her, and he'd liked it.

Awareness of their surroundings returned. Chase dragged his thoughts away from Faith's embrace and smiled at the priest. Then taking Faith's arm, he escorted her down the aisle, nodding to his friends as he went.

Those who'd attended followed them outside to wish them well.

"Luke, you did a good job with the flowers," Chase told the boy. He had enlisted Luke's help to find her a bouquet.

The boy beamed up at him and confided, "I think she liked them."

"I do, too." He winked at him.

"Miss Faith looked beautiful."

"Yes, she did," he agreed.

"Will you join me for dinner?" Padre Rodriguez invited the newlyweds. "Cara has prepared something special."

"Thank you, Padre," Chase said, glad to have a chance to visit with him for a while longer — and also glad that he wouldn't immediately be left alone with Faith in their small room. Theirs was to be a marriage in name only, he reminded himself sternly.

"Luke, you're coming, too, aren't you?" Chase asked him.

Luke looked respectfully up at the priest.

"Of course, Luke is coming with us! This is a celebration."

The dinner was delicious, and the company was delightful. Padre Rodriguez gave the blessing over the meal. Then as the food was served, he began to regale Faith with stories about Chase from his childhood. He recounted his adventures and misadventures, leaving Chase groaning.

"I've been trying to set a good example for Luke," Chase laughed with a rueful shake of his head. "I thought the past was past."

"It's good to let Luke know you're not perfect," Padre Rodriguez told him with a smile. "He worships you enough as it is."

"Chase isn't perfect?" Luke asked, deliberately looking shocked.

"Good boy," Chase told him, and they all laughed.

"That's right. You're a Ranger. That makes you very close to perfect, if you weren't already," Faith added, smiling at him with open warmth.

Their gazes met.

Chase went quiet, just staring at her. It was as if the entire world had suddenly faded away and the two of them were alone. Faith was beautiful. He realized then and there that he wanted her badly — more than he'd ever wanted another woman. He realized, too, that he couldn't have her — married or not. They had an agreement. He had to abide by it.

Faith had listened with interest to all the stories about Chase, and she found herself more and more intrigued by this man who was now her husband. He'd had a hard time growing up without a father, but he'd had good friends, loving friends like Padre Rodriguez who'd been a positive influence on him.

Distantly, Chase heard Padre Rodriguez bidding everyone good night. He tore his gaze away from Faith.

"Will I get to see you before you leave in the morning, Chase?" Luke asked as he appeared at his side.

"Of course," he promised. "And thanks for all your help."

"Yes," Faith put in as she joined them. "The flowers were perfect."

Luke grinned. "I'm glad."

The priest came to speak with them. "Will you join me for a drink, Chase?"

Chase glanced toward Faith, not sure whether he should leave her alone or not, but Cara was drawing her away.

"I'll be along shortly," he called to her.

She smiled back at him in understanding as Cara went with her to their room.

"Is there anything you need?" Cara asked. "I've arranged for a bath for you."

"Oh, thank you." Faith was delighted. The thought of soaking in a tub was wonderful.

"We want you to be perfect for your new husband when he comes to you tonight," she added with a knowing smile.

Faith almost stopped walking. *Perfect for her new husband.* The memory of his exciting kiss pulsed through her, and she pushed it away. She and Chase had an agreement. Theirs was a marriage in name only.

Cara saw the hesitation in her and hurried to reassure her. "Do not worry. He loves you. All will be fine."

"I know," Faith answered, but she felt unsure, especially after the way Chase had looked at her following their kiss. It had almost seemed as if he could see into her very soul and had known what she was feeling. It had unnerved her.

When they reached the room, Faith found that the bath was ready for her.

"Will you need anything else?" Cara asked.

"No. I appreciate all your kindness." Her words were heartfelt.

"It's good that you came here to be married. This is Chase's home."

Cara gave her a shy, knowing smile as she left.

Faith closed the door after her and turned to the tub. She would have liked to linger in the warm bath, but she knew she had to hurry. Chase would be returning to the room soon. It would be best if she was finished with her bath and already in bed when he got there.

Chapter Fourteen

Faith stripped off her clothes and sank down in the water. It felt wonderful. She lay back and closed her eyes in pure enjoyment. She allowed herself only a few minutes of leisure, then forced herself to start washing. When she finished, she toweled herself dry and slipped into the nightgown she'd bought in town.

Faith looked down at herself and gave a slight shake of her head as she turned back the covers on the bed. This was hardly the way she'd expected her wedding night to be. She'd thought she would be in a beautiful nightgown, waiting breathlessly for her husband to come to bed and make love to her. True, she was waiting for her husband and she was breathless — but it was because she was nervous, and the gown she was wearing was plain white cotton, hardly a garment meant to entice a man's desire.

The thought was foreign to her — enticing a man's desire. She'd shared a few kisses with John during their courtship, but she had never experienced anything beyond that. She truly was still an innocent. She'd been very lucky to have escaped from the renegades. Had she been held captive much longer, her innocence would have been brutally stolen from her.

A shudder wracked Faith as she remembered the looks on the Indians' faces when they'd torn her clothing. Even now, the memory of their hands upon her had the power to leave her trembling. She thanked God again that she'd gotten away and that she'd found Chase.

Chase — her husband —

Faith found herself smiling as she thought of him. She had enjoyed watching him with his friends at the mission and especially with Luke. It was obvious the boy thought the world of him, and she was sure the feeling was returned. Chase's manner seemed to change when he was with the boy. His expression seemed less guarded and he laughed more. She decided that she definitely liked to hear him laugh.

She'd liked his kiss, too.

That thought came out of nowhere, surprising Faith even as she accepted that it was true. She slipped into bed as she relived that moment when their vows had been sealed and his mouth claimed hers. She had never known a man's kiss could be so wonderful. Certainly, she'd never expected such tenderness from Chase.

Chase was a strong man, a virile man, a man of action. But that kiss had revealed a whole new side of him — and it was a side that she wanted to know more about.

Faith worried about what she should do if he came to her tonight and told her that he'd changed his mind about their agreement. She swallowed nervously at the thought.

She wondered if she'd be able to refuse him —

She wondered if she wanted to —

They had taken their vows before God. Chase was her husband.

Images of him played in her mind. She saw him as he'd looked that first night sitting alone in front of his campfire, looking like a warrior. She remembered, too, how it had felt when he'd captured her as she'd tried to steal his horse. He'd held her pinned against him to subdue her. His body had been hard-muscled and powerful. She had been helpless against his strength.

Faith knew now that Chase would never use his strength against her. Now he used it to protect her. He had been her champion against the renegades and against the drunks in town. He had even married her to give her a chance at a new life, a life untainted by her captivity. He had made her his wife — and then he'd kissed her.

Chase's kiss —

Its sweetness haunted her. The tempered passion of his embrace had spoken of desire barely reined. For a moment, Faith wondered what it would be like to experience the full joy of his lovemaking. She knew a little about what happened between a man and a woman, and as she tried to picture herself loving Chase — lying with him, caressing him, kissing him — she felt a heat rise deep within the womanly heart of her, and she quickly pushed the erotic thoughts away. She was the one who'd insisted on a marriage in name only.

Faith lay tensely in bed, awaiting her husband's coming.

Chase sat opposite Padre Rodriguez in his office, savoring a glass of whiskey. It had been some time since they'd had a chance to talk in private, and he was enjoying these moments with the man who had been the main guiding presence in his life.

"Your bride is a lovely woman," the priest remarked.

"I'm glad you approve."

"I do. I hope everything works out for you in Sidewinder. It's not going to be easy facing your father again."

"He means nothing to me," Chase said coldly. "Who knows? Maybe he'll be dead before I get there."

The priest shot him a look of disapproval. "Never stop praying for Tom McBride. There's always hope that he'll see the error of his ways. Just the fact that he's sent for you this way shows a real change of heart on his part."

"Maybe." Chase shrugged. "I wouldn't even be going if I hadn't heard that Sherwood was in the area. Bringing him in is the only thing I'm concerned about."

"Be careful," Padre Rodriguez cautioned. "Your job is a dangerous one, and you've got a wife now, you know."

"I know."

At Padre Rodriguez's mention of Faith, she drifted into Chase's thoughts. He envisioned her waiting for him now in their marriage bed. He quickly pushed the image from his mind.

"Where do you plan to settle down after

you've taken care of your business in Sidewinder?"

"I've still got my land near Los Santos." He honestly hadn't thought that far ahead. He was used to living day to day and only having to take care of himself. He realized now that that would have to change.

"Will you stay a Ranger?" the priest asked perceptively, knowing it would be hard for Chase to have a wife and family and keep his current way of life.

"I don't know. I hadn't thought about it." Chase was honest. It had never occurred to him when he'd proposed to Faith that he would have to give up his work. Maybe it would be better if he stayed a Ranger. It would keep him away from home and away from the temptation of her.

He drained his whiskey and got to his feet.

"I've kept you long enough from your beautiful bride," Padre Rodriguez told him with a smile. "It's your wedding night. Go along with you. I'll see you in the morning before you leave."

"Good night, Padre, and thank you for everything."

"My pleasure, Chase. It truly is my pleasure."

The older man stood and walked Chase to the door. He gave him a reassuring pat on

171

the back as he sent him off to his wife.

Chase started toward the room, but his pace was not quick. He would have stayed longer with the priest if he could have, but to linger any more would have seemed strange. As Padre had said, it was his wedding night. Faith was waiting for him.

Chase prided himself on being a confident man, but right now he was most uneasy, and that was an unusual emotion for him. He knew Faith had married him only because she had had no other choice. The fact that she'd wanted theirs to be a marriage in name only emphasized that. He would have to put the memory of her kiss out of his mind. He'd never expected it to be so sweet or so arousing.

Unbidden excitement stirred within Chase, and he fought it down with an effort. What passed between them tonight when he joined her in the bedroom would be no different from when they were on the trail. Their marriage didn't really change anything.

Chase reached the room and went in, closing and locking the door behind him. One lamp was burning low, and Faith was lying in the bed, her golden hair splayed out around her on her pillow. She had the covers drawn up to her chin, and her gaze was wide-eyed upon him. She looked alluring and innocent at the same time, and the heat of forbidden desire hit him full-force.

Damn! He'd never felt this way about a woman before!

He clenched his jaw against the powerful need that centered low and hard and hot within his body. His gaze lingered on her, tracing the swell of her breasts beneath the sheet. He swallowed tightly and tore his gaze away.

"You're back," she said quietly.

His expression grew dark, but she didn't know why.

"Yes."

"Is something wrong?" Faith asked, worried that he was angry about something.

"No. I was just trying to decide where to sleep. I'll take the floor."

"There's no need. There's plenty of room in the bed."

At her words, he shot her a surprised, questioning look.

Faith realized her implication and blushed.

Quickly she amended, "I mean, you can sleep on top of the covers, and I'll sleep beneath them. There's no reason for you to sleep on the hard floor." She shifted to the edge of the mattress, offering him most of the bed. She made sure to keep the covers up high. "I can scoot over farther, see? It's very comfortable."

Chase realized Faith was such an innocent that she had no idea how seductive she looked just then. She was his wife. She was inviting him to her bed, making room for him, offering him his rightful place beside her, and yet he wasn't to touch her. He bit back a growl of frustration. Sleeping across the campfire from her had been difficult, he wondered how much rest he was going to get lying next to her with only the thin blanket separating them.

He grunted his reply and began to unbutton his shirt. That done, he sat down in the chair and took off his boots and socks, then stood up and stripped off his shirt. He was very aware that her gaze was upon him, following his every move.

Faith was watching Chase undress, her gaze riveted on the hard, tanned expanse of his chest when he shed his shirt. It came to her in a revelation that Chase was a beautiful man. There wasn't an ounce of spare flesh upon him. He was hard and lean, and standing before her as he was, she couldn't take her eyes off of him.

And then he reached for his belt buckle and started to unfasten it, and her gaze dropped lower.

Though he still had his pants on, Faith could see proof of his arousal. She blushed and closed her eyes, unsure if he was really going to completely undress or not. She had never seen a naked man before, and she wasn't quite sure what she was supposed to do when he took off his pants.

Chase swore silently to himself and quickly turned away from her.

"You can relax. I'll keep them on."

He refastened his buckle and turned down the lamp. Desire was strong within him, but he controlled it.

"Good night," he growled as he stretched out beside her on top of the covers.

The softness of the bed felt good to him, but he didn't want to move for fear of accidentally touching Faith. He lay rigid, staring up at the ceiling. The ache in his body was powerful, and he hoped it would ease up enough so he could get some sleep. He needed the rest. Forgetfulness would be welcome.

"Good night," Faith whispered back, feeling it was finally safe to open her eyes again.

She kept her gaze on Chase's face, not wanting to risk looking any lower down his body. Though she knew he'd kept on his pants, there was something about the powerful, tanned width of his chest that lured her. She did so want to reach out and touch those hard muscles, so it was better not to tempt herself.

Feeling this way was foreign to Faith. She'd never been physically attracted to a man before. It was an awakening for her, and the power of her feelings frightened her, even as they drew her to him.

Faith lay quietly, studying Chase's profile in the dark shadows of the room, committing to memory his chiseled features and the lean line of his jaw.

She let her eyes drift shut, still feeling a bit nervous about lying next to him, yet at the same time, feeling safe because it was Chase beside her. Her lips curved in an innocently sensual smile as she thought about the proof of his arousal.

Did he really want her?

It surprised her to think that he did after he had so readily agreed to the marriage in name only. She had thought he didn't care about her in that way, that he had only married her to help her and not because he truly wanted her.

Cara's words about Chase loving her slipped into her thoughts and gave her pause. He didn't love her. He couldn't love her. They didn't really know each other that well yet. They were still practically strangers.

They'd only been together for a few days. She had known John for several years and had thought she loved him. She had thought she could marry John and be happy, but she'd been wrong — terribly wrong. How, then, could she be sure so quickly that she could find happiness with Chase?

The memory of his kiss was her answer.

Faith clutched the covers more tightly to her breast and closed her eyes again. She needed to go to sleep and stop thinking about how wonderful his kiss had been. Once it was morning, everything would be back to normal. The tension between them would be gone, and they'd be on their way to Sidewinder again.

Silently, though, Faith did offer up a prayer of thanks to God for bringing Chase into her life.

Chapter Fifteen

Sleep claimed Faith quickly, secure and comforted as she was by Chase's presence beside her.

Chase was not so lucky.

As the hours passed, he lay on the soft bed, every fiber of his being aware of Faith slumbering peacefully next to him.

He wanted rest.

He needed rest.

But the soft sound of her breathing and the sweet scent of her kept Chase awake and aware of her every move. He was tempted to turn toward her and watch her sleep, but he knew better. He was barely in control of his desire as it was. There was no reason to subject himself to such torment.

Chase knew he'd been far better served sleeping across the campfire from Faith. He wished he were there now.

Muttering to himself, Chase shifted

uncomfortably on the bed. He turned his thoughts to Sidewinder and what he was about to face when they arrived there. He supposed the first thing he had to do was seek out the attorney who'd written to him and find out exactly what was going on out at the Circle M.

Chase wasn't looking forward to any reunion with Tom McBride. Why the man wanted him at the Circle M after what had passed between them all those years ago was beyond Chase. Tom McBride had made his feelings clear when he'd thrown him off the ranch, and there had certainly been no reason for them to change in the time that had since passed. If Chase had cared, the letter might have interested him, but he didn't care. He hadn't since the day he'd been ordered to leave and never return.

Blackie Sherwood entered his thoughts, and Chase frowned in the darkness. Somehow, some way, he was going to track the outlaw down. If Sherwood had a connection with Malone there in Sidewinder, he was going to find it. Chase knew it would be best to start with the sheriff and find out exactly how Malone had been killed. Details from his captain had been sketchy. He didn't know a lot right now, but he intended to find out everything. If he was going to find the murderer, he had to be prepared.

Thoughts of work were easing the tension in his body, and Chase was glad. He felt some of the tightness in his shoulders relax. He would concentrate on his assignment and mentally plan what he was going to do. He shifted position, seeking more comfort, as he plotted his moves to find Sherwood.

It was a mistake.

Disturbed by his movements, Faith grew restless in her sleep. She stirred and threw off the covers. Then she flung one arm out wide across Chase's chest, her hand coming to rest dangerously near his belt buckle.

Chase's breath caught in his throat. Her hand on his flesh was a firebrand, searing him. He bit back a groan of pure sensual torment as he glanced over to see if Faith was awake. But she slept on, unaware of the chaos she was wreaking upon him.

Unable to help himself, Chase let his gaze sweep over her. She was wearing a plain white gown, and the pure simplicity of it enhanced her beauty. There were no frills or ruffles or satin bows. The gown softly molded to her slender body, revealing every sweet, lush curve. His gaze was hungry upon her, and the power of his need for her grew even more demanding.

Chase found he wanted to take Faith in

his arms and clasp her to him. He wanted to strip away the garment that shielded the perfection of her body from his view. He wanted to kiss her lips and then trace a path lower. He wanted to —

Chase brought himself up short as he almost started to reach for his sleeping wife. Sweat beaded his forehead. In frustration, he closed his eyes and tried to think of other things, but the feel of her hand resting so warmly on his stomach tied him in knots. It was almost his undoing.

Desperate for relief, he knew he had to move her hand. There was no other way he could lie there and keep his sanity. Ever so cautiously, he reached over to gently take her hand in his and shift her arm away from him.

At the contact, Faith sighed audibly, and, though she did draw her arm away, snuggled even closer to him. The movement unintentionally hiked her gown up higher, baring her long, lovely, shapely legs to his view.

Chase swallowed tightly and imagined himself caressing the silken length of her thighs before he moved between them and —

Lord, help me!

Chase offered up a prayer of true desperation as he tore his gaze away from Faith. He was in abject misery. His body was on fire with the power of his passion. He had never felt this way before, and it was taking all of his considerable willpower to control the need to be one with her.

And then he saw it.

His salvation!

The bathtub!

The tub was sitting in the corner of the room, and Chase was almost certain that the water in it would be good and cold by now.

If he was to stay in control of his nearly runaway passion, he knew what he had to do.

Slowly, without disturbing Faith, Chase edged away from her and slid from the bed. He wasted no time in shedding his pants. Gritting his teeth, Chase stepped into the tub and sank down into its icy embrace.

A muffled groan escaped Chase, and he gripped the sides of the tub tightly as the shock of the cold water knifed through him. It was torture — pure and simple. It took him a long minute to finally feel free of the driving passion that had possessed him. He stayed in the water a little longer, wanting to make sure he was in complete control before he tried to go back to bed.

Chase didn't understand why his desire

for Faith was so hard to control. He'd been tempted by women many times in his life, but Faith was the only one he'd ever wanted this badly.

Chase frowned at the thought, confused by his own feelings. One thing he knew for sure: Once they were on their way to Sidewinder, he was going back to sleeping across the campfire from her. It would be easier on him that way.

Chase stood up and stepped out of the tub. He quickly dried off and then donned his pants again. Cured of what had ailed him, calmer but weary, he moved back to the bedside. As he stood there, gazing down at Faith, she stirred and moved back onto her own side of the bed again. He looked gratefully heavenward before lowering himself onto the bed.

Exhaustion finally claimed him.

He slept.

Hours later, Faith awoke feeling rested and refreshed. She started to stretch and then realized where she was and who she was with. Her eyes flew open, and she saw Chase lying next to her. She was surprised that she'd slept so soundly. She watched him sleep and realized with a bit of surprise that she liked having him this close. Her gaze settled on his features, relaxed now in slumber.

Faith felt a great urge to move closer to him and press her lips to his, but she held back. Chase hadn't even wanted to kiss her when he'd come to bed. He'd shown no interest in her. She'd thought the kiss they'd shared at the ceremony had been something special, but obviously it hadn't meant anything to him.

Faith sighed and told herself that this was the way she'd wanted it. He had offered her his name and his protection. He hadn't offered her his love.

His love —

Did she want his love?

Did she love him?

Was it possible to love him after so short a time?

Faith wasn't certain, but she'd never felt this way before, not even with John. There was something very special about Chase. Had he stolen her heart so quickly?

As she lay there pondering the truth of her feelings for Chase, he woke up. She found herself staring into his eyes, mesmerized by the power of his regard. It almost seemed as if he could see into the very depths of her soul. A warmth spread through her. She smiled at him.

"Good morning," Chase said in a low, gruff morning voice.

To Faith, he sounded sexy and very, very male.

"Morning," she replied, watching and waiting to see what he would do next. She was completely disappointed when he quickly rolled away, distancing himself from her, and got up.

"We have a lot to do today, so we'd better get going," Chase told her. He kept his back to her as he went to the small washstand.

Opening his eyes to find Faith lying there watching him had jarred Chase. Not that it was unpleasant to have her at his side, but the feelings that had jolted through him were unsettling. He'd finally managed to get himself under control the night before; he wasn't going to get carried away again.

Faith was beautiful.

She was desirable.

She was his wife.

She was forbidden to him.

That was what he had to keep reminding himself. He was finding it quite easy to forget their agreement when he was caught up in the heat of wanting her.

Chase didn't allow himself to look at her again until he'd finished washing and dressing. He sat down to pull on his boots and glanced her way. When he did, he was in for a surprise. She'd risen from the bed and was standing there watching him, modestly holding the blanket wrapped around her. She looked almost like a goddess to him, swathed as she was in the blanket with her hair tumbling down around her shoulders in a mass of soft, golden curls.

"How soon do you want to leave?" Faith asked.

"Padre Rodriguez will want us to have breakfast with him, and he usually eats early. It's probably about six-thirty now."

"I'll hurry and dress."

"And I'll go tend to our horses and find Padre. Just come to the rectory when you're ready."

With that, Chase gathered up all his things and left the room. He needed to get away.

They met and breakfasted with Padre Rodriguez. They had just finished the meal when Cara came to tell them that Luke was waiting outside to speak with Chase. It was time for them to leave, so they all went out to see Luke together.

The boy was standing by the horses. His expression was stoic as Chase strode over to speak with him.

"You're leaving now?"

"Yes. Faith and I have to be in Sidewinder

186

soon," he explained.

"I could go with you," Luke suggested. "Padre Rodriguez would let me, I know."

Chase loved the boy, but knew he couldn't care for him and hunt down Sherwood, too. "I'm sorry, Luke, but I'm on an assignment. I'll be working on Ranger business when I'm there."

"Oh." It was a quiet, accepting, yet heartbroken reply.

"You are going to behave yourself while I'm gone, aren't you?"

"Yes, Chase. I'll be good."

"Of course he will," the priest put in as he joined them. "Luke's a big help to me around here."

"I'm proud of you," Chase told him.

Luke looked up at him adoringly. "You are?"

Chase clapped him on the back. "I am, and I'll be back to see you just as soon as I can arrange it."

"I'll be missing you, Chase," Luke said soberly, and then in a spontaneous move, he threw his arms around him and gave him a fierce hug.

Chase knelt down and returned the embrace with heartfelt force. "You be good, now."

"Yes, sir."

Chase stood, his expression revealing his sadness at leaving the boy again.

Faith saw the exchange and was touched by the obvious love they had for each other.

"I'm going to miss you, too," she told Luke. "And thank you again for the beautiful flowers yesterday."

Luke nodded as he stepped back and watched them mount up. Padre Rodriguez came to stand by his side and put a reassuring hand on his shoulder.

"Go with God," the priest told Chase and Faith. His gaze caught and held Chase's. He knew Chase was facing a difficult time, but he also knew that he was a strong, intelligent man. He would handle whatever troubles came his way.

"Thanks, Padre."

Chase lifted his hand in farewell as they rode from the mission.

Chapter Sixteen

Chase usually enjoyed riding cross-country. He liked the solitude and the peace of the untamed land, the sense of being as one with nature. This trek to Sidewinder with Faith, though, was changing his mind. Being in such close contact with Faith every minute of every hour of every day was taking its toll on him.

Chase supposed if he hadn't been so aware of her in a sensual way, the trip would have been long, but uneventful. As it was, each mile was proving torturous to him — especially when Faith rode ahead of him. His gaze was riveted on her. The way she sat her mount, the slender curve of her waist and the movement of her hips were driving him to distraction. She had plaited her hair and was wearing it in a single, thick braid down her back, and he found he longed to untangle the braid and run his fingers through the silken, golden length of it. He wanted to —

Jerking his thoughts back to reality, Chase forced himself to think about his upcoming "family reunion" just to distract himself and keep his desire under control. He went over in his mind what he knew about Tom McBride's family and tried to decide how he was going to deal with his two half-brothers and half-sister. Not that he really considered them family. As far as he was concerned, he had no family except for Faith, and even she didn't really count.

Or did she?

He frowned as he looked over at Faith, who was riding by his side. She noticed his glance and smiled at him. It was an honest smile, nothing contrived, simply a warm smile, and Chase's confusion mounted as he felt a stirring deep within him.

Was Faith his family now?

Did he have a "real" family?

He looked away, scowling as he tried to answer his own questions. Putting his heels to his horse's sides, he quickened their pace. They'd reach Sidewinder tomorrow. He had to concentrate on his assignment.

Faith wondered why Chase suddenly looked so fierce, but she didn't say anything. The pace he'd set for them didn't encourage conversation. It was obvious that something was bothering him, and she thought he was probably worried about tracking down the outlaw.

The long miles seemed almost endless, passing in a blur of heat and dust. It was getting late, and Faith knew they would have to stop to make camp soon.

The first night out, Faith had been surprised when Chase bedded down across the campfire from her. After sharing a bed the night before, she'd thought he would sleep right beside her, but he'd made a point of distancing himself from her. It was an unspoken rejection, but a rejection just the same. And it had hurt, no matter how much she'd tried to pretend to herself that it didn't.

Another half hour passed before Chase brought his horse close to hers.

"There's a small creek not too far ahead. We'll camp there for the night."

Faith smiled at the news of having a creek nearby. "Good. I need to take a bath."

Chase tensed at her statement and started off again, trying to ignore the vision her words brought to mind.

Faith followed his lead. The miles passed more quickly for her now as she anticipated taking a bath that night. It was going to feel real good to be clean again.

They reached the area where Chase wanted to camp, and Faith was delighted to see that the stream was running fresh and clear. There was even a small pool that looked deep enough to bathe in. Dismounting, they began to set up camp. She could hardly wait to finish eating dinner so she could take her bath.

Chase's mood was less than pleasant as they ate their dinner in relative silence. He could tell that Faith was eager to take a bath, and she'd be doing it practically right there in front of him. Then tomorrow when they reached town, he would have to deal with the McBrides. Between Faith and her bath and the thought of dealing with the McBrides, he was annoyed and restless.

Chase scowled blackly. He wished there was somewhere he could go to lose himself, but alone as they were on the range, he was trapped as fully as if he were chained. He had to stay close in case she needed him. He hoped to hell that she didn't. The farther he stayed away from her, the better.

Faith looked up to see his dark expression. She didn't know why he seemed so angry, but she figured a little time alone would do him good.

"I'm going to take my bath now. Is that all

right?" It was just starting to get dark, so she knew she had enough time to finish before night fell.

Chase grunted in response and turned to sit with his back to the stream.

Again, Faith couldn't imagine why he was so gruff all of a sudden. If his mood hadn't improved by the time she returned, she would ask him about it and try to draw out of him whatever was troubling him.

Gathering up her few personal things, Faith hurried down to the stream. She used some bushes for privacy and quickly undressed, then hurried into the water. The chill of the stream was refreshing after the long, hot day riding, and she gloried in its coolness. Glancing up toward the campsite, she saw Chase still sitting there with his back to her, his posture straight, almost rigid.

Faith grabbed up her soap and forgot about his bad mood for a few minutes. She hummed in delight to herself as she scrubbed off the trail dust and washed her hair. It was only a small stream, but it felt luxurious to her. With great regret, she finished bathing and stepped up out of the water. She toweled herself dry and quickly dressed again. Another glance at Chase proved that he hadn't moved in the time she'd been in the water. Faith didn't understand why she was disappointed.

Chase had been ready to scream in frustration as he listened to Faith singing in the water. In his mind, he could see her — her wet hair shimmering around her shoulders, her naked body glistening. It had taken all of his willpower to stay right where he was, facing away from the stream. The temptation to turn around and watch her had been powerful; even more powerful had been the need to throw off his clothes and join her in the water.

But he hadn't.

She wanted a marriage in name only.

Only when he heard her coming back to the campsite did Chase allow himself to relax a bit.

"That felt wonderful," Faith told him as she sat down beside him before the fire. She pulled her comb out of her saddlebag and began to work at the tangles in her wet hair.

Chase didn't respond, but shifted his position so he was facing the fire again.

Faith truly was concerned about how quiet he'd become. She knew they were going to arrive in Sidewinder tomorrow, and she figured he was probably thinking about what was to come. Not sure what to expect, she bravely decided to broach the subject, just to get him talking.

"Tomorrow is the big day," Faith said.

"Yes, it is," Chase said tersely.

"Do you have any idea what's going to happen once we get to Sidewinder?" she asked.

"Yes, and we need to talk about it." Chase realized she had no idea how complicated the situation was. He knew he couldn't avoid telling her the whole truth any longer. He had to explain to Faith exactly what they were going to be facing in Sidewinder. He glanced over at her to find her gaze upon him, her expression watchful and questioning.

"Is there something you haven't told me about?" Faith asked worriedly.

"There are some things I've kept from you that you need to know before we get there." He paused, gathering his thoughts, then went on. "I've already told you about my mother and how I was raised at the mission. What I didn't tell you is that I did go to see my father once about ten years ago — "

"Padre Rodriguez told me what happened to you on that visit," she admitted, wanting to be completely straightforward with him. "It must have been terrible for you."

"It was." Chase's voice was flat, all the pain and rejection of that time returning to haunt him. "Especially when I returned home and found out my mother had died while I was gone."

Faith saw a flicker of pain in his eyes, but it was quickly masked. Her heart ached for him. He had led such a lonely, solitary life. "Riding to the ranch to try to see him was a very brave thing for you to do."

He shrugged. "It would have been better if I'd stayed by my mother's side."

"You didn't know that at the time, though. You were only trying to please her."

"I know." Sadness shadowed his features. He had wanted to make his mother happy, and he'd failed.

Faith's heart ached as she stared at him, seeing his pain, wanting to ease it for him. Chase had been so young when all this had happened to him. It still amazed her that he had grown into such a fine man despite all the hardships he'd had to face.

"You don't have to have any contact with your father while we're in town, do you?"

"Yes," Chase answered in a flat voice. He dug in his saddlebag and pulled out the letter from Tom McBride's lawyer. "Here, read this. It'll explain everything to you."

She took the letter from him, and when she finished reading it, she looked up. "It sounds like your father wants to make

196

amends with you, like you have some kind of an inheritance coming to you."

"I don't want anything from Tom McBride, and I really don't want any kind of a relationship with him or his 'real' family. I'll play along and suffer through this reunion, but only because I can use it as my excuse for being in town while I try to find Sherwood. It'll be worth every miserable minute of being in the McBrides' company if, in the end, I can put Frank's killer behind bars."

"Why do you suppose your father wants you back now? Do you think he wants to make amends for the way he treated you before?"

"I don't know, and I don't care. It doesn't matter. If I hadn't heard that Sherwood might be in Sidewinder, I wouldn't even be making the trip."

"I understand." She was sympathetic. "What do you know about your father's family?"

"He was married to a woman named Emily, and they had two sons and a daughter. I don't know what happened to his wife, though, for according to that letter, it looks like he's married to somebody named Clare now."

"But you do have two brothers and a

sister," she remarked thoughtfully.

"They're nothing to me," Chase said harshly, and he meant it. The less he had to deal with any of them, the better.

"Have you ever met any of them?"

"I haven't wanted to, but I'll probably have to now."

"I never had any brothers or sisters."

"Me neither."

"You're very much a loner, aren't you?"

"Up until now, I have been."

For a moment, their gazes met.

"Having me along isn't going to cause you any trouble, is it?"

"No. In fact, your being with me will help. It makes it look like I really am in town on family business."

"Good. I wouldn't want to cause you any trouble while you're on an assignment."

"You won't. I'm just telling you all this about the McBrides so you know who we'll be seeing and why. I hope it won't take me long to get information on Sherwood. I don't want anyone in town to suspect the truth of why I'm there."

"If you find out where Sherwood is hiding out and go after him, what should I do? Should I wait for you in Sidewinder?"

"That'll be the best way to handle it. That way I'll know you're safe and protected in town, and I won't have to worry about you."

"Would you . . . worry about me?" Faith asked softly.

Chase looked at her in the firelight. "You're my wife, Faith."

His words struck at the very heart of her. Until that moment, she'd wondered if he'd given any thought to their wedding vows at all. Other than the one kiss they'd shared after the ceremony, Chase had kept his distance from her and made certain to give her all the privacy she needed — and more.

Now, as Faith stared at him, she saw a trace of some emotion in his eyes, yet she couldn't quite put a name to it. He looked cautious and at the same time hopeful, and she wondered if maybe —

Faith reached out to Chase and gently touched his cheek.

"Do you know what a good man you are, Chase McBride?" she asked quietly in a sweet whisper, her gaze warm upon him.

They were just a breath apart as she spoke, and she was glad. Suddenly she knew what she had to do.

She wanted to kiss him.

She needed to kiss him.

Ever so slowly, ever so gently, she leaned toward him and pressed her lips to his.

Chapter Seventeen

Chase held himself completely still as Faith unexpectedly kissed him. He didn't want this to happen. He had to stop her now, before he had to take a bath himself — and not just for the sake of cleanliness. The trouble was, he didn't know if the stream water was as cold as the bathtub water had been back at the mission. Chase allowed himself to enjoy her kiss for a moment longer, then took her by her upper arms and held her slightly away from him.

"Don't, Faith," Chase ordered in a hoarse voice.

"Why not?"

"Don't do anything you're going to regret," he warned her.

She looked up at him, her eyes wide. "Kiss me, Chase. I won't regret it."

"You don't know what you're asking."

"Yes, I do. Please, Chase."

He could no more have denied her than he could have stopped breathing.

She was his wife —

Chase's mouth captured Faith's in a powerful possession. He kissed her deeply, tasting of her sweetness and her passion. Taking her in his arms, he crushed her to his chest. He lay back upon his bedroll, taking her with him, and Faith gasped at the contact between them, so intimate. She fit against him perfectly, her breasts and hips pressed tightly to him. The proof of his need was hard against her, and she reveled in the knowledge that he did desire her.

"Chase — " Faith whispered his name and threw her head back as his lips left hers to explore the arch of her throat.

Excitement tingled through her as he pressed hot kisses down her neck. He paused only long enough to unbutton the blouse she wore. Brushing aside the garment, he pressed his lips to the pale flesh bared to his gaze. Her chemise still shielded the crests of her breasts from his caresses, but that didn't stop him from exploring them through the garment. At the hot touch of his mouth, Faith arched upward, offering herself to him, wanting more, needing more from him. She held his head to her, then shrugged the straps of her chemise from her

201

shoulders and completely bared her breasts to his kisses.

Chase's caresses ignited fires within her. She had never been so aroused, and she surrendered willingly to his lovemaking, helping him, encouraging him.

Chase was a driven man. Never before in his life had he wanted to possess a woman the way he wanted Faith. He worked at helping her undress. He needed to see her beauty, wanted her unclothed before him so he could explore each and every glorious inch of her body with his kisses and caresses. She was everything he'd ever wanted in a woman and more. She was innocence and beauty and passion and excitement.

He wanted to be one with her.

He was driven by a need as old as time itself to bury himself deep within the womanly heart of her and make her his in all ways, to claim her for his own.

For just an instant, sanity cautioned Chase and doubts assailed him. For all his life, he'd controlled his passion and desire. He'd saved himself, holding back, fearful of fathering a child who would be doomed to suffer as he had throughout his childhood. But no longer.

Faith was his wife.

Chase pushed the doubts aside.

He drew away from her only long enough to help her slip out of the last of her clothes. Neither of them spoke, but their gazes were locked as she tore away the barriers that separated them. When at last she lay naked before him, Chase's gaze went hungrily over her, taking in the fullness of her breasts, then moving lower to visually caress the flatness of her stomach and the heart of her womanly passion. Her legs were long and shapely, and he longed to have them wrapped around his waist as he made her his own.

Chase ached with the power of his need. The heat within him was so fierce that he felt as if he were about to explode. He moved to take her in his arms again, but she stopped him.

"No — I want to see you, too."

He wasted no time taking off his clothes.

Faith's gaze was hungry upon him, visually caressing the sleek power of his chest and shoulders as he threw off his shirt. She couldn't wait to touch him. She grew a bit nervous as he stripped off his pants, and her first sight of him unclothed made her catch her breath. She realized he was a magnificent specimen of a man, but she was unsure what to do next.

Chase could see the uncertainty in her

eyes as he came back to her, and for a moment he feared she might have changed her mind. When Faith welcomed him with open arms and a warm, sensuous smile, his fears were erased.

"You're beautiful," she whispered as she drew him close, cherishing the hardness of his male beauty against her.

They surrendered to the heat of their need. Their passion overpowered them, driving all thoughts of harsh reality from their minds. They only knew that they wanted each other as desperately as they needed to breathe, and they wouldn't stop until their hunger for one another had been sated.

Faith and Chase wanted to go slowly, to cherish each moment of their time together, but their passion would not let them.

Desire had no logic.

Desire demanded action.

They responded, clinging together, kissing and caressing. It was physical, this thing between them, and they gave in to its power. With each touch and kiss, their need grew until there could be no delaying any longer.

They had to be one.

Chase had never known such bliss. He'd never realized how beautiful making love could be. He realized, too, though, that it wasn't just any woman who could excite him this way and make him lose control. It was only Faith. He wanted to lose himself in her innocence and loveliness. He could bury himself in the depths of her and never regret it for a moment. He rolled with her, bringing Faith beneath him.

Faith wanted Chase even closer. Mindless in her arousal, her instincts urged her to open to him, and she did. Chase came to her, fitting himself to her in love's most intimate embrace. He shuddered, reveling in the intimacy of his position. Faith reached down and led him to the heat of her. A shudder wracked him as ever so slowly he began to thrust forward. He gave a guttural groan as he sought the depths of her womanhood and breached the proof of her innocence. He made her his for all time. The feelings that surged through him were powerful. He had never known such intimacy or such ecstasy. It was as if they had been made only for each other.

Faith caught her breath as Chase possessed her. She went still as she came to understand the joining of their bodies and the power of their union. He had conquered her, yet she had claimed him. Then there was no more time to think as Chase's lips sought hers in a passionate kiss that swept away anything but the need to seek love's ultimate pleasure.

Instincts drove them. Chase began to move in love's age-old rhythm, and Faith met him in that sensual dance.

They were one.

The glory of their love drove them on in the pursuit of passion's peak. It burst upon them in a moment of pure rapture as they strained together. Their hearts spiraled to heaven and beyond as they clung together, awed by the power of what had passed between them.

Afterward, they lay wrapped in each other's arms, glorying in the beauty of their loving. Neither spoke, fearful of ruining the moment — so special, so thrilling.

Chase moved first, starting to shift away from her, but she held him tight, wanting him to stay close. He surrendered to her unspoken demand, their bodies still joined as one. He reached out only to pull the blanket up over them. His mouth sought hers in a gentle kiss; then, together, they rested.

Chase's thoughts were chaotic as he lay with Faith. He had never known that loving someone could be so perfect, but it had been. The moment he'd moved within her had been soul-shattering for him. He'd been lost, caught up by the fierce emotions that had driven him. There had been no turning back. He had sought and given pleasure, and it had been ecstasy for him.

So this was what it was all about —

Chase was now even more glad that he had waited for this moment — for Faith. Their lovemaking had been perfect.

As he lay in the circle of her arms, reliving in his mind their loving, he was shocked when he felt the need stirring strongly within him to have her again.

Faith was lying with her eyes closed, marveling at the sensations that had flooded through her. She had never known that making love could be so sweet. When Chase began to move within her again, she was surprised. She'd had no idea that he would want her again so soon, but she wasn't about to object.

Reaching up to embrace him, she caressed his back and shoulders, then let her hands drift lower to his waist and hips. She urged him on, gasping in delight as he quickened his pace. His hands were upon her, arousing her, tracing paths of fire over her sensitive flesh, and she responded ardently, a slave to the passion he had awakened within her.

They came together in a crescendo of excitement, kissing and caressing each other until that rapturous moment when reality disappeared and it was only the two of them, soaring to the heights of ecstasy.

Exhausted, they fell blissfully asleep in each other's arms.

Chase awoke first just before sunup. During his sleep, he had moved to Faith's side and he lay there now, reflecting on all that had happened. All night he had been caught up in the heat of his passion. Now with the cold light of dawn, sanity was returning, and with it came the reality of what he'd done.

There was no denying that he'd enjoyed every minute of making love to Faith, but he couldn't help wondering why she had suddenly wanted him. She had been the one who just a few days before had insisted on a marriage in name only. Then last night after he'd told her about what was going to happen in Sidewinder, suddenly she'd wanted to make love to him.

A sickening feeling overcame him as he recalled just when she'd reached out to him. He wondered if she had only come to him because she'd been feeling sorry for him. And if that was the truth, he damned well didn't want her sympathy.

His life was just fine as it was. He didn't need a wife who pitied him for any reason. He was perfectly happy.

Memories of losing himself in her embrace taunted him then, and he amended his "perfectly happy" thought. He was as happy as he could be. He cared about Faith, but he didn't want her sympathy.

Chase found himself wondering what he did want from her, and right now he wasn't sure. Certainly, he'd enjoyed the sex they'd shared. He'd enjoyed the intimacy he'd had with her, for he had never known that feeling before.

Warmth stole through him as he thought again about the night just past, and he knew he had to get up and get away from Faith. She was far too tempting lying beside him, asleep and vulnerable as she was. He had only to reach out to her and they would both be lost for hours to come. He couldn't let that happen. Not again, so soon. He had to come to grips with what had passed between them the night before. He had a lot of soul-searching to do.

Instead, he was going to concentrate on Ranger business.

Today they would reach Sidewinder.

It was time for him to start tracking down his man.

Faith came awake slowly with a smile on her lips, but it quickly faded when she

realized that Chase was no longer by her
side. She opened her eyes and looked
around, wondering where he'd gone, and
spotted him down at the water's edge. Clad
only in his pants and boots, he was standing
tall and proud with his back to her. Her
heartbeat quickened at the sight of him. He
was darkly tanned and corded with muscle,
and she recalled all too vividly how much
she'd enjoyed touching him last night. She
almost called out to him, but decided
against it, wanting just to relax and enjoy the
view for a moment.

Faith's smile returned as she realized how
much Chase looked like a warrior this
morning. A few days ago, the thought would
have terrified her, but today it sent a thrill
coursing through her. He had proven himself to be a warrior — but he was her warrior. He was her defender. He had fought
battles for her and he had kept her safe. He
was her husband.

A myriad of emotions assailed Faith as she
faced the reality of what had passed between
them throughout the long, dark hours of the
night. The power of her emotions frightened
her, for she wasn't sure how to deal with
them. She had made love to Chase, and it
had been wonderful, but did she dare let it
continue? Had last night been one single

night of weakness for them? Would the light of the new day make them both realize that they'd made a terrible mistake in giving in to their desire?

Chase turned toward her then as if sensing she was awake, and across the distance their gazes met. His expression was guarded and remote. Faith knew immediately that despite their hours of loving, nothing had really changed between them.

A part of her was glad, for she knew that if Chase touched her again all would be lost. Yet even as she accepted that their lovemaking shouldn't have happened, a part of her cried out for the warmth and tenderness of the man who had loved her through the long, dark hours of the night.

Chapter Eighteen

Sidewinder.

Chase looked around as he rode slowly down the main street of the town with Faith by his side. Things had changed since he was last there. The town had grown some, but it seemed the main growth had been in saloons. The place looked rough and more than a little untamed. It was mid-afternoon now, and he was glad it was still daylight. From the look of things, it would get pretty wild around town at night.

Glancing at Faith, Chase could see how tense she'd become. He wanted to reassure her, but he couldn't. Sidewinder matched its name — it was low-down and dangerous.

Ahead, Chase spotted the sign for the Sidewinder Hotel and reined in before it.

"Here we are," he said grimly as he dismounted and tied up his horse.

"Welcome home," Faith said as she, too,

climbed down and took care of her mount.

Chase gave a harsh half laugh at her remark. "This has never been my home."

"I knew there was something I liked about you," she returned, managing to smile at him.

"Let's see about getting us a room."

He led the way inside, ignoring the open stares they were getting from the townsfolk. He had deliberately taken off his Ranger badge. The fewer people who knew what he did for a living, the better. If Sherwood was anywhere around, Chase wanted to catch him unawares.

The hotel was run-down but seemed clean as they crossed to the desk. A young man was sitting behind it. He glanced up, saw Chase, and went back to what he was doing.

"My wife and I need a room," Chase said.

"We don't have any vacancies," the clerk answered without even bothering to look at him again.

Chase stiffened, long accustomed to such treatment. "The name's — "

"I don't care what your name is or anything else about you. We don't have any rooms for your kind, so just go on and get out of here."

"Why — " Faith was outraged at the way

213

the man was treating Chase. "Where's the manager?"

"He's busy."

"I'd like to speak with him," she demanded.

Chase was watching her, admiring her spirit, but he had dealt with this man's kind before and knew what they were up against. "We can leave, Faith. It's all right."

"We will not — "

A bespectacled old man came out of a backroom behind the desk. He frowned as he looked from his clerk to Chase and Faith. "Afternoon, folks," he said. "I'm Damon Winters, the manager. Is there a problem? Can I help you?"

"We'd like a room, but your clerk said you didn't have any." Chase took charge before Faith could say anything.

"I'm afraid he's mistaken. We do have one vacancy."

"Good. We'll take it. I don't know how long we'll be staying, though."

"Fine." Winters turned the registry around for him.

Chase signed in and pushed it back across the desk to the manager. He noted the startled expression that overcame Winters when he read the entry.

"You're really a McBride?" Winters looked

up at him sharply. He could tell that the stranger had Indian blood in him, so his name was a real shock.

Chase nodded tersely as their gazes met. Winters saw the blue eyes and had no doubt about who the stranger's father was.

"Well, I'll be," he muttered, turning away and busily picking out a key for the couple. He wondered how old Tom had managed to come up with a son who looked like this, but then he knew all about Tom McBride and his whoring ways. Nothing surprised him much anymore. Hell, everybody in town knew how Tom used to be before he'd married Clare. "Here. It's room twelve. Go upstairs and straight down the hall. Your room is the last door on the right."

There had been more rooms available than that one, but Winters figured he'd put them in the back where nobody would see them.

"Thanks." Chase took the key and led the way up the stairs.

"Friendly place, Sidewinder," Faith said wryly as she followed him.

"It's only going to get better."

The room was small and minimally furnished. There was a double bed, a chair and a washstand. Chase stared at the bed for a minute, then quickly looked away.

215

Memories of the last time he'd shared a real bed with her assailed him. He didn't have time for those kinds of thoughts right now. He had business to take care of, and besides there wasn't space enough for a bathtub of cold water in the small room.

"Will you be all right alone for a while?" Chase asked.

"I should be. Why?"

"I need to talk to the law here in town and see if anyone has heard anything about Sherwood." He went to his saddlebags and took out the letter.

"I hope everything goes well for you."

"So do I. When I get back, we'll go see the lawyer, Hanes. Be ready." He strode from the room without looking at her.

She stared after him for only a moment, feeling dismissed, then went to lock herself in. Turning back, she found herself staring at the bed and thinking about the night to come. It would be interesting, that was for sure. Faith set about getting as comfortable as she could.

Chase had seen the sheriff's office on his ride into town, and he strode toward it, eager to start hunting down Blackie Sherwood. He wanted the killer to pay for his crime. Chase opened the door to the office and went in to find a rather heavyset man sitting behind the desk.

Sheriff Paul Scott looked up as he heard the door open. He suspiciously eyed the stranger who walked in, wondering what he wanted. The man looked like a half-breed, and Scott didn't particularly like dealing with his kind. He knew they could mean trouble.

"Something I can do for you?" Scott asked, leaning back in his chair. His expression was anything but welcoming.

"The name's Chase McBride. I'm a Ranger, and I wanted to talk with you about Terry Malone."

"You're a Ranger?" He was skeptical.

"That's right." Chase took out his badge and showed it to the sheriff.

"Why ain't you wearing it?" Scott pressed.

"That's part of what I have to talk with you about. Can I sit down?"

The lawman gestured toward the chair in front of his desk, his manner more respectful now. "You said your name's McBride. You any relation to Tom?"

"Yes, but that's not why I'm here. This is Ranger business."

Scott nodded. "What can I help you with?"

"I understand that Terry Malone was killed in a shoot-out here?"

"That's right, it happened down at the Roundup Saloon. He was a bad one, that Malone."

"His friend Blackie Sherwood is, too. He's the only one left of the gang that robbed the bank in Foster and then killed a Ranger at their hideout afterward. Headquarters thought he might be heading this way since Malone showed up here. I was wondering if you'd seen him or heard anything about him being in the area."

"No. Not a word. It's been quiet, and I like it that way."

"Have you been looking for Sherwood?"

"Hell, no," Scott answered quickly. "I don't go looking for trouble. It finds me often enough as it is."

"Well, if you hear anything about him, let me know. I'm staying at the hotel for now."

"You going to be in town long?"

"I don't know. I've got some business to take care of out at the Circle M."

"I tell you who you should talk to." At Chase's interested look, the sheriff went on. "Tanner McBride. I don't know what relation he is to you, but he was involved with that gang. Hell, there were even rumors that he was in on the bank robbery. The law there arrested him, but they had to let him go 'cause they couldn't prove anything. Of course, that night at the Roundup, Tanner was one of the ones shooting at Malone. He hit him, too. Damned if he didn't."

"What was going on at the Roundup?"

"Miss Callie's brother had been killed in that bank robbery. She came here looking for Tanner to try to find Malone. When she heard that Malone was in the saloon, she got a gun and went in after him. Damned fool woman! She shoulda come an' got me!"

"Maybe she thought there wasn't time. She sounds brave to me."

"Brave or stupid. Take your pick!" the sheriff sneered. "It was ugly that day — Miss Callie getting shot and all. But Malone got his, and that's what mattered."

"Who's Miss Callie?"

"You ain't too close related to the McBrides, are you?" he remarked snidely. "She's Tanner's wife. They just got married not too long ago, soon as she'd recovered from her wound."

Chase was tempted to tell him what he thought about being related to the McBrides, but he controlled the urge. "I've been out of touch a few years."

"Old Tom isn't looking too good, from what I hear. I guess it's good you showed up for a visit. What are you? A cousin or nephew or something?"

Chase looked at the sheriff levelly as he answered, "I'm Tom McBride's son."

"Well, I'll be damned." The sheriff was shocked by this news. He hadn't heard any rumors about a bastard son. He wondered how Tanner was going to feel when he found out about him.

"I'd appreciate it if you would keep our conversation here private. The fewer people who know I'm a Ranger, the better." Chase sounded authoritative and in command.

Sheriff Scott quickly agreed. "Whatever you say."

"I appreciate your help," Chase told him as he stood up.

"If I hear anything, I'll let you know."

Chase walked outside, realizing that he was very much on his own in his search for Sherwood. The lawman in Sidewinder was going to be of little use to him.

He headed for the hotel. It was time to get Faith and meet with the lawyer.

Faith had grown restless as she awaited Chase's return. There was only so much she could do to pass the time in the small room all by herself with nothing to read. She'd grown more and more tense about Chase's situation as she paced about. It was obvious from his serious manner that he was concerned. She wasn't sure if he was worried about tracking down Sherwood or his upcoming reunion with his family. Neither one was going to be easy for him. She was lost in thought when she heard someone try the doorknob.

"Faith — I'm back."

At the sound of his voice, Faith hurried to unlock the door and let him in.

"How did your meeting go?" she asked.

"The sheriff hadn't heard anything about Sherwood," he answered.

"So he was no help at all to you?"

"I did learn one very interesting thing. Tanner McBride was involved with this gang at one time. When Malone was shot here in town at the Roundup Saloon, Tanner was one of the men doing the shooting." He quickly filled her in on everything the sheriff had told him.

"Do you think Tanner may have an idea about where Sherwood is hiding out?"

"I don't know, but I intend to find out just as quickly as I can. Are you ready to go meet the lawyer?"

"Yes."

"Let's go, then. It's getting a little late and I want to catch him before he closes his office for the day."

As they left the hotel, Chase looked even more serious as he spoke to her. "Just in case this Hanes asks us how we met and when we married, I think we need to agree on the right way to tell him about our past and our courtship — without lying."

Faith realized he was once again protecting her, and a wave of warmth went through her. "Thank you."

"For what?"

"For trying to protect me again."

"We're starting a whole new life. There's no reason to dwell on the past."

"Well," Faith began, touched by his words and by his sentiment, "I think it's safe to say that we've been married less than a year and that when we met we knew right away that we were meant to be together. That's not a lie, either. I mean, who else would we have been with but each other out in the middle of nowhere like that?" She was grinning at him conspiratorially.

"I like the way you think, woman," he said, returning her grin. "But how did we meet?"

"How about, fate just threw us together? That we met one dark, starry night and have been almost inseparable ever since?"

"That sounds good. I don't know if anyone will even ask, but just in case, I want to be ready."

"This isn't going to be easy for you, is it?"

"I'm not looking forward to it, if that's what you mean, but I have to do it. Especially now that I know Tanner might have some information on Sherwood. I've got to talk to him and see what I can find out. The sheriff said he was out at the Circle M, so one way or another, it looks like we will be going to the ranch soon." Inwardly, he grimaced at the thought.

"I'm sorry, Chase."

"For what?" He frowned.

"I can only imagine what it's going to be like for you when you go back to the ranch."

He shrugged. He was ready for whatever was to come. Tom McBride might think he'd shown up for an inheritance, but Chase knew that he was using McBride for his own purposes. He truly didn't want or need anything the man had. He was here to avenge Frank. That was all.

They reached the lawyer's office. The sign on the door read WILLIAM BENTON HANES, ESQ. Chase opened and held the door for Faith to enter.

The office was small and sparsely furnished, but everything was neat and in order. Bill Hanes was sitting behind his desk hard at work when he heard the door open. He looked up as they came inside. He had never seen the woman before. He wondered who she was. The man who came in behind her was tall and dark. There seemed something familiar about him, although he couldn't say exactly what. But when he made eye contact with the stranger, a jolt of instant recognition shot through him. He knew without a doubt that he was facing Chase McBride.

"Good afternoon, folks. I'm William Hanes. Can I help you with anything?"

"I'm Chase McBride, and this is my wife, Faith. I'm here in response to the letter you sent me," Chase told him, watching the lawyer closely, trying to judge his reaction.

Bill Hanes came around from behind his desk to shake hands with Chase. "It's a pleasure to meet you, Mr. McBride — Mrs. McBride. Please have a seat."

He waved them into the chairs before his desk, then went to sit down, too.

"I am glad you're here. When I hadn't heard anything back from you, I didn't know if my letter had reached you or not."

"I was out on an assignment. My captain held it for me at our headquarters."

"Good, good. Your father will be very pleased to know you're here."

Chase was hard-pressed to keep his expression bland and his words civil as he responded, "Somehow, I find that very hard to believe."

"It's true. He wants his family around him now. It's important to him."

Chase gave a rueful shake of his head. "Why now, after all these years?"

"As I mentioned in the letter, Tom McBride is dying. It is his wish to bring his family together."

Chase was cool as he looked at the attorney. "The last time I was here, I was told I wasn't part of his family."

"Time and circumstances have a way of changing a man," Bill explained slowly. He couldn't reveal anything more. "Can you make the trip out to the Circle M in the morning? I can send word tonight that you're here, and we can reunite you with your father first thing tomorrow."

"That will be fine," Chase answered. "Do you need anything else from me?"

"No, not at this time. Where are you staying while you're here in town?"

"We're at the hotel."

"If there are any changes, I'll contact you there. Otherwise, shall we plan to meet here around nine o'clock? We'll all ride together in my carriage, if that's all right with you?"

"We'll be ready."

Chapter Nineteen

Bill Hanes sat at his desk, staring down at the missive he'd just written to Tom.

> Dear Tom,
> This is to inform you that your son has arrived. I will be accompanying him and his wife out to the ranch tomorrow morning.
> I remain,
> William Benton Hanes, Esq.

That would do it. Tom would know just by his phrasing who was there.

He gave a shake of his head as he imagined the scene to come when Chase faced Clare for the first time — not to mention the rest of the family. If nothing else, it was going to be interesting.

Sealing the letter in an envelope, Bill went down to the stable to hire one of the hands to ride out to the Circle M and deliver it for him.

Clare saw the rider coming in and wondered who'd be paying them a visit so late in the day. It was almost dark. She went out on the porch to greet the newcomer.

"Evening, Mrs. McBride. I'm Ed Taylor. Mr. Hanes hired me to deliver this to your husband."

"Thank you." She came down the steps to take the envelope from him so he wouldn't have to dismount, but his next words stopped her.

"Oh, no, ma'am. I can't give it to you. Mr. Hanes said I was to see that your husband got it himself."

Clare's expression had been welcoming. She was a beautiful woman and was used to getting her way with men. At his refusal, the look in her eyes turned icy.

"My husband is sick in bed. I'll make sure he gets it right away," she promised.

"I'm sorry, Mrs. McBride, but Mr. Hanes said I was to give it only to your husband, that I should hand it to him myself."

Clare gritted her teeth against the rage that threatened. She was coming to despise Bill Hanes. She managed a tight smile as she spoke. "Come on inside, then. I'm not sure

Tom's awake, but I can wake him for you. He's not well, you know, and he needs all the rest he can get."

She was hoping the man would feel sorry for Tom and agree to turn over the letter to her.

"Thanks." Ed dismounted and prepared to follow her indoors.

Thwarted, and more than a little curious about the content of the lawyer's letter, Clare led the way inside and up the stairs to her husband's room. She made it a point to stay as far away from Tom as she could during these last days. His condition disgusted her, so she had the mute cook Tiny tend to his needs.

Tom's illness irritated Clare. It had been dragging on for what seemed like forever. Deep in her heart, she wished Tom would just die and get it over with. He had been a robust man, but the illness had ravaged him. She could barely stand to look at him anymore. The only good thing about the whole situation was that she'd discovered what a good actress she was. Tom had no idea about the truth of her feelings. She had him completely fooled, and she was proud of it.

"Wait here just a moment while I make sure my husband is up to your visit," Clare told the messenger.

Forcing herself to smile again, Clare quietly opened Tom's bedroom door and went in. She was disgusted at the thought of even having to speak with Tom, but she disguised her emotions with practiced ease.

"Tom, darling," she said softly as she stared down at the emaciated man lying unmoving on the bed.

Tom heard her voice and opened his eyes. He pinned her with his blue-eyed regard. "What?"

The quickness of his response belied the weakness of his body. His flesh was failing him, but his mind was as sharp as ever.

"Bill Hanes has sent a messenger with a letter for you. He's here now and wants to see you."

Tom nodded, the look in his eyes keen. "Get him in here!" He waved one hand weakly toward the door. "What are you waiting for? There might be news!"

Clare opened the door to admit the young man.

"What is it? What have you got there?" Tom demanded.

Ed stared down at the dying man, trying not to let his shock show as he handed over the lawyer's letter. He'd never seen anybody in this condition before. Tom McBride was nothing but skin and bones. He bore little resemblance to the man Ed remembered seeing around town. Tom's eyes, bright and penetrating as they were, seemed sunken in his skull. When Tom grabbed the letter from his hand, Ed stepped back quickly.

"Go on. Get out of here," Tom ordered, seeing the man's reaction to his condition.

"I'm supposed to wait for an answer from you," Ed said awkwardly.

Tom gave a grunt as he quickly tore open the envelope. He pulled out the letter and read it once, then reread it just to be sure.

"I'll be damned," he said, glancing over at Clare. "He's back, and he's married."

"Who is?" Clare asked cautiously.

"My son. Bill's bringing him out here tomorrow morning." He looked back at the lawyer's messenger. "Tell Bill Hanes that I'll be ready and waiting for him."

"Yes, sir."

Ed started from the sickroom and Clare went after him to show him out.

"Clare!" Tom called to her.

She looked back. "Yes, Tom?"

"Come back up here after he's gone. I want to talk to you."

"Yes, dear," she promised as she left.

She saw Ed from the house, then delayed as long as she could before going back upstairs. She was trying to gain control of her runaway emotions before she faced Tom.

She was furious.

Obviously, Tom's oldest son Stone had returned.

She wanted to scream her frustration.

She wanted to rant and rage.

Instead, she controlled her fury with an effort and prepared herself to speak with her husband. She was smiling by the time she went back into his room. She had found one thing to improve her mood: If nothing else, Stone's return would draw Tanner, Tom's youngest son, back up to the house, and she would enjoy that very much.

Clare had been in love with Tanner for years now, and even though he'd married recently, she still believed the day would come when she would have him for her own. She would act the part expected of her with Stone, but her thoughts would be only on Tanner and how she was going to get him in her bed.

Clare entered Tom's room to find him lying there with his eyes closed, looking like a corpse. The only disappointing thing to Clare was that she could see the rise and fall of his chest. She cursed her luck. He was still alive.

"Yes, Tom. Did you need something else?" she asked.

His eyes opened and he pinned her with a sharp stare. "Send word to Tanner. Tell him I want him here at the house tomorrow morning. Tell him his brother's coming home."

"I'll let him know." She hid her delighted smile at his order.

Tanner couldn't ignore or refuse his father's request. Tanner would be there in the morning.

Clare only hoped that he left his wife, Callie, back at the line shack where they were living. They'd refused to move into the main house after their wedding and had been staying there instead. It was quite a ride out to the cabin, and Clare resented that he was so far away from her. She wanted him close. She wanted to be able to see him — to spend time with him — to touch him —

"I need to rest," Tom said in a weakened voice as he closed his eyes again.

Clare's thoughts were jerked back from what she wanted to do to Tanner once she got him in her bed, to reality. She was forced to push her erotic thoughts of her husband's youngest son from her mind. "I'll be back to check on you later."

Clare left the room to seek out her servant Manuelo. She would send him to Tanner with the message from his father. Then she would wait in great anticipation for Tanner's arrival.

After Faith and Chase left Bill Hanes's office, they stopped to eat at a small restaurant in town. It was beginning to get dark when they finished and started back to the hotel.

The sounds of drunken rowdiness coming from the saloons echoed through the streets of town. Chase wondered why the sheriff didn't keep a tighter rein on things. Then he remembered their earlier conversation, and he had his answer. *Sheriff Scott didn't go looking for trouble.* No doubt, Chase thought, he just holed up in his office and didn't come out unless somebody got shot. Chase was real glad that he wasn't the law in this town. It wouldn't be easy cleaning up this place.

As they neared the hotel, two drunks staggered out of a nearby saloon. They were shouting vile threats at each other. Suddenly one of them went for his gun. Gunfire erupted. Shots were fired wildly.

Chase reacted instinctively. He grabbed Faith and pinned her against the side of a building, shielding her body from harm with his.

The impact of having her in his arms was sudden and powerful. Chase was stunned.

All day long, he'd forced himself to concentrate on business, but now, having her so close, his desire returned in a heated rush.

Faith fit perfectly against him, and Chase remembered vividly how ecstasy had been his when he'd lost himself deep within her. A fire of need flamed to life within him, and he gritted his teeth as he tried to fight it down. He was relieved for more than one reason when the shooting finally stopped, and he could move away from her.

Chase still kept Faith behind him as he turned to see what had happened. One of the drunken gunfighters was down, but not dead. The other was standing over him, still shouting at him. Men from the saloon came running out to see what had happened and broke the two apart. Chase forced himself to step even farther away from Faith.

"Is it over?" she asked in a nervous voice.

"Yes."

"Thank you," Faith said, her eyes wide as she gazed up at Chase. Being held so close to his heart had sent a shiver of awareness through her, and she longed to go back into his arms and stay there. Only in the haven of his embrace did she feel safe from the ugliness of the world. He was so strong and handsome, and she was beginning to realize that she wanted to be close to him — always.

"You're all right, aren't you?"

"I'm fine," he answered more tersely than he'd meant to as he fought against the primal need that was destroying his self-control and rendering him mindless.

Faith knew nothing of his tormented thoughts. She heard just the coldness in his voice and believed that Chase had held her only to protect her from the gunfire. That was all.

"Is the sheriff going to come and see about all the shooting?"

"Eventually, but I don't think Sheriff Scott is too worried about his town getting shot up this way. It probably happens every night, from the look of things."

"Do you think he's hiding?"

"I wouldn't doubt it. He's outnumbered, and he knows it." Chase wasn't sure whether to feel sorry for the lawman or to fault him for the sorry state of the town.

Chase knew it was safe now, and he shepherded Faith toward the hotel. As he walked by her side he kept wondering how he was going to keep his hands off of her tonight. Just being close to her for that short period of time had been painful for him. He knew he couldn't lie beside her in the hotel room bed tonight without making love to her. She was beauty and innocence and everything he'd ever wanted in a woman, but she didn't want him.

The thought of watching Faith get ready for bed was pure misery for him, so Chase decided to avoid it. He ushered her upstairs to their room, then unlocked and held the door for her to enter, but did not go in himself.

Faith wondered at his action, but said nothing as she stepped into the room.

"I'm going down to that saloon for a drink. You'll be safe here while I'm gone. Just lock the door."

She was hurt, feeling almost as if he were abandoning her. She turned back to look at him and saw his closed expression. "Aren't you tired?"

Chase was exhausted, but he wasn't about to admit it. "No. That saloon is so wild, I think I may be able to find something out about Sherwood's whereabouts. So go on to bed. I'll probably be back late."

He left, closing the door, then waited outside in the hallway until he heard Faith turn the lock. Satisfied that she was safe from others, and from himself, Chase made his way to the saloon.

The sign out front of the building said Roundup Saloon. Chase guessed it was the busiest place in town, judging from what the sheriff had told him and from what he'd witnessed earlier. He went in and walked up to the bar, ignoring the stares he got from the patrons. He was used to it, and he didn't care.

"Whiskey," Chase ordered.

The bartender quickly placed a glass before him and poured him a healthy splash.

"Thanks." Chase pushed money across the bar.

"New in town?" Barney, the bartender, asked.

"Just got in today."

"Well, welcome to Sidewinder," he said before moving off to wait on someone else.

Chase took a deep swallow of the potent liquor. He didn't need a lot, but he needed enough to dull the ache within him. He had thought controlling his sexual urges had been difficult before, but now that he'd known the power of loving Faith, it was practically impossible. Being one with her had been his heaven — and now abstinence was proving to be his hell.

"What are ya doin' servin' his kind in here?" a sloppy, hostile drunk demanded of the barkeep.

Barney knew the man and wanted to ignore him. "I don't know what you mean by 'his kind,' Isaac."

"He's a damned breed, Barney! Can't you tell?"

"The only thing I noticed was that he paid me for his drink. Now, how about I buy you one?"

"But he's a filthy half-breed and you're servin' him!" Isaac protested loudly, drawing a lot of attention to himself.

Chase wanted to ignore him but knew better than to turn his back on a drunk who was looking for trouble.

"That's right, Isaac. I did serve him. He isn't causing me any trouble. You are."

"I want him out of here!" Isaac charged at Chase in a blind, drunken attack.

Chase turned, drew his gun and hit the drunk on the head, knocking him out before he could land a blow. He collapsed at Chase's feet.

Chase had reacted so quickly and so efficiently that even the piano player stopped playing to stare at him.

"Damn!" Barney muttered, then added, "Somebody get Isaac out of here!"

Chase slowly, deliberately holstered his gun, then turned back to the bar and drained his drink.

"You want another one? On the house?" Barney offered.

Chase nodded.

Barney refilled his glass. "Good job handling Isaac."

"I didn't want any trouble. I only wanted a drink."

"Enjoy." Barney smiled at him with respect, wondering who this man was.

Two very pretty saloon girls came to stand by Chase, one on either side of him.

"Evening," they said in unison.

"Ladies," Chase returned.

"I'm Marcy."

"And I'm Rita. Do you want to have some fun tonight?" the girl invited knowingly.

Chase took another drink, then smiled down at both of them. "I appreciate the offer, but I'm a married man."

"That don't stop the other men here," Marcy said, her gaze hot upon him.

"Sorry, ladies. Good night."

He nodded to the barkeep and quit the saloon, deciding that he'd already attracted too much attention to be able to get information about Sherwood.

Marcy and Rita watched him go, then turned to Barney.

"Who was that?" they both asked, intrigued and excited by the handsome stranger.

"I don't know. He never said his name."

"Well, I sure hope he comes back soon,"

Marcy said longingly.

"Hell," Rita put in with a coarse laugh, "I hope he has a big fight with his wife. The lucky girl."

They all joined her laughter, then turned back to business.

It had surprised Chase that he wasn't the least bit tempted by the saloon girls' offers. They were pretty women.

But there was only one woman he wanted — and that was Faith.

Chase went back to the hotel and quietly let himself into the room. He'd been hoping that Faith would be asleep when he returned, and she was. As carefully as he could, he undressed, except for his pants, and lay down on top of the covers.

Beside him, Faith slept quietly.

What he didn't know was that earlier she'd softly called his name in her sleep.

Chapter Twenty

Chase had never suffered physical torture in his life, but between spending the night lying in bed with Faith and not touching her and riding to the Circle M just now to confront Tom McBride, it certainly felt like it. As each mile passed and they drew closer and closer to the man who had fathered him, Chase's mood grew ever blacker. If he'd been given a list of places he didn't want to be and hell was number one, the Circle M would have been a very close second. Only knowing that Tanner McBride was somehow connected to the man responsible for Frank's death kept him from riding away.

But there could be no leaving.

He would stay — for Frank.

Chase was going to handle his reunion with Tom McBride just like he handled everything in his life — head on.

Chase didn't know how he was going to

handle Faith, though. The night by the campfire when they'd made love, she had come to him. Since then, she had made no move toward him and he was convinced that she regretted what had passed between them.

"So, tell me about the McBrides," Chase ventured, finally asking the question he'd been avoiding all morning.

"How much do you know?" Bill returned.

"Not a lot. I know my father has two legitimate sons and a daughter, and his wife was named Emily, I believe. But in your letter you mentioned that he's now married to someone named Clare."

"Yes. Emily died tragically some time ago and Tom has remarried. Tanner is the younger of his two sons; he's come back home already."

"Why did he ever leave?" Chase couldn't imagine why anyone would want to go away from a spread as nice as the Circle M. He was puzzled by the sudden strained look that crossed the lawyer's face.

"There was some trouble — "

"With the law?" he asked.

"No, no, nothing like that. Tanner and his father had a falling out of sorts after Emily died, so Tanner left. He's been gone for quite a while now. Lauren and Stone, too."

Chase was amazed that Tom had alienated his own children. "Anything I need to know about?"

Again Bill looked uncomfortable. "I guess you'll hear about everything eventually anyway." He paused to gather his thoughts. "Tom always believed that Tanner was responsible for Emily's death. She was killed in a wagon accident. Tanner was supposed to have fixed the wheel, but when it fell off, Emily was thrown from the wagon and died. To this day, Tanner swears he made the repairs. It wasn't long after the funeral that Tom married Clare, and things got complicated. Tanner took off first. Lauren went back East, and then Stone left, too."

"So the old man's been alone for a while," Chase said thoughtfully.

"Clare's with him. When he found out he was dying, he had me send out the letters. He doesn't look good, and Doc Pierce doesn't know how much longer he can hold out. It's hard seeing a man who was as big and strong as Tom waste away like this."

Chase remembered his own reaction to the news that Tom McBride was dying and wondered how his other children were reacting. He was going to find out shortly.

"Will Lauren and Stone come back?"

"I'm not sure yet. I've had correspondence from Lauren, but I haven't heard anything from Stone."

"There's still time left."

"Yes, according to the letter, but I don't know if Tom can hold out that long."

Faith had been listening in silence to their conversation, and was slowly coming to understand just who and what they'd be facing when they reached the ranch house.

"What's his wife Clare like?" she asked. She'd noticed that the lawyer hadn't said much about her. She wasn't sure if it was deliberate or accidental.

Again Bill hesitated, as if measuring his response. "Clare is a very beautiful woman," he began, carefully picking his words. "She's much younger than Tom."

Faith thought she understood. "I take it she's the reason his children left."

"Not that they were children anymore. Stone and Tanner were full-grown men. Lauren was still young at the time — I think she was fourteen. She went away to school," Bill finished. "Chase, I think you and Stone are about the same age."

Chase nodded in response. Despite all the information the lawyer had just given him, none of it explained why the old man wanted him there. Why did Tom McBride suddenly want a relationship with his bastard son? The son he'd denied all these years?

"There's the ranch house," Bill said as they topped a low rise. The buildings were spread out in the valley before them.

The main house itself was a two-story structure. There were a barn, bunkhouse, corral and other outbuildings. The Circle M seemed to be a well-maintained and successful ranch.

Chase stared down at the scene below, fighting down the anger that welled up within him. He told himself that what had happened long ago no longer mattered.

This wasn't about his mother.

This was about finding Blackie Sherwood.

Chase girded himself for the confrontation to come.

"Let's go see my father," Chase said in a cold but determined voice.

Clare was sitting alone in the parlor, looking out the window toward the corral, hoping to get a glimpse of Tanner, who was working the horses. He had ridden in earlier that morning in response to his father's command.

Clare had been thrilled when she'd seen Tanner riding up alone.

She'd deliberately unbuttoned one more button at her bodice. She wanted to entice him. She wanted to lure him to her and make him forget all about the little bitch he'd married.

And then Callie came riding in behind him.

Fury had filled Clare, and she was still angry now, over an hour later. She wanted Tanner, and some day, some way, she planned to have him all to herself. It was just a matter of time.

Clare was lost deep in thought as she pictured Tanner coming to her willingly. Then she caught sight of the carriage coming. Forcing her thoughts back to reality, she stood and went out on the porch to welcome Stone home.

As the carriage approached, she recognized Bill Hanes. She smiled grimly, disgusted that Stone had chosen to come back. She wanted them all to stay away — except Tanner. She didn't want to have to share the inheritance she'd earned by marrying Tom and bedding him all these years.

The carriage drew closer, and Clare was soon frowning. Try as she might, she did not recognize the man who was riding with the lawyer. She wondered if Stone could have changed that much. True, the man had dark hair like Stone, but there was something different about him.

Clare's expression darkened even more as she waited. Her gaze never left them as the carriage rolled up to the house and stopped.

"Good morning, Clare," Bill Hanes said as he climbed down and tied up the carriage horse.

"Where's Stone?" Clare demanded without preamble or small talk. Her gaze was riveted on the man and woman in the carriage. She didn't know either of them. The man was a complete stranger to her. She was certain she'd never seen him before in her life, for if she had, she would have remembered him. His black hair, high cheekbones and dark tan spoke of Indian blood, and there seemed to be an almost dangerous edge to him. The woman beside him she dismissed as unimportant.

"Stone's not here, Clare," Bill explained patiently. "I haven't heard from him yet."

"But in your letter — you said Tom's son was here," she said accusingly.

"And he is," Bill answered quietly. "Clare, this is Tom's son Chase and his wife Faith."

"Excuse me?" Clare went pale at the news, her eyes flashing fire. There were only Tanner and Stone and Lauren to share the wealth with — not this stranger, too! This had to be some terrible kind of mistake or perhaps a sick joke on the lawyer's part. She stared at the man he'd called Chase and then realized — those eyes — those blue eyes —

"This is Tom's son," Bill repeated slowly and calmly.

She whirled around to face him, her hands on her hips, fury etched in her expression. "You mean to tell me that Tom slept with a squaw?" The thought made Clare's flesh crawl and she wanted to scream.

Chase had heard enough. He could tolerate most insults, but no one insulted his mother.

"He didn't sleep with just any squaw. He slept with my mother." Chase paused for effect and then added, "And now he's sleeping with you."

Clare gasped in complete and utter shock at his comment.

Before she could recover and attack again, Bill took control.

"If you'll excuse us, Clare, Chase has come to see Tom. We'll go on in."

He quickly ushered Chase and Faith inside, leaving Clare standing on the porch, ready to kill. She glared at them as they moved past her. They ignored her.

"Faith, it will be best if you wait in the parlor. Tom only wants to see Chase," Bill directed, showing her into the room. "I'll be back down in a few minutes. Make yourself comfortable."

"Thanks," Faith answered, taking a seat. She hoped he was a man of his word and would return quickly. She certainly didn't want to be left alone with Clare. What little she'd seen of the woman had convinced her that she wanted nothing to do with her.

Bill returned to Chase and started up the stairs to the second floor, expecting him to follow. But Chase remained standing in the hall, his gaze locked on the study.

Painful memories of the way he'd been treated the one and only other time he'd been there were assailing Chase. The study door was open and he could easily see inside. Nothing seemed to have changed since last he was there. He hadn't been welcome then, and Clare had just made it quite clear that he wasn't welcome now. Instead of being hurt by the rejection, Chase felt an immense sense of satisfaction knowing that he didn't care if he was welcome or not. It truly didn't matter to him if his father liked him.

Chase followed the lawyer up the steps.

Bill stopped before a closed bedroom door and then knocked quietly.

"Tom?" he called softly.

"Who is it?" came a gruff response from inside.

"It's Bill Hanes. I've got someone here I think you want to see," he said.

He opened the door and stepped inside to find Tom lying in bed looking even worse than the last time he'd seen him. Tom was a shadow of his former self. Even so, he had a look of almost feverish excitement in his eyes as he faced Bill.

"He came?" Tom demanded eagerly. "Chase is here?"

"Yes, he is," Bill said. "Are you ready to see him?"

"Damn right I am," he answered, looking toward the door.

"I'll get him for you," Bill said, opening the door to admit Chase.

Tom lay in his bed watching the door, anxious to know what was happening out in the hallway. Bill accompanied Chase when he stepped into the sickroom.

"Thanks, Bill," Tom said, dismissing him without a thought. "I need some time alone with Chase. Can you go get Tanner for me? It's time he met his brother."

"I'll get him up to the house as fast as I

can," the lawyer promised, quickly absenting himself from the room.

Tom gazed at his son, and he smiled a victorious, taunting smile. Chase looked as though he'd grown into a fine man. Tom knew about his involvement with the Rangers and wondered how that had come about.

"It's good you showed up," Tom said sarcastically. "It should be quite a celebration."

"What celebration?" Chase countered. Sick though he might be, Tom McBride was still not a man to trust.

"My funeral, of course. You're going to be damned glad to be rid of me once I'm gone, aren't you?"

"I didn't give a damn if you were alive, so why would I care if you're dead?"

"Then why are you here?" Tom challenged.

"Curiosity," Chase said, shrugging. "But what I don't understand is why you sent for me. The last time I was here, you threw me off the ranch and ordered me never to come back. Why did you have this sudden change of heart after all these years?"

Tom managed a hoarse bark of laughter. "All in good time, son. All in good time."

At his use of the term "son," Chase stiff-

251

ened. His father had never acknowledged him until this moment, and now it was a little late.

Tom's tone was shrewd as he continued, "You'll see when your other brother and sister show up."

"You mean the rest of your 'real' children, don't you?"

"They're related to you, whether you like it or not. Now, go on. Get out of here," Tom ordered tersely.

"You don't have to throw me out this time. I'm glad to go." He headed for the door.

"There is one more thing, Chase."

"What?" He stopped and looked back.

"You know the terms I set forth in the letter. You are required to stay here, with me, on the Circle M."

Chase gave a slow, disgusted shake of his head. "I'm married. My wife's with me."

"Fine. Bring her, too. There's plenty of room here in the main house."

The thought of living under the same roof with Tom and his wife Clare wasn't the least bit appealing. "Why do you want me here now?"

"I already told you — all in good time. You'll find out when the others arrive." Tom was feeling quite smug, believing that he was controlling Chase, and it showed.

"I hope they get here fast." And Chase meant it. The only thing that kept him from walking away and never looking back was knowing that Tanner was there. He needed information from him to go after Sherwood.

Chapter Twenty-one

Faith looked up as Clare joined her in the parlor. Having already had a taste of her "hospitality," she was ready. She fully understood now what Bill Hanes had been trying to tell them on the ride to the ranch.

"You have a lovely home," Faith said, trying to be civil.

"You would think so, if you're used to living in a tepee." Clare was in a murderous rage. She was determined to make this woman and her bastard husband as miserable as she could.

Faith continued to smile at her. "Actually, I've never been in a tepee, have you?"

Clare ignored her comment as she sat in the chair opposite her and went on. "Faith, you seem like a nice young woman. I'm finding it hard to believe that you would marry a half-breed bastard." She gave an exaggerated shudder. "Whatever possessed you to do it?"

"We were meant to be together. It was fate."

"Fate? It sounds more like a curse or a nightmare," she sneered. "And you actually let him touch you? He's a half-breed, for God's sake! I can't imagine — just the thought is repulsive to me."

Anger was growing within Faith, but she used it wisely, matching Clare insult for insult. "I'm sure Chase would find the thought of touching you repulsive, too."

"Why, you — !"

Bill came down the stairs just then and interrupted the exchange. "I've got to find Tanner. Tom wants him here at the house to meet Chase. Do you happen to know where he is?"

"He was down at the corral a few minutes ago," Clare offered.

Bill looked from Clare to Faith and sensed the tension between them, but said nothing more. He went to find Tanner, leaving the women alone again.

Clare turned a cold-eyed glare on Faith, all pretense falling away. "We'll never have to worry about him touching me, because I won't let him anywhere near me."

"You're right, we'll never have to worry about that because he wouldn't be interested." Faith's smile was real. "I love my husband, and he loves me. He wouldn't even think of looking at you in that way, let alone touching you. You are, after all, his father's wife."

Clare was not used to being attacked this way. She was still young and beautiful, even if she was married to a dried-up, dying old man. Her anger increased as she faced this slut who'd married Tom's bastard son and now wanted part of her inheritance. She wanted to throw Faith out of the house, but knew she couldn't.

The shock of learning that Tom had fathered a half-breed son was still eating at Clare. She found herself wondering how many other bastard McBrides there were out in the world and how many of them would be showing up at the ranch to stake a claim on what should have been hers. It had been infuriating enough to know that she had to share the ranch with Tanner, Stone and Lauren, but the addition of another son to that list outraged her all the more. She wished Tom would just drop dead right now. She couldn't guarantee how she was going to react to him the next time she had to go into his room. The thought of his bedding a squaw made her flesh crawl.

Her thoughts were filled with hatred.

Then the front door opened.

And Tanner walked in.

Clare rose to her feet. Her heartbeat quickened at the sight of him. *Tanner* — He was tall and dark-haired and the most compelling man she'd ever seen, and she wanted him desperately. Bill Hanes was right behind him and so was his wife Callie, so Clare had to take care not to let her feelings for Tanner show. She wanted to strip off his clothes, throw him down right there in the front hall and make love to him endlessly, but she couldn't — not yet. Her day was coming, though, she was certain of it. Tanner would be hers.

"Bill said Pa wanted me up here at the house," Tanner said as he moved toward the parlor. He wanted to take care of whatever his father needed and leave the house again as quickly as he could. The less time he spent around his stepmother, the better. It was then that Tanner saw the young woman sitting on the sofa. "Hello," he said politely.

Faith smiled up at him, noting the blue eyes that marked him unmistakably as Chase's kin. "You must be Tanner."

"Yes, and you're . . . ?"

"Faith. Faith McBride," she answered.

"You're Stone's wife?"

"No, I'm — "

257

At that moment, Chase started down the stairs. Tanner turned at the sound of his descent to see who was coming.

He expected Stone.

He was prepared to see Stone.

Chase paused for a moment, then descended the rest of the way to the hall. He walked toward the man he knew must be Tanner and put his hand out. "Tanner, I'm Chase McBride."

Tanner stared at him openly. "You came."

"You knew about me?" Chase was surprised.

"I saw you that day when you and Pa had the fight, but I wasn't quite sure just who you were at first. It took me a while to figure it out." Tanner reached out and took his hand in a firm handshake. "That was a long time ago, though. It's good to finally meet you."

Their gazes met and locked as each man assessed the other, and neither found the other wanting.

"This is my wife, Faith," Chase said.

"And this is my Callie," Tanner responded.

The two women greeted each other.

Clare stood by, her temper barely under control. In her mind, she sneered, *My Callie.*

"You knew about him?" Clare blurted out

to Tanner in a disgusted voice, her tone accusing. "And you didn't tell me?"

"It wasn't my place, Clare. If you want to be mad at anybody, be mad at Pa or Bill, here. He knew about Chase, too, but he didn't say anything."

Clare turned her hostile glare on the lawyer.

"Attorney-client privilege, Clare." Bill defended himself easily, not worried about her anger. She was not his client; Tom was.

"And how many more *wonderful* surprises do you have in store for me?" she asked sarcastically.

"I'm not at liberty to say."

"We've got a lot of catching up to do," Tanner told Chase with a grin.

"There should be time. I just found out that Faith and I are supposed to live here on the ranch." Chase glanced toward Faith, hating to break the news to her this way. He was glad, though, that he was going to be thrown together with Tanner. There were a lot of questions he needed to ask him about Malone and Sherwood.

"Here? Tom wants you to stay here?" Clare shrieked.

"That's what he said." Chase shrugged. "We can move in tomorrow. You're already living here, aren't you, Tanner?"

Clare fell silent in utter shock and disbelief. How could Tom do this to her? He wanted to bring a filthy half-breed into her house!

"We're living up at a line shack."

"Why aren't you staying here at the main house?" Chase asked. He'd hoped to have Tanner close by so he could talk with him easily.

Tanner looked at Callie. "We just got married and wanted some privacy. If Pa needs us, he can send one of the men up to the shack. I'm usually working with Jeb and the hands anyway, so I'm around pretty regular. Now that you're here, you can help us, too."

"That'll be fine. I'm looking forward to getting to know you better," Chase said, and it was no lie.

"Me, too," Tanner said. Then he turned to his stepmother. "Clare, tell Tiny that we'll all be staying for dinner."

"I don't have room for everybody," she refused coolly. She wanted the damned half-breed out of her house — the sooner, the better.

"Don't worry. I'll go tell Jeb to have the hands eat down at the bunkhouse tonight. We'll have plenty of room then," he said, dismissing her concern without a second thought.

Being thwarted by Tanner didn't help Clare's mood. "I'm going up to speak with your father."

Leaving them behind, she moved toward the steps. Her back was rigid as she struggled to maintain her dignity in the face of such adversity. It wasn't easy.

Tom had been expecting Clare, and he wasn't disappointed. As exhausted as he was from his meeting with Chase, he still was ready when she came barging into his room. She didn't even bother to knock, and he knew she was furious. It was just what he'd expected from her.

"Tom! How could you do this to me?" Clare demanded as she shut the door behind her and stormed to the side of his bed.

"Do what to you?" he asked, looking up at her. She was a magnificent-looking woman with her blond hair and fair coloring. As she stood angrily before him, her breasts heaving, he thought her more beautiful than ever. Fire flashed in her eyes, and her cheeks were high with color. He wanted her in the worst way, but he knew he didn't have the physical ability to take her anymore. He had been a man of enormous carnal appetites; being rendered weak and impotent by his illness made his life a living hell.

"How could you bring that . . . that thing into my home . . . our home!"

"What are you talking about?"

"I'm talking about that Indian — that half-breed," she declared in disgust. "I will not have him living here. He's a vile, filthy man, and I can't bear to have him in my house!"

Tom managed a smile at her, which he knew only angered her more. "That vile, filthy man is my son, Clare."

"By an Indian woman!" She looked at him with condemnation and outrage. "How could you?"

"It was easy," he said with a grin, remembering his lusty younger days. "Morning Sun was a damn pretty woman."

"She was an Indian! A squaw!"

His smile broadened as he remembered. "She would do anything to please me. I liked that about her."

"And she gave you a half-breed son you never wanted or acknowledged until now!" Clare shot back.

"How do you know if I acknowledged him or not? I sent money to support him. I'm his father. There's no doubt about that. Didn't you see his eyes?"

"Yes, I saw them, and Tanner said that he'd seen him before — "

"So he remembered him, did he?" Tom was thoughtful, recalling that day long ago.

"Yes. He said that Chase was here at the ranch and you'd beaten him and thrown him off."

"He was demanding I go see his mother. Emily didn't know about her, and I was through with Morning Sun, so I told him to get the hell out. I didn't want anything to do with Morning Sun anymore."

"That's how you always treat women, isn't it? You use us as it pleases you and then throw us away when you're tired of us."

"I've never gotten tired of you, Clare. Even now" — he reached out and snared her wrist in a viselike grip to pull her down to him — "even now I want you. Seeing you mad like this stirs my blood."

"But, Tom — your condition — " The thought of making love to him made her feel sick, and the strength with which he held her surprised her. She feared he might actually try to take her right now, and she wouldn't have been able to bear it.

"To hell with my condition." His free hand sought the swell of her breast as he pulled her down for a kiss.

"Tom — please don't force me to let that half-breed live here with us," she pleaded as she relaxed a little and gave herself over to his kiss. She wanted to gag, but faked enjoyment. She'd always gotten her way with him by giving him what he wanted.

"Don't tell me what I can or cannot do in my own home, Clare," he said when he broke off the kiss.

"But you've always taken care of me, and as sick as you are, I'll be afraid, having someone like him living under the same roof with me. What if — ? What if he tried to rape me or — "

He interrupted her. "Chase may be a half-breed, but you have nothing to be afraid of. Chase is a Ranger, Clare."

"He's a Ranger?" Her shock was real, and she pulled back to look down at him.

"That's right. At least one of my sons has done something I can be proud of."

"But that wife of his — she's so disrespectful to me."

"I've never known anyone more capable than you of handling people, Clare. I'm sure you'll get along fine with them once they've settled in."

"I wish I was as sure as you are." She tried to sound frightened and pitiful, hoping he would worry about her.

"Chase is not the one I'm worried about," he said in a strange voice, then drew her back down to him. It had been so long since he'd made love to her, and he wanted her badly.

Tom held Clare close, enjoying the feel of her breasts crushed against his chest. His mouth claimed hers in a hungry kiss. He felt a stirring of excitement within himself, and for a moment forgot that he was sick, forgot that he was no longer a man.

And then the attack came.

Suddenly his breathing grew labored, and he began to gasp and choke. Clare escaped his hold and stood over him, watching as he trembled visibly. His face turned white, and fear was visible in the depths of his eyes as he strained to draw a breath.

In her heart, Clare wished this would be the end of him, that he would die right now, but her expression showed only sympathy and worry. After a moment, the attack let up and Tom's breathing eased.

"Thank heaven you're all right," she told him, taking his hand and holding it to her breast. She thought if just kissing her had brought on such a serious attack, why not see what else she could stir up. "I was so afraid — "

With what was left of his strength, Tom jerked his hand away from her. "Get out of here. I need to rest."

"All right. I'll check on you later."

He turned his head away from her, not

bothering to respond.

Clare let herself out of the room. She was still annoyed about Chase. Try as she might, she hadn't been able to convince Tom to send Chase and his witch of a wife away. If nothing else, though, she knew she wouldn't have to worry about Tom trying to bed her again. Those days of submitting endlessly to his passion were over.

Chapter Twenty-two

"Chase is a Texas Ranger," Bill Hanes announced as they sat at the dinner table.

Tanner's expression changed subtly at his statement, and Chase was very aware of it.

"You must lead an exciting life," Callie offered.

"It has its moments," he responded. "And there are times when I wish it wasn't quite so exciting."

"I'm surprised they let you join," Clare said scathingly.

"The Rangers know a good man when they see him," Faith put in, immediately coming to his defense. "And Chase is one of the best trackers around."

"Of course, he would be a good tracker, considering how he was raised." Clare was still trying to come to grips with what Tom had done to her by so openly bringing his bastard into the family. What upset her even more was that Tanner seemed to be warming to him. She wondered what he was thinking; Chase was going to be taking some of his own inheritance.

"I'd say Chase should be proud of what he's accomplished," Tanner said, irritated by Clare's hateful remarks.

Chase was surprised both by Faith's defense of him and Tanner's support. He hadn't expected it. He glanced at Faith to find her gazing warmly at him. "I had friends who encouraged me."

"And you had Padre Rodriguez," Faith put in with a gentle smile.

When the others looked confused, Chase explained how he'd been raised at the mission. "He kept me out of trouble until I left right after my mother died."

"You were lucky to have him," Callie remarked.

"Looking back, I guess I was, but at the time I didn't think so. He was strict."

"How did you and Faith meet?" she asked. "You're gone for long periods of time on your assignments, aren't you? It must have been difficult for you to be together."

"Ever since the moment we met, we've been practically inseparable," Faith offered.

"Our first meeting was accidental, but I'm

real glad it happened," Chase added.

"I was engaged to another man at the time, but after being with Chase and getting to know him, I realized I couldn't marry anyone else and be happy."

No one seemed to notice that they hadn't given any specific details of their courtship.

"I can't believe your parents let you marry him," Clare put in icily, thinking Faith had acted like a slut. She felt sorry for Faith's original fiancé. From the way Faith spoke, Clare thought she had probably been bedding the breed while she was engaged to another man.

A silence fell over the table.

"My parents are dead," Faith said quietly, "but I'm sure they would have approved of Chase. He's a very special man." She gazed at her husband, her expression one of open adoration. Then she looked at Callie. "How did you meet Tanner?"

Callie blushed. "It's a long story."

"We've got time," Faith answered easily. She found herself warming to Callie, but she wasn't sure what to think about Tanner after all that Chase had told her about his connection with the Malone gang.

"I came to Sidewinder looking for Tanner."

"So you knew him before?" Faith asked.

"No. I'd never met him, but you see, my brother had been killed in a bank robbery in Foster."

"I'm so sorry." Faith's emotion was honest. She knew what it was like to lose family tragically.

"So am I. He was a good man and didn't deserve what happened to him," Callie replied. "Tanner was arrested right after the robbery, but then the sheriff let him go because no one could prove he was really a part of the gang. I came here to find him, hoping to learn who had murdered my brother."

"That was so brave of you." Faith was impressed.

"I used a made-up name and took a job working as a singer at the Roundup Saloon. I didn't want Tanner to know who I was, just in case he really was one of them." She paused to look over at her husband. "We were attracted to each other from the start, but it wasn't until Terry Malone showed up here at the Circle M that everything was finally resolved."

"The leader of the gang came here? To the ranch?" Faith asked, pretending to be shocked by this revelation and hoping to help Chase find some of the answers he was looking for.

"Yes," Tanner broke in. "Malone and I had been friends in the past. He'd saved my life one time, so I owed him. I let him stay here on the ranch, but I told him to lay low and stay out of trouble. He claimed it was Blackie Sherwood who did the shooting at the bank, and at the time I believed him, because I knew how trigger-happy Blackie was."

"Why did they arrest you in Foster?" Chase asked, wanting to hear his version of what had taken place there.

Tanner looked him in the eye as he answered, "I'd been drinking with them, and I was drunk. They asked me to hold the horses for them in an alley, and I did it. What I didn't know was that they were robbing the bank. I got arrested, while they got clean away."

"That must have been terrible for you — trying to prove your innocence," Faith said sympathetically.

"It was," Tanner agreed. "Malone was a wild man sometimes. He proved that when he came here. He didn't stay out of sight like I told him. He went into town."

"And I found out he was there," Callie added in satisfaction.

"Why don't you tell everyone just how stupid you really were?" Clare said snidely, wanting to make Callie look bad. "Instead of going to the law like a sensible person, she got a gun and followed Malone into the saloon all by herself! She almost ended up dead!" Clare was wishing that Callie had died from the gunshot wound she'd gotten in the shoot-out. It would have been so wonderful to have Tanner all to herself.

"You went after Malone by yourself?" Chase was shocked by the thought of this sweet, innocent-looking woman trying to bring in a dangerous man like Malone.

"He'd killed my brother. There was no time to go for Sheriff Scott. I didn't want to risk letting Malone get away after I'd worked so hard to find him. I had to bring him to justice. He and his two partners, Slim and Blackie, even killed a Ranger while they were on the run after the robbery."

"Clare said you were almost killed. What happened?" Faith asked.

"I was shot at the saloon, but Tanner showed up just in time to save me — and to shoot Malone."

"Were you badly hurt?"

"Yes. It took a month for me to recover. I'm almost back to normal now."

"Thank God you're alive."

"I have thanked God many times — for

saving me and for giving me Tanner," she said, looking at her husband.

"So you two really haven't been married very long," Faith said, amazed that she and Callie were both new brides. She, however, couldn't let anyone know the truth of her marriage.

"No, not very long at all, but I'm loving every minute of it. I can't imagine a life without Tanner now."

Chase had been sitting back, listening to the exchange. "If you got Malone, whatever happened to Slim and Blackie? I heard the news about the Ranger being shot at headquarters."

"Slim was killed in the shoot-out with the Rangers, but no one knows anything about Blackie," Callie told him. "I'll be glad when he's dead or behind bars, too."

"I couldn't agree with you more." Chase listened carefully, but he was watching Tanner as he spoke. Tanner's expression revealed nothing.

Tiny, the cook, came into the room carrying plates heaped with food and set them on the table.

"It took you long enough," Clare complained. She didn't like Tiny and didn't hesitate to try to make his life miserable.

The cook looked at her, but didn't respond to her complaint.

"Well, hurry up! We're hungry," she carped.

Clare was in a hurry to get the meal over with. She wanted them all out of the house as quickly as possible. She was sick of listening to them, and she was miserable having Tanner so close and not being about to touch him. She physically ached with the need to be in his arms.

Tiny returned to the kitchen as those seated at the table began to dig in. He came back a few minutes later with several more dishes, then disappeared from the room again.

"Tiny's an idiot," Clare said in annoyance. "If I wasn't so desperate for help with Tom in the condition he's in, I would have fired him long ago. I can't stand his silence."

"Why would you fire him? His cooking is good, and if he's quiet, he's not causing you any trouble," Bill Hanes pointed out.

"He seems sneaky to me. I don't trust him."

"Tiny's no idiot," Tanner told them. "He knows how to communicate. He knows Indian sign language."

The cook returned with one last dish of food and was just starting from the room when Chase reached out and touched his arm to stop him. Tiny quickly looked at him, his expression questioning. Without hesitation, Chase used the sign language he'd learned from his mother's people to introduce himself and Faith. There was a long pause as Tiny looked from Chase to Faith and back. Then he nodded and answered him, welcoming them to the ranch. They communicated for some moments, their hands moving quickly. When Tiny left the dining room, he seemed quite pleased with himself, for he was smiling.

"I should have realized that you would be able to 'talk' to him that way," Clare said, looking at Chase. "You people do that kind of thing all the time, don't you?"

Chase met her gaze. He was used to people with her superior attitude, so nothing she had to say bothered him in the least. "Yes. We do."

Clare thought it had been bad enough that Tiny and Tanner communicated that way, but now that Chase was doing it too, she was fuming. She fell silent, pretending interest in her food. As soon as dinner was over, she was going to find Manuelo. He was her personal servant, and completely dedicated to her. She knew what she wanted done, and she was certain he would take care of it. He had never failed her yet. She smiled slightly to herself, wishing the meal was over.

"Well, I think it's time we headed back to town," Bill said as they finished the last of their food.

"What time do you think you'll be arriving tomorrow?" Tanner asked Chase.

"I think we can take care of our business in town and be here by noon."

"I'll be watching for you."

Chase, Faith and Bill stood to go. Tanner and Callie accompanied them outside, but Clare did not. She disappeared out the back door to look for Manuelo. She had no desire to keep up the pretense of being cordial to the bastard and his woman. If she could have found a way to keep them out of her house forever, she would have.

Chase stood with Tanner by their horses.

"Tiny was right about Clare," Tanner remarked, having interpreted some of what Tiny had signed to Chase. "Watch out for her. She can mean trouble."

"Tiny seems to understand a lot about what's going on."

"He's intelligent. He just can't talk. Clare's always underestimated him."

"Thanks for the insight. It's going to be interesting living here in the main house, that's for sure."

Chase, Faith and Bill climbed into the carriage, ready to make the trip back to Sidewinder.

Tanner stood back with Callie and watched them drive away. None of them noticed Clare standing behind the ranch house, watching the carriage move off, her expression one of loathing and hate, her fists clenched at her sides.

"I wish there could be more than one carriage accident around here without causing any suspicion," she muttered to herself as she started off to find Manuelo.

Clare found him in the bunkhouse eating with the rest of the hands. At the first sight of her, Manuelo hurried to her side to see what she wanted.

"I heard what happened today," he told her.

"And you're going to help me do something about it. I will not have that bastard in my house taking any part of my money. Where did he come from? Out from under some rock? I want you to get rid of him as soon as you can — and her, too. I can't stand either of them, and I want them gone."

"What do you mean by 'get rid of him'?" Manuelo asked cautiously, a worried look in his eyes.

"I don't care what you have to do to get rid of him. Shoot him, stab him, bury him alive — it doesn't matter. I just want him dead and gone!" Clare knew that was the only sure way to be rid of him.

Manuelo's expression turned to one of utter shock at her words. She had ordered him to do many things before, and he had never questioned her judgment — until now. This time he had to. "Senora Clare — this Chase — he is a Texas Ranger. I cannot kill a Ranger!"

"I never thought you were a coward, Manuelo," she said sarcastically.

"Chase is a lawman. There is a difference, Senora."

"You won't do this for me? You won't help me when I need you the most? And after all I've done for you." Clare knew just how to play Manuelo to get what she wanted out of him.

"I will see what I can do."

"Look into Chase's past. Maybe there's someone who has a grudge against him and would like to get even. Surely there's someone out there who can help us get rid of our 'problem.' "

"Yes, Senora," he replied, but still he worried. This wouldn't be simple. He would have to think it through carefully and make

278

sure that whomever he found to do his dirty work would be trustworthy and deadly. He could afford no mistakes, dealing with a Texas Ranger.

Chapter Twenty-three

"How do you think it went?" Bill asked Chase as they made the trip back into town.

"As well as could be expected," Chase answered.

Chase still wasn't sure how to refer to Tom. He wasn't comfortable calling him "Pa," and "Tom" seemed too distant. He would have to wait and see how things went once they'd moved in.

Not that Chase was looking forward to living on the ranch. Judging from the way Clare had acted today, it was going to be hell on earth while they were there. Chase glanced over at Faith. He'd been touched by the way she'd defended him earlier at dinner. He would have preferred to cut and run with her, but he couldn't. He had to be close to Tanner. He had to find Sherwood, and it looked like Tanner might be the key. He couldn't just up and leave. He owed Frank.

"Tom's not looking good."

"No, he's not. Is there anything the doctor can do for him?" Chase asked.

"No. His illness is terminal. He won't be recovering."

Chase fell silent, not sure how to respond. His initial response when he'd received the letter was still his prominent feeling. He wondered if that would ever change.

"Will I ever get to meet him?" Faith asked.

"I'm sure he plans to meet you," Bill advised her. "He's a very sick man. Just be patient with him."

Both Faith and Chase were glad when Bill dropped them off at the hotel.

"I hope everything works out for you," Bill told Chase as they parted company.

"So do I," Chase answered, thinking of Frank again and wanting his revenge.

They shook hands, and then Faith and Chase entered the hotel and went up to their room.

Faith said nothing more until the door was locked behind them. Only then did she turn and look at her husband, her expression serious.

She took a moment to really study Chase — seeing him as the man who'd rescued her — who'd saved her — the man she'd married. Chase was so tall and handsome. Her heartbeat quickened as she stared up at him. Her gaze went over his chiseled features, committing to memory the male beauty of him — the high cheekbones and the startling blue of his eyes.

Faith finally admitted to herself that she wanted him — in all ways. She couldn't tell him, though, for she knew Chase didn't really want this marriage. Still, the thought of lying in his arms again, sharing his kisses, excited her. Their one night of loving had been perfect, and she needed that again. She wanted that again. She wanted to touch him and caress him and hold him deep within her. Only then would she be sure that he wanted her and needed her. Only then, when they were one, would she believe there was any hope for their future together. She wondered how to entice him to make love to her this night. It had been a long, difficult day for him — a savage day, really — and she didn't know how he was feeling.

"Is something bothering you?" Chase asked, aware of her scrutiny and wondering at it.

"Well, yes . . ." she said hesitantly.

He was suddenly worried that, having met the McBrides and listened to Clare all day, she didn't want anything more to do with him. He stiffened slightly, preparing himself for the worst. "What is it?"

"I don't know about you," she began, "but I cannot stand Clare."

"Clare?" Chase repeated dully. He'd expected her to tell him that she was through with their marriage and wanted to leave.

"She is a nasty woman, and I'm not looking forward to moving in at the ranch and being forced to see her every day. Is there any way we can live somewhere else, like here in town, and still do what you need to do?" she asked hopefully.

Relief flooded through him.

"No. According to my father's terms, I have to be there at the ranch, and believe me, I don't like the idea either," he answered. "I could speak with Tom about it and see if it would be all right for you to stay here in town, if you want."

"No, I couldn't do that," Faith protested. "I'm your wife, and I'm going to stand by you — no matter what. If you have to suffer through living on the Circle M, I'm going to live there, too."

"Are you sure, Faith? It's not going to be pretty — especially knowing how Clare feels about me — and you're going to be caught in the middle of it."

"Who's to say she wouldn't be just as bad

to me if I lived in town? At least, this way we'll have each other."

The thought of having someone else besides himself to rely on was new to Chase, but he found he liked the idea — especially since it was Faith.

She added, "Who knows? Maybe I can help you find Sherwood. Did you like the way I got that information about the Malone gang out of Callie?"

"You surprised me, that's for sure, but don't even think about helping me with Sherwood. The man's a killer."

"Maybe I could start riding with you. We could be a team. Do they have women in the Texas Rangers?"

"Forget it. I don't want you in any danger."

"You're just tired of rescuing me, that's all," she laughed, and suddenly realized how good it felt to laugh again. It had been so long. She went on quickly, "I do have an idea how we can avoid living in the main house with Clare, though, if you're interested."

"What is it?"

"Have you ever lived in a tepee?"

"Yes," he answered cautiously.

"Do you know how to build one?"

"Why?"

"I want you to put one up out in front of the house at the ranch." She quickly related the conversation she'd had with Clare in the parlor. By the time she was done, they were both laughing.

"Faith — " Chase was suddenly serious.

She looked up at him, wondering what had chased away his laughter.

"Thank you for defending me today."

Faith suddenly realized that no one had ever supported him before. "Well, you're always defending me, and besides, I was right," she said, lifting her gaze to his. "What I told them was the truth. You are a good man and a great tracker. You're my protector. You're my warrior."

He was surprised by her words. Most whites were disgusted by his Indian heritage. "You want me to be your warrior?"

"Yes," she answered simply.

Chase couldn't help himself. He reached out to her, touching her cheek. Unable to resist any longer, he took her in his arms and drew her near. He wanted to feel the sweet softness of her pressed against him. He wanted to hold her close. He didn't know how he had lived his whole life without Faith. She accepted him unconditionally. She completed him. She made him whole.

Faith slipped her arms around him and

embraced the solid power of his body. He had become her strength, her rock. Without him, she would have been lost. He had saved her and protected her, and he was still trying to shield her from the ugliness of life every chance he could. She ached with the need to be one with him, to show him how much he meant to her.

Chase swept her up in his arms and kissed her passionately as he carried her to the bed. Faith looped her arms around his neck and returned his kiss in full measure. He laid her upon the bed and followed her down, not wanting to be apart from her for even a moment. Being in her arms was heaven for him. He needed her desperately.

Their clothes were suddenly a terrible barrier. With eager hands they stripped away the garments that kept them apart. There was no time for kisses and caresses. Their need was too great. They had to be one.

Faith opened to Chase, drawing him to her and arching against him. He needed no further encouragement to claim her as his own. He sought the sweet heat of her and was lost even as he conquered. They moved together in love's age-old rhythm. They wanted only to please each other. When their passion burst upon them, they clung together, lost in the ecstasy that was theirs and theirs alone.

They loved long into the night, giving and taking, until they surrendered in their sensual exhaustion to sleep, Faith curled against Chase, safe in his embrace.

Chase awoke at first light. He lay still, cherishing the warmth of her delicate body curved so tightly against him. Memories of their loving brought a slow smile to his face, and he knew he would never want to take a cold bath again. Making love to Faith was much more satisfying — and enjoyable.

He let his thoughts drift to the day to come. The move out to the ranch would not be pleasant, but it had to be done. He smiled at the thought of living in a tepee in front of the big house on the Circle M. The idea had its appeal. At least there, they would have some privacy from Clare. Before they went out to the ranch, though, there was one other thing he needed to do — take Faith shopping. She had only a few clothes to her name, and he wanted her to have a decent wardrobe before she came under Clare's constant scrutiny.

Chase lay quietly in bed with Faith, enjoying the peace of the time they had there alone. In just a few short hours, they would be with the McBrides, and he doubted they would find much peace during their time there.

Faith awoke to find herself nestled against Chase, one arm flung possessively across his chest. The thought made her smile, and it was the smile of a very satisfied woman. Their hours of loving had been wonderful, every bit as exciting as the first night they'd come together, and she wondered distantly if their loving would always be so perfect.

"Good morning," Chase said in a husky voice. He'd been watching her sleep, all the while remembering her wild responses to his caresses through the long, dark hours of the night.

Faith ran her hand across his chest in a seductive move. "Is it?"

His response was immediate and definite.

It was some time later when they finally left the bed to face the new day.

"There's one thing I want to do before we go out to the ranch," Chase told her as he got dressed.

"What?"

"After we have breakfast, I want to take you shopping. You need more clothes."

Faith looked momentarily stricken. "I — I don't have a lot of money left."

"I do," he said firmly. "I want you to get everything you'll need."

"But I don't want you to — "

"You're my wife, Faith. It's only right that

288

I pay for your clothes." He sounded a little irritated. The fact that she balked at the idea of his buying her clothing hurt him unexpectedly.

"Well, thank you," she said softly. "I'll finish getting cleaned up and then I'll be ready to go."

"I'll go pay for the room and meet you downstairs."

Faith watched him go and wondered why he'd seemed so angry all of a sudden. Not wanting to displease him any more, she hurried to wash and dress.

An hour later they had already visited a dress shop and purchased several day gowns for her. The selection had been slim. Most of the gowns the store carried were for the women who earned a living in the saloons of Sidewinder. Faith had insisted that they go to the general store next.

"Morning, folks," the owner said. "I'm Hiram Wiggins. Can I help you with anything?"

"I'm just looking right now," Faith told him. She knew exactly what she wanted and headed straight toward the men's and boys' clothing section.

Chase had no idea what she was after, so he stayed at the counter talking to the storekeeper.

"I heard you were a McBride," Hiram said. "And a Ranger, too. It's good to have you here in town."

Chase was surprised and a bit annoyed, especially since he'd asked the sheriff not to tell anyone about his profession. "News travels fast in Sidewinder. Where did you hear all that?"

"Bill Hanes is a close friend of mine. I saw him the other night and he told me you'd come to town. How's Tom doing? I heard from the doc that he's real sick."

"He's not good, but I guess there's always hope." Chase was a little relieved to know that the sheriff hadn't been the one talking. Though he'd seemed useless, at least he knew when to keep his mouth shut.

It only took Faith a few minutes to pick out the right size, and she was ready to go. She joined Chase at the counter and laid a pair of boy's pants down on it.

"That's all I need for now," she told Chase.

He frowned at her choice. They would certainly be too small for him. "A pair of pants?"

"I used to wear them at home all the time, especially when I worked the horses. I thought maybe I could help out at the ranch."

Hiram looked a little shocked by her purchase, but said nothing. As far as he was concerned, a sale was a sale. They had money. He'd sell them the pants.

"Well, it was nice meeting you folks. Come back anytime."

They left the shop and went to get their horses, ready to make the trip out to the Circle M. They kept the pace slow, not the least bit in a hurry to take up residence there.

"What are you planning to do about Tanner and Sherwood?" Faith asked.

"I'm not sure yet. With Malone showing up here the way he did, there's always hope that Sherwood will follow, but there's no guarantee. I'll have to win Tanner's trust. Then maybe he'll tell me something that will help me track Sherwood down."

"I like Tanner," she remarked thoughtfully. "And I really like Callie. I still can't believe she went after Malone all by herself. The fact that she married Tanner convinces me that he really wasn't involved in the robbery in Foster. If Callie thought for a moment that Tanner had had something to do with her brother's death, there's no way she would be with him right now. Why don't you just tell Tanner the truth? Maybe he'd help you."

"I'd like to think that, but I can't be sure. Not yet. Maybe in time. Like he said, he owed Malone, so he let Malone stay on the Circle M. Who's to say he doesn't owe Sherwood, too?"

"You're right, but it would be good if you two could work together."

"This is Ranger business. I'll handle it."

Faith let it go for now. He had little trust in people, and she understood why. He had been a solitary man for most of his life.

They reached the top of the low rise where the ranch could be seen spread out below them.

"We're here," Faith said.

"Are you ready?" Chase looked at her.

"Yes," she answered, and they rode down to the Circle M.

Chapter Twenty-four

Clare was not at all pleased with the way things were going. She'd tried again that morning to convince Tom to send the bastard and his wife away. She'd suggested having Chase live at the line shack and bringing Tanner back to live with them at the main house, but Tom had gotten very angry with her and had refused. She had left him, frustrated and furious herself. Oh, how she would have preferred to have Tanner there with her!

Chase and Faith had arrived from town shortly after her fight with Tom. After settling in their room, Chase had gone down to the stable to meet the hands.

Clare was waiting impatiently now for his squaw to make an appearance. Faith was taking so long coming downstairs that Clare was beginning to wonder if she was going to hide in her room forever. Not that that was a bad thing. She really wanted nothing to do with Faith. If the woman disappeared off the face of the earth that very instant, it wouldn't be too soon.

As she bided her time, Clare kept thinking up different ways she could torment the newcomers. She hoped Manuelo could arrange some terrible accident for them soon, but if not, she would drive them away herself using any means possible — and she did mean any, Clare wanted them gone — out of her life and Tom's. It was enough that Lauren and Stone would probably show up soon. Having this bastard thrown in only made things even more complicated. And she didn't like complications.

After Chase had left her, Faith finished unpacking and then changed clothes. As she pulled on the pants, she began to feel like her old self again for the first time since the tragedy of the renegade raid. She hoped Chase didn't mind her dressing this way. She knew some people would think pants on a woman outrageous, but she only found them practical. And since Faith wanted to spend as much time working with the horses as she could, practical seemed the way to go.

Wearing a shirt and her new pants, Faith pulled her boots on and then went to stand before the small mirror over the washstand to brush out her hair. Instead of letting it fall freely about her shoulders, she pulled it back and plaited the long, golden tresses into a single thick braid. She managed to give her reflection a reassuring smile before leaving the room. Faith hoped she wouldn't see Clare on the way out of the house. She wanted to stay away from her. It was going to be difficult enough putting up with her at mealtimes when they were forced to be together. She certainly didn't want to spend any extra time with her.

"So you finally decided to come downstairs, have you?" Clare's voice rang out caustically from the parlor as Faith hurried down the steps.

Faith cursed her luck that the other woman would be sitting there like a predator just waiting for her to make an appearance. Taking a deep breath, she steadied herself.

"Yes, I had to unpack our things before I could go down to the stable with Chase," Faith said as she paused in the doorway.

"Oh, my God!" Clare exclaimed when she saw Faith's attire. "Well, this certainly answers all my questions."

Faith frowned. "What questions?"

"About you — and about your half-breed

husband, but now it all makes sense. This explains everything!" She made a point of eyeing Faith critically from head to toe, smirking as she did so.

"What are you talking about?" Faith asked.

"Your husband likes you to look like a boy! That's why you're dressed that way and wearing your hair back like that. I wondered what the attraction was between the two of you and now I understand! I mean, you are so plain, and you dress so poorly. But if this is what you normally wear, I suppose you did consider yourself dressed up in your split riding skirt yesterday, didn't you? And here I thought you just had no fashion taste at all."

Faith rarely felt like hitting people, but Clare was proving to be the exception. Somehow she controlled the urge. "Clare, I've known you a little over one day, and you've already managed to make me wish we'd never met."

"So pack up and leave," Clare said coldly with a smile that matched.

"I don't want to be here any more than you want me here. But your husband decreed that Chase and I have to live on the ranch. That is the only reason we are here, Clare, so I suggest you learn to accept it and stay out of my way — and out of my husband's way."

"You just remember — this is my home!" Clare snarled.

"I doubt I'll be able to forget that, even for a moment."

"Good, because you don't belong here — not you and definitely not that half-breed bastard you call a husband!"

"I don't know a lot about this family, and you know what? I'm glad. The little I have learned certainly explains why Tanner and his brother and sister left here after Tom married you."

"Tom loves me."

"I don't know why."

Clare gasped at her insult. "You wouldn't understand true love. You and Chase deserve each other."

Faith suddenly found herself smiling at the woman. "Why, Clare, that's the nicest thing you've ever said to me. Chase is a wonderful man. He's one helluva Ranger, and I'm proud to call him my husband. Now, if you'll excuse me, I'm going down to the stable to see if they can use any extra help." She started out the door, then out of pure spite turned back to see Clare watching her with a malevolent expression. "And just to put your mind at ease, Clare, I am absolutely certain that I'm all the woman Chase needs, so you don't have to be concerned."

Faith walked out of the house, glad to be away from Clare and eagerly looking forward to finding her husband. In the distance down by the corral, Faith caught sight of Chase talking with several of the ranch hands. She realized again just how blessed she was to have him, and she quickened her pace.

Chase was deep in conversation with the Circle M's foreman, Jeb Riggs, and Zeke, one of the hands, when he noticed Faith coming down from the main house. He did a double take and stopped in mid-sentence to watch her walking toward him. He was completely caught off guard by the sight of her wearing the pants she'd bought in town.

"I see your wife's coming," Jeb remarked as he turned to follow Chase's gaze. He smiled, admiring Faith's shapely form and her bravery in wearing the pants. There were few women around who could get away with it. He found he liked her already. "She looks like she's ready to go right to work with you."

"Damn, Jeb," Zeke said, staring at Faith with open male appreciation. "I don't know how much work me and the boys are going to get done with her around. I ain't never seen a woman wearing pants before."

"Easy, Zeke. This is a lady you're talking about," Jeb cautioned, "and she's Chase's wife."

Zeke glanced at Chase, a bit shamefaced. "Sorry." He didn't want to anger Chase Mc-Bride. There was something about the fellow that marked him as a dangerous man.

Chase nodded at Zeke, his gaze still riveted on Faith as she closed the distance between them.

Faith realized as she drew closer that Chase was staring at her, his expression unreadable. She wondered if something was wrong, but greeted him with a smile, then looked at the other two men.

"Hi, I'm Faith, Chase's wife. It's a pleasure to meet you."

"It's a pleasure to meet you, too, ma'am. I'm Jeb, the foreman of the Circle M, and this is Zeke." Despite his rough exterior, Jeb was a true gentleman at heart. His smile was warm and welcoming.

"I'm ready to work, so if there's anything you need me to do, just let me know," she volunteered.

"You know ranching?" Jeb was surprised.

"Oh, yes. I was raised on one."

"We need all the help we can get around

here," Jeb said. "I was just telling Chase how shorthanded we are. I put Tanner to work when he showed up. I know he'll be glad for any help he can get."

"We're ready whenever you say the word," Faith said.

"You haven't seen much of the ranch, have you, Chase?"

"No."

"Well, let me and Zeke get a couple of horses ready for you, and we'll take you out and show you around — give you the grand tour."

"We'd appreciate that."

The two men went off to the stable, leaving Faith and Chase alone.

"Is something wrong?" Faith asked him, trying to gauge his mood. It was hard to tell from his stony expression what he was thinking.

"Are you sure you want to wear those?" Chase's voice was tight as he stared at her pants. He had always thought her attractive, but seeing her this way made him even more aware of her as a woman. The pants fit her perfectly, and he was unable to look away from the sweet curves of her hips and long legs. He could tell that the other men had noticed, too, and he was feeling a bit jealous of her.

"Do the pants bother you that much?"

"Yes — me, and the others."

"They're really very practical," Faith told him. "Especially if I'm going to be working around the stable, and, believe me, I want to be out here with you. There's no way I can stay in that house with Clare day in and day out. But if you honestly don't like them on me, I guess I could work in my riding skirt."

"I didn't say I didn't like them on you. I like them too much. That's the trouble," he remarked, fighting down the urge to carry her back up to the house to their room and have his way with her right then and there.

"Oh." Faith unexpectedly found herself blushing and feeling a bit disconcerted at his honesty. She did love the freedom wearing pants gave her, but she had been so protected on her family's ranch that she had never had to worry about things like this before. "If you think I should go change, I will — "

"No. Never mind. If you're comfortable, wear them. Just stay close to me for the first couple of days until the men around the ranch get used to seeing you this way."

Faith smiled at him. "It will be my pleasure staying close to you."

A surge of awareness jolted through

Chase, and he knew he had to distract himself. "Let's go see if we can help with the horses."

Faith walked ahead of him into the stable, and Chase found he couldn't take his eyes off the gentle sway of her hips. He couldn't decide if the pants were the best purchase he'd ever made — or the worst.

Clare saw Chase and Faith ride away with Jeb and Zeke, so she knew it was safe. She summoned Manuelo and sent him upstairs to search their room, while she stayed downstairs to make sure they didn't return unexpectedly.

Manuelo quietly mounted the staircase and let himself into the bedroom. He went through their every possession with practiced ease, looking for something he could use against them. He searched each drawer as well as their saddlebags, but found nothing that could help him. In frustration, he returned to Clare where she awaited him in the parlor.

"Well?" she asked anxiously.

"I am sorry, Senora, but I found nothing. They have very few possessions with them. When they get back from their ride, I think it will be best if I stay around them. I will listen, and I will watch and wait, and I will follow. Soon I will find what it is we need to be rid of them."

"I knew I could count on your help."

"Always, Senora."

Manuelo left Clare and went to wait for Faith and Chase to return. He had to come up with a plan to eliminate them without leaving any clue that he or Senora Clare had been involved.

It was several hours later that they returned with Jeb and Zeke to the stable. Manuelo was ready. He made his way to the stable to speak with them.

"Hey, Manuelo — what are you doing down here?" Jeb asked, surprised by his unexpected appearance.

"I have finished my work at the house and saw you ride in. I came down to see if you needed anything."

"No. Zeke and I were just showing Chase and Faith around the ranch. Have you met them yet?"

"No, Senor Jeb. Although I had heard that they were here," he replied.

Jeb made the introductions. "Manuelo mostly helps Clare up at the main house."

As they tended to their horses, the conversation centered on the state of things at the ranch.

"So tell us what it's like to be a Ranger,

Chase," Jeb urged, changing the subject.

"It's a hard job, but a rewarding one," Chase began.

"How'd you manage to get time off to come here?"

"I'd just brought in the Lawson gang, so I had some time off coming to me," he told them. It wasn't an outright lie, it was more of a half-truth. He had brought in the Lawson gang and the Rangers did owe him a day or two off, but certainly not the months he'd be spending in Sidewinder.

No one noticed the sudden spark of interest displayed by Manuelo at his words.

"They were very dangerous, weren't they?"

Chase nodded. "They were some of the worst West Texas has ever seen. It's good to know that they're safely behind bars now in the Los Santos jail."

"How long until you have to report back?" Jeb asked.

"Not until I've taken care of things here," he answered elusively.

"Well, it's good to have you here, Chase McBride. Welcome home."

Chase's expression was suddenly strained. "I don't know if I would call this 'home' yet."

"You're family now. That's good. I remember that day you were here years ago," Jeb admitted, looking him square in the eye.

"So do I." His voice was flat.

"Times have changed. We've all changed. Maybe things will work out better now."

"We'll see."

Manuelo hid a smile. Things were definitely going to work out better for Senora Clare now, that was for sure. He had just gotten the information he needed. It would take a few weeks to put his plan into action, but once he did, Senora Clare would never have to worry about this half-breed again.

Chapter Twenty-five

"Clare!"

The sound of Tom's shout came to Clare as she sat in the parlor, but she chose to ignore it. When he continued to call out to her, she grew annoyed. She got up to go out on the porch. She paused only to look up the stairs in the direction of his shout; then, disgusted at the thought of always being at his beck and call, she went on outside, paying no attention to him.

Unbeknown to Clare, Tiny had come out of the kitchen and had seen her deliberately ignoring her husband's call. Tom sounded upset, so Tiny waited until Clare had gone out of sight, then hurried up to see if he could help Tom in any way.

"Clare! Where the hell are you?" Tom shouted as loudly as he could. He wanted to talk to her, and he wanted to talk to her now. He'd been calling for her for so long that his strength was beginning to fail him.

The door to the bedroom opened, and Tom was pleased — for a moment. Then Tiny entered.

"Dammit, Tiny, I don't want to talk to you. I want Clare! Where is she?" Tom snarled. "Get her in here. Now!"

Tiny had been worried as he'd hurried up the stairs, but seeing that Tom was only angry, he nodded his understanding and went to get her. Clare was right where Tiny had known she would be, sitting peacefully on the porch well out of earshot of Tom's shouts. Motioning to her, Tiny made it clear that her husband wanted her upstairs.

"Oh — was Tom calling me?" she asked with fake innocence.

Tiny nodded, angered by her insincerity.

"I guess I'd better go see what's wrong with him," she said and slowly made her way up to the bedroom. She'd been hoping Tom would wear himself out calling for her and pass out from the exhaustion, but thanks to Tiny, she was now forced to play the dear, devoted wife.

"Yes, darling, what is it? Tiny came to get me," Clare said sweetly as she swept into the sickroom. It took all her considerable willpower to keep her expression loving as she stared down at Tom.

"Where the hell have you been?" he demanded in a raspy voice. The fire of his anger was burning in his eyes, but his breathing was labored.

"Why, I was sitting out on the porch. What do you need? Can I get you anything?" she asked, trying to soothe him.

"I want you to go get Chase and his wife. I haven't met her yet and I want to see them both."

"I haven't seen them for a while. They were down at the stable a while ago."

"Well, go get them," he demanded.

Fury at being helpless in the face of his power filled her. "Of course, darling. I'll go right now."

Clare all but stormed from the house. She knew the bastard and his wife were out there somewhere, but why she had to be the one to go find them was beyond her. Initially, she had rejoiced at the news that Tom was terminally ill, but she had never realized she would end up being his slave this way. Clare consoled herself with the knowledge that it would be over soon. The last time Doc Rogers had been out, he'd told her that Tom wasn't doing well at all and he didn't know if he was going to last much longer.

The thought brought a smile to Clare's perfect features.

When she reached the stable, she found Chase and Faith in conversation with Jeb.

"I'm sorry to interrupt you, but your father wants to see you, Chase."

Chase was surprised to see Clare in the stable and even more surprised by his father's request. "What does he want?"

"He didn't say, but he did ask that you bring Faith with you," she answered, giving Faith a deliberate once-over look. She wondered what Tom was going to think of her pants. It just might prove amusing.

"We'd better go up," Chase told Jeb. "What time do you want us to be ready in the morning?"

"We'll be riding out about seven," the foreman told him.

They agreed to meet him then, and headed back up to the house, following Clare, who'd gone off without them.

Chase and Faith exchanged puzzled looks at the prospect of seeing Tom McBride. When they reached the house, Clare was already upstairs with Tom.

"They'll be here in just a moment," Clare was assuring her husband.

"You wanted to see us?" Chase asked as he entered the room with Faith following behind him.

"Yes, dammit! Get the hell in here!" Tom

snapped, his blue-eyed gaze hard as he glared at Chase.

"There are ladies present," Chase countered. "Watch your language."

Tom looked from Clare to Faith. When he saw that she was wearing pants, his eyes widened a bit and his mouth twisted into an ugly smile. "I only see one lady in here."

Faith wasn't surprised by his attitude. In fact, she was ready for it. She smiled brightly at him in return. "Why, thank you, Mr. McBride. It's lovely to meet you, too. I'm Faith."

Clare stiffened, not about to put up with the implied insult. "I think my husband was referring to me."

"Get out of here, Clare," he said. "I want to talk to my son."

Clare left the room and closed the door behind her. She did not go downstairs, but lingered in the hallway outside the door to eavesdrop on their conversation.

Tom looked at Chase again. "You dare to lecture me on manners when you didn't even bother to bring your wife in here to meet me all day?"

"You weren't in any hurry to meet her when I spoke with you earlier," he countered.

"That was then." He looked over at Faith,

studying her. "Is there a reason you're dressed like a common ranch hand?"

She met Tom's gaze straight on, not the least intimidated by him. If anything, she was angry with him for the way he'd treated Chase all his life. She wasn't about to let him cow her. She wouldn't give him that power over her. "I'm dressed this way because it's comfortable and because I intend to earn my keep around here while we're living on the Circle M."

Tom gave a derisive snort. "What can you do? You're only a woman."

"You'd be surprised," Chase answered. "She's quite a woman — and a lady."

Tom glared at them both. "If she's such a lady, what's she doing with the likes of you?"

Faith could see that Tom's words were angering Chase, so she smiled at her husband. "I married Chase because he was the answer to my prayers."

"You wanted to marry a half-breed bastard?" Tom struck with ugly force.

Faith countered without pause. "I wanted someone who was strong and honorable. Chase is that and more. His Indian blood makes him a better man, not a lesser one, and whether he's a bastard or not isn't important. His parents made that choice — his mother and his father. He had no say in the matter."

"You think you're pretty smart, don't you, girlie?" Tom said sarcastically.

Faith met his gaze without fear. "I'm smart enough to know a good man when I see him." She was tempted to add *and I only see one good man in this room,* but she kept the thought to herself.

"Get out of here. Both of you."

Chase was more than glad to go, and Faith was right beside him.

Clare had heard the end of the conversation and had rushed downstairs so she wouldn't be caught listening at the door. Tiny was setting the table, so she knew it was almost time for the evening meal.

Dinner passed quickly. Jeb and the ranch hands came up to the house to eat, and the talk over the meal centered on the work they would be doing the next day.

Clare was bored out of her mind as she listened to their discussion. It annoyed her that Jeb and the men were so taken with Chase and Faith. They had accepted them as easily as they'd accepted Tanner back into their midst. The only thing that kept her from screaming was her secret knowledge that Manuelo was on his way to take care of things for her. It might take a few weeks, but he had never failed her yet. She could last another few weeks, she was certain.

Clare was very glad when dinner was over. The men left, and Chase and Faith finally went upstairs to their room, leaving her alone. Tiny had tended to Tom, so there was no need for her to see him again, and now the rest of the evening was hers to do with as she pleased. Her only regret was that Tanner wasn't anywhere around, but at least she had her fantasies about him to keep her occupied.

Chase was quiet, lost deep in thought, as he and Faith made their way to their bedroom. He was glad that Clare had given them the room at the back of the house. The farther he stayed away from Clare and Tom McBride, the better.

Faith was walking slightly ahead of him as they moved down the hallway, and his gaze was inevitably drawn to the natural but enticing sway of her hips. As gentle-spirited as he knew Faith to be, her defense of him to Tom had amazed him. He had never had anyone defend him so openly or so ardently before, and he wasn't sure how to react. He thought about her words, allowing himself to wonder for just a moment if she'd meant them. He finally decided Faith was just playing the role they'd agreed on, and that she really hadn't meant anything she was saying.

Even so, Chase wondered how much acting had gone into their lovemaking. He wondered if she'd just been playing a role then, too. He hoped not. He hoped she'd wanted him as much as he'd wanted her. The memories of the times he'd made her his own stirred his passion. He had fought to keep his desire for her under control all day, but now they were going to be alone in their own room.

Faith entered the bedroom first. He stepped in and locked the door behind them.

"You don't trust Clare either?" Faith asked, turning to smile at him when she heard the lock turning.

"This has nothing to do with Clare," Chase answered in a deep, husky voice as he went to her.

"It doesn't?" Faith was surprised, gazing up at him.

"No, but it does have everything to do with us."

Chase didn't say another word. He lifted one hand to tenderly touch her cheek as he bent to kiss her. He captured her lips in an exchange that fanned the fire he had been fighting to control. Urging her against him, he dropped his hands to cup her hips as he'd wanted to do all day and lifted her to grind her against the power of his need.

Faith gasped aloud at the excitement of being clasped so tightly to his hard, lean body. She linked her arms around his neck, clinging to him, never wanting to let him go.

Somehow they managed to move to the bed and fall upon its soft width. With eager hands, they stripped away their clothing. Chase took extra care as he drew her pants down over her hips and slipped them off her. He caressed the shapely length of her legs.

When at last there was nothing keeping them apart, they came together in a fiery mating, their need for one another taking them to the heights of ecstasy. Their pleasure burst within them and filled them with pure delight.

Exhausted, but enraptured, Chase and Faith lay together in silence, limbs entwined, sharing sweet, soft kisses. They treasured the intimacy of being alone, safe at last in the haven of their room.

Never before in his life had Chase allowed himself to need another person. He realized now that he was truly glad Faith was there with him. It was wonderful to hold her this way, to wake up in the night and have her by his side. Remembering what she'd said to

Tom about him, he was both pleased and confused. He wondered if there had been a double meaning to her words. She'd said he was the answer to her prayers, but she could have been talking about just praying for someone to help her escape the raiding party. He didn't know, and for some reason that troubled him.

His last thought as sleep claimed him was how perfectly she fit against him.

Blackie Sherwood did not like being hunted by the Texas Rangers. He realized now he should have thought about that before he'd gunned down the Ranger that day at their hideout, but all he'd cared about then had been escaping and saving his own ass.

Now here he was, broke and damned near desperate. Blackie knew he had to find Terry Malone. Together they could pull off another robbery somewhere and get some money, maybe even make a run for Mexico if they had to.

Blackie had been trying to figure out where Malone would have gone to hide after the shoot-out. The only place he could remember his friend mentioning was Tanner McBride's ranch near Sidewinder. Malone had told him how Tanner owed him and how Tanner was due to come into a big inheritance. Blackie figured Malone had probably gone there to sit tight and wait things out.

Blackie knew what he had to do. He'd go find Malone and stay with him until things quieted down.

Blackie Sherwood rode for Sidewinder.

Chapter Twenty-six

"Are you ready?" Jeb asked Tanner.

"As I'll ever be," Tanner responded, his expression grim, but the look in his eyes one of excitement.

With that, Jeb released his hold on the horse's head and got the heck out of the way. He high-tailed it to sit on the fence and watched with avid interest as Tanner fought to bring the powerful steed under control.

The black stallion wasn't about to be conquered. Determined to remain untamed, it began to twist and buck in a wild attempt to dislodge Tanner from its back.

They had been working at breaking horses all day, and they'd been very successful. This last stallion, however, was proving to be the biggest challenge. Jeb was beginning to suspect it was a mule in disguise.

Tanner stayed in the saddle, hanging on for all he was worth, but the stallion was relentless. Spinning quickly in tight circles, it used all its power to try to unseat Tanner. And it did. Tanner went flying from the horse's back and landed heavily in the dirt, his body as battered and bruised as his self-esteem.

"That is one ornery critter," Jeb remarked with a muffled laugh to Chase, who had come to stand on the other side of the fence to watch all the action. Jeb didn't want Tanner to hear him laughing, but it was hard to hide his amusement.

"The stallion definitely has a mind of his own," Chase agreed. "Hey, Tanner! You want me to give him a try?"

Tanner turned to glare at his half-brother from where he sat in the dirt. He was tired of humiliating himself and was more than ready to watch Chase take a turn at making a fool of himself. "He's all yours, brother. Enjoy."

Chase nodded and climbed over the fence. "Come on, Jeb."

Jeb went with him; he would hold the horse while Chase mounted. Tanner summoned enough strength to get to his feet. "I'm getting out of harm's way."

Chase smiled at him. "I like that — 'harm's way.' If I do saddle-break him, we'll call him 'Harm.'"

Tanner just gave a painful laugh as he took a seat atop the fence to watch Chase in action.

Jeb cornered the stallion, while Chase took up the reins. The horse rolled its eyes and laid its ears back as it tried to back away from them.

"Easy, Harm, I'm not going to hurt you," Chase muttered softly as he stroked the magnificent animal's neck.

The stallion gave a nervous snort and stood still as if waiting for the inevitable.

Jeb grabbed the horse by the ear and held its head in an unyielding grip as Chase mounted him in one smooth move.

"Let him go, Jeb," Chase said in a quiet voice. He held the reins in a steady, powerful grip, ready for whatever action the horse had in mind.

After Jeb let him go, Harm stood quietly for a moment as if pondering the best way to rid himself of this man who dared to try to ride him. Then, in a frantic move, Harm spun sideways and bucked at the same time. Chase was glad that he had a firm hold on him. He weathered the storm of the stallion's best efforts, clinging to the powerful animal, moving with him as he desperately tried to unseat him. He talked to Harm in a low, soothing voice, trying to calm his fears and win his trust. The battle was waged for over fifteen minutes as Chase refused to be thrown despite the animal's fierce attempts. Finally, Harm surrendered to the man's mastery. He stood in the center of the corral, sweaty and trembling from exertion.

"You did it!" Faith called out in amazement. She had been working in the stable and had come out to see what was going on.

"Only because I wore him out for Chase," Tanner put in with a laugh as he came to stand with her, still knocking the dirt and dust from his clothes.

"I'm sure that was it. He looked worn out, I could tell," she agreed good-naturedly. They had been at the ranch for nearly a week now, and she was finding herself more and more drawn to Tanner. She knew that Chase was feeling the same way.

Chase rode the stallion over to where they were standing, and Jeb came to join them.

"What do you plan to do with him?" Chase asked, keeping easy control of the stallion now that he'd established his mastery.

"Why? You want him?" Jeb asked.

"I'll buy him, if you're selling," Chase said.

"He's yours. Take him. He's a gift."

"I'll pay for him," he insisted.

"We'll worry about that if and when you ever leave the Circle M," Jeb said.

Chase did smile then. He wheeled Harm around and circled the corral several times to get him used to being ridden.

"That is one good-looking piece of horseflesh," Jeb said in pure admiration of the stallion and Chase's ability.

"Yes," Faith agreed absentmindedly. She was thinking how handsome Chase looked riding the magnificent stallion. Her heartbeat quickened as he rode back toward where they were standing.

"Tanner — you want to give it another try?" Chase invited, his grin almost evil.

"I think I'll pass. I'm just glad we saved him for last. It would have been a real long day if we'd started off with him first." He was moving kind of slow as he spoke. "Where did you learn to ride like that?"

"I lived with my mother's people for a while after she died. They taught me a lot."

"That explains it," Tanner said admiringly.

Clare had come out to sit on the porch and from there she could see the corral. When Tanner had mounted the wild stallion, she'd risen to her feet to watch him. She'd wished in her heart that she had been the one Tanner was mounting. The idea of being ridden by Tanner had brought a smile to her lips. The horse had thrown him then, and Clare had to bite back a horrified scream. Only when Tanner got up and dusted himself off did relief flood though her.

Clare had watched Chase mount the wild stallion next. She'd begun hoping against hope that the horse would accomplish what she could not. Manuelo had been gone for a week now. When anyone asked about him, she simply said he'd gone away to take care of personal business. She was growing more and more irritable as each day passed. At any moment, she kept expecting Bill Hanes to show up with both Lauren and Stone in tow, making her life even more miserable than it already was. She was very, very disappointed when Chase tamed the stallion and rode it around the corral like a calm saddle horse. Silently, she cursed the horse for its weak will. There was no man alive who could break her as easily as that horse had been broken.

In disgust, Clare went back inside the house to get ready for dinner. The following day, at least, she'd have some peace and quiet. Faith was supposed to go visit Callie at the line shack, and Chase and Tanner were going to town for supplies. She paused, wondering if there was some way she could arrange for Chase to stay on the ranch while she went with Tanner, alone, into Sidewinder. The possibility lifted her spirits.

And then she heard Tom's call.

"Clare! I need you!"

She knew there would be no trip into town for her — no time alone with Tanner. She was trapped on the Circle M with an old, dying man.

Her fists clenched in frustration, she started up the steps to see what he wanted. Clare told herself it would only be a few more months — just a few more months.

Chase was tired but feeling good as he finished taking care of Harm.

"You all set to head into town in the morning?" Tanner asked as Chase came to where he was talking to Jeb.

"What time do you want to leave?"

"The earlier, the better. We've got quite a lot of supplies to load up. So we're going to be there awhile."

"I can be up and ready to ride by six A.M."

"I'll be waiting for you. Faith, should I tell Callie that you'll be out to see her for sure?"

"Oh, yes. I'm looking forward to it," Faith told him.

"Good. I'll see you first thing in the morning." Tanner mounted up and rode out, ready for a quiet night with his wife.

Jeb joined Faith and Chase. They stopped to wash up at the water pump and then went on up to the house, ready for dinner.

The meal was a pleasant one, for Clare had little to say this night. That pleased everyone else. Talk turned to Chase and his mastery of the stallion he'd named Harm. They all laughed at his choice of a name for the animal. Several of the men had tried to ride Harm with no success.

"I'm surprised you all are so impressed by his ability," Clare finally said, sick of listening to them sing Chase's praise. "He is half Comanche, you know."

Her snide comment brought silence to the table, until Faith spoke.

"Which half, Clare?" she asked politely.

Clare shot her a murderous look as the men laughed. Clare got up and left the table. No one missed her after she'd gone.

A short time later, Chase and Faith made their way upstairs. They didn't know where Clare had gone, and they didn't care. The farther away from them she stayed, the happier they were.

"Have you learned anything more from Tanner about Sherwood?" Faith asked as they got ready for bed.

"No, but I'm hoping this trip into town will give us some more time to talk." They had been riding together, working on the ranch, but there had always been other hands with them.

"Do you think he knows anything?"

"I don't, but you never know, especially after Malone."

"I'll talk to Callie tomorrow, too. Maybe I can learn something that will help you."

"I hope so. The longer it takes, the harder it will be to track him down."

"Chase — I was wondering . . ." she began, then paused, unsure how to continue.

"What?" He looked at her expectantly.

"What are we going to do if you don't find Sherwood here? Do you have a plan?"

Chase frowned slightly. He had always lived his life from day to day, assignment to assignment. He'd never had any long-range plans except to stay alive. "I'm going to find him. Don't worry."

He knew that wasn't the real question she was asking, but he didn't offer anything else. He couldn't. He had no idea where the future would take them. He had never been married before. He had never had to plan for anything beyond the immediate.

And now here he was — with a wife.

The reality of it struck him then.

What would he do once he'd brought Sherwood in?

Would he go on another assignment? And if so, what would he do with Faith? He had no home to speak of, only some land he owned near Los Santos. For years now, he had just roamed from town to town, taking care of Ranger business. He'd had no one to answer to except his captain. No one to worry about except himself.

And now that had all changed because of Faith.

Confused, Chase quickly undressed and bedded down without looking at Faith again. He had never been in this situation before, and he wasn't quite sure what to do. Troubled, he pretended to be asleep as she undressed and slipped into bed beside him.

Faith lay awake, surprised by the sudden change in him. She had thought he would want to talk more tonight, but she'd been wrong. His silence bothered her — and the fact that he hadn't kissed her. She supposed he was worried about catching Sherwood.

Longing to be close to him, lying in the circle of his arms, Faith glanced over at Chase, but he seemed to be asleep. She felt a little lost as she turned down the lamp and then snuggled beneath the covers and closed her eyes.

Beside her, Chase lay unmoving, but awake. Until now, until Faith, his future had always been just the next day. He'd never allowed himself to think farther ahead than that. Those days, he realized, were over.

His sleep, when it came, was troubled and restless as his mind warred with his heart.

Chapter Twenty-seven

Manuelo had made the trip to Benton quickly. He knew Senora Clare was frantic, and he wanted to put her fears to rest.

He'd taken a room at the local hotel, then sought out the busiest saloon and gone in for a drink. He was there to listen, to watch and to learn everything he could about what was going on in town. He had made his plan on the ride there. Now all he had to do was find the right way to put it into action.

"What'll it be?" the barkeep asked.

"Whiskey," he answered, paying him when he set the glass before him.

"You're new in town, aren't you?"

"Just passing through," Manuelo told him.

"So you ain't here for the big trial?"

"What trial?"

"The Rangers brought in the Lawson gang, and their trial starts the first of next

329

week. They're a bloodthirsty bunch, and it'll be good to watch them swinging when the judge and jury get done with them."

"I never heard of the Lawsons."

"Where have you been?" the barkeep said, surprised by his ignorance. "They've been causing trouble all over West Texas for more than a year now. They're nothing but a bunch of cold-blooded murderers. There isn't a soul alive who's going to miss them once they're gone."

Manuelo nodded. "It's good you've got them behind bars."

"Oh, yeah. The sheriff even hired an extra deputy to make sure they don't escape."

"Good lawman?"

"Sheriff Burke is one of the best," the barkeep agreed. "But I tell you, that Ranger who tracked them down and brought them in is the one we should thank."

"I've always heard the Rangers get their men." Manuelo was wondering if the barkeep was talking about Chase, and he quickly got his answer.

"There isn't any doubt about that with Chase McBride. The Lawsons met their match in him. Hell, Ben and Jay Lawson and Carlos, the Mexican who rides with them, were all vowing to get even with McBride. But I got news for them. It ain't going to happen. Not the way the sheriff's guarding them. They're locked up good and tight."

Manuelo took a deep drink as the barkeep moved off to wait on someone else. Manuelo was glad to be alone. He needed time to think. It was good to know that there was an extra deputy working at the jail. That might complicate things a little, but not too much. He'd just have to kill two lawmen instead of one during the jailbreak. He must make sure there were no witnesses.

After he finished his drink, Manuelo left the saloon and made his way through town. He located the jail and managed a quick look inside as he passed by. He could see that the cells were in back, separated from the front office. That was good — real good.

Manuelo strolled around back and crept unseen through the dark alley to the back of the jail. He wanted to make sure he knew where everything was before he made his move. There was a barred but open window high on the jail wall. He moved as close as he could to it before tossing a single small pebble through it.

He waited.

Nothing happened.

He found another small stone and threw it through the window. The second pebble found its mark, and he heard a muttered curse from inside.

"I am here to help you," Manuelo whispered in Spanish to the prisoners.

There was a long silence; then one of the men answered, his voice barely audible.

"Who are you?" the man replied in Spanish just in case anyone else was around listening.

"A friend."

"We have no friends."

"Yes, you do. Do you want to get out of there?"

"What the hell do you think?"

"Then be ready. Tomorrow night. But there is a price for your freedom."

"What?"

"Chase McBride. I want him dead."

"That'll be our pleasure."

"Be ready. I will be back."

Manuelo moved away into the night. He returned to his hotel room and made a mental list of everything he was going to need for the Lawson gang — horses, money and supplies enough to get them to Sidewinder. If everything went as planned, this time tomorrow night the Lawsons would be on their way to seek revenge on Chase McBride.

The following morning, Manuelo left the

hotel, bought the supplies he needed and pretended to be leaving Benton. He checked at the stable and saw horses there he could steal to use for the escape.

It would not be easy, but he would do it.

It was for Senora Clare.

That was all that mattered.

Senora Clare's mother had been kind to him and had helped him when he'd been in need. He owed it to her to take care of Clare in the same way. He would do whatever was necessary to make her happy.

Manuelo rode a short way out of town and found a secluded spot to pass the time. He would be on his way home in a few hours. He hoped Senora Clare would be pleased with what he'd accomplished. He hoped, too, that the Lawson gang was as deadly as the bartender had said they were.

Sundown had come none too soon for Manuelo. He'd waited as long as he could, wanting the town to be settled for the night. Then he'd headed back in. It had taken longer than he'd expected to get the horses, but, practiced thief that he was, he'd managed it without incident, tying them up, saddled and ready, in the alley behind the jail.

Now Manuelo was ready to put his plan into action. Pretending to be drunk, he made his way to the street and staggered through the door of the jail, confronting the deputy sitting at the desk.

"There's trouble down at the saloon!" he told him, slurring his speech.

"What kind of trouble?" the deputy asked as he jumped to his feet.

"There's been a shooting!"

The deputy was unsure exactly what to do. The sheriff had ordered him to guard the office while he went to take a look around the town. "You'll have to go get the sheriff. He's out on the streets somewhere. I've got to stay here and guard the prisoners."

"But the men doing the shooting could get away! You have to do something!" Manuelo moved closer to the deputy, wanting to lure him from behind his desk. "They could be riding out right now!"

Finally the deputy came around his desk, and Manuelo made his move. In one perfect motion, he drew the knife he kept in his belt and stabbed the deputy. The lawman didn't even make a sound as he fell to the floor. Manuelo found the key to the cell and dragged the deputy in the back where the prisoners were anxiously waiting for him.

"Good job! He didn't even scream!" Ben Lawson said.

"Who the hell are you, anyway?" Jay Lawson asked, studying Manuelo, wondering why he wanted them loose to go after McBride.

"It doesn't matter who I am. It only matters that you get out of here before the sheriff comes back. Everything you need is in the alley. Let's go."

Manuelo let them out of their cells and led them out of the office by way of the back door. Everything was as he'd left it.

"Here's some money for you to buy whatever else you need to get McBride." He took most of the cash he'd brought with him and handed it over to the Lawson brothers.

They took the money greedily, stuffing it in their pockets.

Manuelo went on to explain where McBride was and how best they could get at him.

"Where can we find you if we need you?" they asked.

"You can't. You don't know me. Just do what you said you were going to do, and everything will be fine."

"What if we just take the money and run?" one of them asked.

"You want to let McBride get away with what he did to you?"

They looked at each other with understanding as they mounted up.

"Go slow riding out. You don't want to

draw any attention to yourselves. I'll be waiting to hear that Chase McBride is dead."

"Like I told you before, it's gonna be our pleasure."

They disappeared into the night.

Manuelo didn't linger. He rode out, too. No one had yet raised the alarm that the deputy was dead, so he knew he'd get a good head start before the real trouble started in Benton. He hoped Senora Clare would be proud of what he'd accomplished. He couldn't wait to return to the Circle M and tell her.

Faith was looking forward to spending the day with Callie. She had seen Chase and Tanner off very early that morning, and then made the trip to the line shack.

Faith liked Callie a lot and hoped that this time they spent together would deepen their friendship. There was no doubt that passing the time with Callie would be more fun than staying around Clare. She was pleased to find Callie watching for her as she rode in.

"Good morning," Callie called out as Faith reined in and dismounted.

"Yes, it is a good morning," Faith responded. She tied up her mount and went to greet Callie on the small porch. "Because

I'm here with you."

"Why, thanks. Come on inside."

The line shack didn't offer much in the way of comfort, but Faith knew that at least here Callie and Tanner had their privacy. She envied them that. The women went inside to sit at a small table in the area that served as the kitchen.

"I'm glad you're here, too. With Tanner gone, it can get a little lonely up here. I keep a gun handy, but you never know what kind of varmint might show up."

"You're afraid here on the Circle M?"

Callie looked at her, her expression very serious. "I know Tanner didn't have a lot to do with Blackie Sherwood, but if Terry Malone showed up here on the ranch looking for him, what's to stop Sherwood from riding in, too?"

"It's a shame Tanner got caught up with that Malone. He must have been a terrible man."

"He was," Callie said, her tone serious, her expression pained. "My brother, Matt, would still be alive if it hadn't been for Malone."

"Well, for your sake, I hope Sherwood gets caught by the law real soon. Once he's behind bars, you'll know that everything is going to be all right."

"I hope so."

"Thank you for having me out here today. I was really dreading staying at the main house with Clare. She is one vicious woman."

"She is special, isn't she?" Callie said sarcastically.

"Special isn't the word I'd use."

"I was being nice," she laughed. "I don't know if you knew it or not, but she wants Tanner."

"'Wants' him?" Faith frowned.

"She's being trying to seduce him for years, but he won't have anything to do with her. She won't leave him alone. That's why we moved up here, to get away from her."

"I didn't realize that."

"Tanner's not interested in Clare at all, but she seems to think of nothing else. She's the reason he left home in the first place. She was trying to get him into her bed and Tom came in. Clare lied and told him that Tanner had made advances to her. Tom was furious. He hit Tanner and told him that he wasn't his son anymore and to get off the ranch. Tanner didn't come back again until he got the letter from Bill Hanes."

"I wonder why Tom wants his children back home now," Faith said thoughtfully. "It sounds like he never really cared about them. Why else would they all have left?"

"One word: Clare. Watch out for her."

"I have been, but knowing this, I'll be even more careful around her."

Chapter Twenty-eight

Chase and Tanner took the buckboard into Sidewinder; they would need it to bring back the supplies. The going was slow, and they had a lot of time to talk.

Chase was surprised by how well he and Tanner were getting along. He hadn't expected to feel welcome at the ranch, and yet Tanner had been most accepting of him, as had Jeb. He'd been wondering why Tanner had ever left the Circle M. It had been his home. He'd had parents who loved him.

"You know, when I was a kid I really envied you living on the ranch. It looked damned near perfect to me when I came here that time."

"Looks can be deceiving, Chase," Tanner said with little emotion. When Chase cast him a sidelong, almost surprised glance, he went on, "There wasn't much to envy after she came — "

"Clare?"

Tanner nodded. "My mother was barely cold in the ground when Pa married her. She turned my life into a living hell."

"I can imagine."

"If you think she's bad by herself, you should have lived here with the two of them." He gave a weary shake of his head. "Our father is one mean son of a bitch. Before my mother died, he made her life a total misery. Your mother wasn't the only woman he used."

"Why did you leave?"

Tanner's expression became strained. "For some reason, Clare wants me."

"What?"

"She's been after me from the moment she moved into the house. She cornered me one day, and when Pa walked in, she told him that I had tried to seduce her. Pa hit me and threw me off the ranch. He said I wasn't his son anymore."

"Where did you go?"

He shrugged. "I went crazy for a while. That was the time when I was with Terry Malone. After a while, though, Malone went his way and I went mine. Strange how things happen, isn't it? I got the letter from Bill Hanes and was getting drunk in a saloon when I ran into Malone again." He paused to look at Chase. "That was the night Malone and the other two robbed the Foster bank."

"You've got real good luck, don't you?" Chase remembered what Tanner had told him about the robbery and being arrested as part of the gang.

"I do now that I've got Callie."

"I know what you mean," Chase said, thinking of Faith.

They talked of general things the rest of the way into town, relaxed and at ease with each other.

Blackie Sherwood was not a happy man as he rode into Sidewinder, but he expected that in the next day or two his life was going to change. Hell, it had to. He looked around the town, liking the fact that Sidewinder seemed to be a wild place. There were lots of saloons and that made him feel right at home. The wilder the town, the safer he figured he'd be for the time being.

The Roundup Saloon looked like the liveliest place at this early hour, so he decided to stop there for a drink before he did anything else. If it was the busiest place in town, he was sure he'd be able to find out what he needed to know about Tanner

McBride and his ranch. With any luck at all, he'd be meeting up with Tanner — and Malone — before the day was out.

That thought brought a smile to his face. He walked through the swinging doors, ready to have a good time. He had enough cash left for a drink or two, and he hoped that by then he'd know what he needed to know.

"Whiskey," Blackie ordered as he sidled up to the bar.

The bartender quickly put a glass before him and poured him a healthy shot. Blackie shoved the payment across the bar and took a drink.

"Good stuff," he said as the whiskey burned its way down to his gut. He needed strong, and strong was what he'd gotten.

"New in town?" Barney, the bartender, asked.

"Yeah, just rode in. It's a hot one out there."

"You like hot?" a sultry female voice asked from behind him.

Blackie turned to find himself staring down at one of the prettiest saloon girls he'd seen in a long time. "Well, sugar, it all depends on whether you're talking about the weather or women."

"You aren't too wrong on my name, big

guy," she told him. "It's Candy — and I am sweet."

"But are you hot?" he asked, enjoying the female attention. It had been a while since he'd had time to think about women.

"I can be whatever you want," Candy purred. "Why don't we sit down and talk about it?"

"I'd like that," Blackie agreed, and he followed her to a table in the back of the room. He was glad she picked one where he could watch the comings and goings of the customers. He always had to be careful, with the Rangers after him.

Behind the bar, Barney just smiled. Candy sure was a hardworking girl.

"So, big guy, where you from?" she asked, pulling her chair close to his.

"Nowhere in particular," he answered.

"Surely you've done something exciting in your life?" She leaned forward, giving him a better view of her ample cleavage.

"Right now, I'm thinking you're the most exciting thing in my life."

"I knew I liked you when you walked in." She laughed, glad that he was proving so easy to handle.

Blackie made his drink last. The reality that he was flat-assed broke made him angry. He wanted to bed this saloon girl, and he didn't even have enough money to do it. He swore silently as he tried to figure out a plan of action. He needed to pull off a job. He needed to rob something, but it would be tricky alone. He wanted to find Terry Malone and get back in business. Once they teamed up again, he'd be all right.

Blackie focused his gaze on the bar, and he realized this would be a good place to hold up. There would be a lot of money in the till of a busy saloon like this. On the other hand, because it was so busy, robbing the place would be hard, and right now he was looking for fast and easy.

"What kind of fun do you have here in Sidewinder?" he asked.

"There's always something going on here at the Roundup."

"I could tell that as I rode in — and by looking at you." He leered at her. "This must be where the action is."

"Sometimes there's too much action, though. There was even a shoot-out here a few months ago. Some outlaw named Malone was killed and a woman was shot. It was downright terrifying."

Blackie hoped his expression didn't reveal the shock and sudden fury that jolted through him. "What happened? Was it a fight over the woman? Or a robbery?"

"No. From what everybody told me afterward, Malone was wanted by the law and the woman came in here after him wanting revenge. Tanner McBride showed up just in time to save her."

"Well, I'm glad it's quiet around here today. I don't need that kind of excitement." His mood had gone completely black. From what she'd told him, Malone was dead, and Tanner had shot him! Blackie had to change his plans and quick. He couldn't trust Tanner — and Tanner had been his only hope.

"What kind of excitement do you need?" She put her hand on his thigh and squeezed.

"How about another drink for right now?"

Chase and Tanner placed their order with Hiram at the store.

"How are things going out on the Circle M? Everything all right?"

"As good as can be expected," Tanner told him. "Pa's not getting any better."

"Sorry to hear that." Hiram nodded toward the merchandise they were loading. "You've got a big order today. You want to pay for it now or put it on the bill?"

"Just bill us for it," Tanner told him. Clare hadn't given them any cash.

"It's run up pretty steep now. Better tell your pa."

"I'll do that, Hiram. Thanks."

They stowed the supplies.

"I want to stop in at the sheriff's office for a minute," Chase said. "My captain said he'd contact me through him if he needed me."

"I'll meet you over at the Roundup, how's that?"

"Fine. I won't be long."

Chase made his way to see Sheriff Scott. He knew the chances were slim that he'd heard anything about Blackie Sherwood, but he had to ask.

"Afternoon, Sheriff," Chase said as he entered the office.

"McBride." The lawman nodded.

"Anything new on Sherwood?"

"Not a thing. It's been real quiet around here, just the way I like it."

"I'll be staying on at the Circle M for a while, so if you hear anything at all, just send word out to me there."

"I'll do that," he told him.

"You got time for a drink? Tanner's over at the Roundup and I'm supposed to meet him there."

"I'm on duty, so I won't be drinking, but I could sure use some time away from this desk." He pushed back and stood up.

Chase was thinking that if the lawman got away from his desk more often, the town might be a lot quieter, but he didn't say anything. They left the office and headed for the saloon.

Tanner strode into the saloon and was greeted warmly by Barney and the owner, Ace. He stood at the bar with them having a drink, relaxing before riding back to the ranch and dealing with Clare and his father again. It felt good to be away from the strain there, and he was glad to be among friends.

"What's this news I hear that there's another McBride?" Ace asked.

"Where'd you hear that?"

"I've got my sources," he answered with a smile.

"Well, it's true. You'll get to meet him. He came into town with me today."

"I'll be damned," Ace said, giving a shake of his head. "If that don't beat all. What do you think of him?"

"He's a good man."

"Don't take after your pa, huh?"

"You got that right." Tanner downed his whiskey and Barney refilled his glass.

"How's Callie?"

"She's doing fine."

"You enjoying married life?"

"You better believe it. I've never had it so good."

They shared a knowing look. Ace had a real fondness for Callie and was glad that she'd found happiness with Tanner.

In the back of the saloon, Blackie went quiet. *Tanner McBride had just walked in!* Blackie sat still, trying to figure out what to do. His first instinct was to back-shoot the son of a bitch from where he sat, but he knew he'd never get away with it. Tanner had shot down Malone, and he deserved no better, but Blackie wasn't big on self-sacrifice. He wouldn't be able to get out of the saloon quick enough to save himself if he started shooting now.

His hand rested on his sidearm. He prided himself on being a great shot. When Tanner left, he'd follow him. After the shooting, there would be enough confusion that he should be able to make his getaway without too much trouble — he hoped.

"I think I'll go see what's taking Chase so long. I want you to meet him."

"I'll be right here waiting for you," Ace said, glad that things seemed to be working out for Tanner.

Tanner paid Barney for the drink and started from the Roundup to find his brother. He did not notice the man who got to his feet in the back of the saloon and followed him.

"Where are you going?" Candy pouted, surprised that the stranger was leaving her without a backward glance.

"I have some business to tend to, woman." Blackie's answer was curt.

Candy was surprised by the sudden change in him. She'd thought she'd have him upstairs in no time, but instead he was walking out on her. She noticed that he seemed cautious as he made his way toward the front of the saloon. She watched as he paused at the swinging doors to look outside, then pushed through. Wondering what was going on, she got up to follow him.

Blackie was ready. Once he was outside, he could take his best shot and then get the hell out of there.

He watched from the saloon doorway as Tanner moved off down the sidewalk. He waited just a moment longer, then boldly stepped out after him. He was ready.

With a sense of dead calm, Blackie went for his gun.

Back-shooting Tanner was perfect.

Malone deserved to be avenged.

Chapter Twenty-nine

Chase and Sheriff Scott had just reached the corner down from the Roundup when Chase saw Tanner come out of the saloon and turn their way. Another man came out of the saloon after Tanner, and Chase's instincts screamed an immediate warning. Something about the man — the way he looked around before following Tanner and the way he was moving — alerted Chase that there might be trouble.

His instincts proved right.

Chase saw the scar on the man's face just as he went for his gun and took aim at Tanner.

"Get down!" Chase shouted to his brother as he drew his sidearm and fired.

Tanner dropped at Chase's shout.

Blackie had gotten off a shot that missed. Jarred by the shouted warning, he turned and fired wildly in the other man's direction.

The sheriff was slow to react, but finally managed to draw his gun and return fire.

Chase dove for cover as he got off two more accurate shots, hitting Blackie squarely in the chest. The outlaw collapsed and lay sprawled and bloodied on the sidewalk.

"Tanner!" Chase got up and ran to where Tanner lay on the ground. He kept his gun in hand. He had to be ready in case there was any life left in Blackie.

Tanner slowly got to his feet. His expression was stunned as he glanced from Blackie's dead body to Chase.

"You all right?" Chase demanded, tense from the excitement and danger.

"Yeah — I'm fine."

Chase knelt down beside Blackie to make sure he was dead. There was no mistaking the scar on his face. Chase had gotten his man. "It's Blackie Sherwood."

"Is he dead?" Tanner asked.

"Yes."

Tanner was frowning as he stared down at Blackie. He realized how close he'd come to dying, and it was unnerving.

He looked Chase straight in the eye. "Thanks."

His brother had saved his life.

Strange, almost foreign emotions welled

up inside of Chase. He and Tanner had come close to dying just now. If he hadn't been paying attention, they would all have been gunned down. He was relieved that Tanner hadn't been hurt, but he was still shaken by the realization that he'd looked death in the face and had been frightened by it. Before now — before Faith — he'd had no fear of death. But now, all that had changed.

"I'm just glad you're all right." Chase clapped Tanner on the back.

Everyone in the Roundup rushed outside to see what all the shooting had been about.

Only then did Chase realize the sheriff wasn't with them. Turning, he saw him lying unmoving a short distance away.

"Tanner, go for the doctor!" he ordered.

Tanner raced off as Chase hurried to the lawman's side. But he was too late. One of Blackie's shots had hit the lawman straight in the heart. Sheriff Scott was dead.

Silently, Chase swore over this senseless loss of life.

This was a moment when he should have been feeling triumphant. Frank's murder had been avenged. Blackie Sherwood was dead. He'd never be killing anybody else again. But Chase felt no joy. He only felt sickened by the innocent lawman's death.

"What happened, Chase?" Hiram, the storekeeper, reached him first.

Chase slowly got to his feet and finally holstered his gun. He gestured toward the dead outlaw. "That's Blackie Sherwood. He was a wanted man. Sheriff Scott and I saw him draw his gun on Tanner. We both fired at Sherwood, but he managed to get off some shots before we hit him. The sheriff's dead."

"Are you and Tanner all right?" Hiram asked. He knew there was nothing more they could do for the lawman.

"We're fine."

"Thank God."

Tanner came back with Doc Rogers then. The physician hurried to tend to the sheriff, but it was too late. There was nothing left to be done for him. He checked on Blackie, but he, too, had gone to meet his maker. Taking charge, the doctor sent for the undertaker.

Hiram helped the doctor take care of everything as people began going back into the saloon.

Tanner went to stand with Chase.

"I was coming to get you," Tanner began. "I had no idea Blackie was in the saloon — let alone in town. I guess I should have been more watchful."

"It doesn't matter. The good news is

you're all right," Chase said.

They stared at each other long and hard.

"You saved my life, Chase." Tanner's voice was intense, matching the fierceness of what he was feeling.

Chase managed a half smile. "I guess you owe me now." He liked the thought.

"I sure do. How about a drink?"

"I need one — at least."

Tanner and Chase walked into the saloon together.

Ace and Barney had not yet returned to their duties. They met them at the door.

"This is your brother?" Ace asked Tanner.

"Yes," Tanner proudly proclaimed. "This is Chase. He's a Ranger."

"You took care of Isaac in here the other night, didn't you?" Barney asked astutely.

"That was me."

"No wonder you're so damned good. You're a Ranger and Tanner's brother." Ace stuck his hand out.

Chase took it in a firm grasp.

"Your drinks are on the house. Did you hear me, Barney?"

"I sure did, boss," the barkeep told him, smiling at Tanner and Chase as he returned to his place behind the bar to serve them.

"I'm glad you're both all right," Ace told them. "It's a damned shame about the sheriff. What are we going to do now for law here in town? Sheriff Scott wasn't much, but he was all we had."

"You and Hiram will find somebody," Tanner said.

"I guess we will," Ace said thoughtfully as he moved away.

Tanner and Chase got their drinks from Barney and went to sit at a table in a quiet part of the bar. They'd had enough excitement for one day. They drank in silence for a while, each lost in thought about what might have happened if Chase hadn't been there at the key moment.

"I wish Callie and Faith were here with us," Tanner said seriously. "If they were, we wouldn't have to go back to the ranch tonight. We could stay here and enjoy ourselves."

"You hate it that much there?" Chase still wasn't used to thinking of Tanner as being unwelcome at the Circle M, too. "I always thought that as a 'real' son, your life had to be perfect."

Tanner shook his head slowly as Candy brought them each another drink. "My mother tried her best to protect us, but she couldn't hide everything from us. We knew how Pa was. We saw how he treated her."

"Your mother must have been special.

Strong, too, to stay with him like she did."

"I guess she believed her wedding vows. Damn, but I still miss her. She was the only good thing about living here."

"How did she die? No one's ever said."

A look of pain and anger crossed Tanner's face at his question, and Tanner downed the drink before him in one swallow before answering.

"Pa swears I killed her."

"What?" Chase was shocked. "What happened?"

"There was an accident. The wheel came off the wagon she was riding in and she died in the accident." He looked at Chase, his expression grim and furious. "I fixed that wheel! But no one believed me except Lauren."

"I believe you," Chase said solemnly.

Tanner sat there in silence before looking up at him. "Thanks."

Candy returned with another round of drinks for them. Tanner took his and quickly took another deep swallow.

"Your father — " Chase started.

"I hate to remind you, Chase, but he's your father, too," Tanner said, interrupting him.

Chase grimaced. "I have trouble thinking of him that way after what he did to my mother." He went on to explain how sick his mother had been, how she'd desperately wanted to see Tom before she died and how he'd refused to go to her. "When I got back to the mission, she'd already died."

"I'm sorry."

"So am I. I never got to tell her I loved her — or say good-bye."

"I understand."

They finished the drinks they had, and Candy brought them each another.

"I think we'd better head back to the ranch after this one," Chase said with a chuckle as he lifted his glass.

"I know." Tanner's grin was a bit lopsided.

They downed their drinks a little more slowly this time.

Chase grew more thoughtful as he considered all that had happened that day. He had come to Sidewinder to get Blackie Sherwood, and he'd done it. That had been his one and only reason for showing up in town, even though he'd used Tom's letter as his excuse. When he went back to Faith, he could tell her there was no reason for them to stay any longer. They could leave the Circle M — and Clare — right away.

It surprised Chase that the thought of never seeing Tanner again troubled him. He frowned in concentration as he tried to sort out his feelings about all that had happened.

"You ready to head home?" Tanner asked.

Chase found himself answering, "Yes."

And he wondered. *Was it home?*

Faith was waiting there for him. *Did that make it home?*

It was getting dark when Faith and Callie heard the buckboard approaching. They had come to the main house for dinner, expecting their men to be back, and had started to worry as time passed and Chase and Tanner didn't return.

"They're back," Faith said as she hurried out onto the porch.

Callie followed close behind her, but Clare didn't bother. The thought of watching Tanner kiss Callie made her furious, so she stayed indoors.

As the two men rode up to the house, Tanner told Chase, "Let's not tell Callie and Faith what happened in town right away. I want to tell Callie later, when we're back at our place."

Chase understood the wisdom of Tanner's plan. It had been a long day, and he just wanted to be alone with Faith. "That's fine with me."

They reined in before the house.

Faith was frowning as she looked at the two smiling men climbing down from the buckboard. Something was going on, but she didn't know what. She had never seen Chase looking so happy before, and she wondered what they'd been up to.

"Evening, ladies," Tanner called out in a courtly manner.

Callie and Faith exchanged a puzzled look.

"It's good to see you," Chase told Faith in a deep voice. His gaze went over her, visually caressing her from the pale silken length of her hair to her sweet, feminine curves. He actually regretted that she'd worn a dress tonight. He'd come to enjoy the sight of her in those pants. He'd been gone only a matter of hours, but in that time much had changed. He wanted to talk to Faith alone, and the sooner the better.

Faith sensed that something was very different about Chase, but she couldn't imagine what. His gaze was so intense on her that a shiver of sensual recognition shot through her. "It's good to see you, too. I missed you today."

"How did everything go in Sidewinder?" Callie asked.

"Same as usual," Tanner answered. "Ace said to tell you hello."

"I should have known you'd pay him a visit," she laughed.

"What's a trip into town without a stop at the Roundup?" he countered. "Chase, help me unload these supplies so Callie and I can leave before it gets too much later."

Chase turned away from Faith and went to help his brother. It didn't take long for them to carry the supplies inside. On the last trip in, Tanner had just put the sacks in the kitchen when Clare appeared before him, blocking the door.

"I missed seeing you today, Tanner," she breathed, looking up at him adoringly.

He stiffened and took a step back, wanting to keep some distance between them. He was on to her tricks and wouldn't put anything past her. "How's Pa?"

"The same," she said with evident disgust. "The next time you go into town, I want to go with you."

"That would be a good idea," he told her.

Her heart skipped a beat at the thought that he actually wanted to be with her. "I'd love that. How soon do you want to go again?"

"Probably not for another week or so."

"We could have a wonderful time there." In her mind's eye, she could see them taking a room at the hotel for half a day and . . . "We could . . ."

"Actually, Clare, the reason I want you to go to town is to settle up the bill you've run up with Hiram at the store. It was kind of embarrassing when he asked us for money today, and we didn't have enough to pay him. I told him I'd let you and Pa know about it so you could take care of it."

The excitement that had filled her turned to ice as the pain of being a woman scorned seared her.

Tanner had been toying with her!

He hadn't really wanted to be alone with her!

"I'll tell your father what Hiram said in the morning," she bit out. She was ready to do something drastic to wipe the smirk off Tanner's face when she heard Chase behind her.

"Callie's ready to leave, Tanner." Chase had realized that his brother wasn't right behind him when he'd left the house. After their earlier conversation, he'd had a feeling about what was going on and had come back to rescue him.

Clare stormed off without a word, disappearing upstairs.

"That's twice in one day you've saved me," Tanner joked.

"You seemed like you were holding your own."

"You can never tell with Clare. You can't trust her at all. Be careful around her, and tell Faith, too."

"She already knows."

Chapter Thirty

Chase stood with Faith on the porch watching Callie and Tanner until they had ridden out of sight.

"Pretty night," Faith remarked, gazing up at the moonlit, starry sky.

"It's a beautiful night. Let's go upstairs."

She was surprised that he wanted to go up already. "Aren't you hungry?"

"Yes," he said seriously, "but not for food."

He gave her a knowing smile as he took her hand and drew her along with him back inside the house. Neither spoke as they went to their room.

Faith didn't know what had inspired this mood in Chase. He was acting very strange.

When they entered the room and locked the door behind them, Chase didn't waste time on words. He simply took Faith in his arms and kissed her, telling her by his embrace all that was in his heart.

"What happened in town today?" Faith asked when he finally broke off the kiss.

Chase held her a little away from him. He gazed down at her, the look in his eyes intense. "Blackie Sherwood was in Sidewinder."

"You were right about him coming here!" she gasped.

"Yes, and thank God I was there when he decided to make his move."

"What happened?"

"He was after Tanner. If I'd been a minute later meeting up with Tanner, Tanner would be dead right now."

"But you got him?" she asked breathlessly, terrified by the thought of what might have happened.

"I got him." Chase nodded, his tone as deadly as his aim had been.

"How did it happen?"

He explained everything, ending with the sheriff's death.

"That's so terrible about Sheriff Scott."

"If I could have done anything to save him, I would have." He was grim.

"I know, but you could have been killed, too." Faith moved closer to him, hugging him, resting her head against his chest, loving the sound of the powerful, steady beat of his heart.

Chase held her, treasuring her nearness. He knew it was time. He had to tell her what had come as a revelation to him that day. The words were torn from him. "Faith — what happened today made me realize something."

Faith waited, not sure what he was going to say.

"I know our marriage started out in name only, but since then everything's changed. I want this to be a real marriage. I love you, Faith."

Her heart swelled with joy, and tears burned in her eyes. "You do?"

"You're the only woman I'll ever want or need," he finished quietly, waiting for her reaction, fearful that she didn't love him. He knew he was a bastard. He knew he was a half-breed and would never fit completely in white society, but no other man would ever love her more than he did.

"Chase — " Faith breathed his name in a sigh as she pulled him down for a kiss. "I don't know what I would have done if anything had happened to you in town today. You're my hero and my husband. I love you, too."

Her words touched him deeply and he gathered her to his heart, seeking her lips in a cherishing kiss that told her everything she needed to know about his devotion to her.

Their desire blazed to life and they moved to lie together upon the bed. It was a moment of complete abandon. Each touch, each kiss built the fire of their need to a raging inferno. They sought to give to each other that ultimate pleasure, wanting only to please, only to satisfy, only to cherish and love and adore.

Chase moved over Faith and made her his own. The moment was tender yet passionate.

"I love you," he told her in a voice husky with emotion.

"I'm glad," she whispered back as she began to move beneath him, enticing him to take her quickly.

Her seductive movements broke what little control Chase had over himself. Mindless in his search for ecstasy, he set a rapturous pace. He lost himself in the beauty of their union. They crested passion's heights together. In the aftermath of their lovemaking, they lay quietly together, awed by the power of what had passed between them. They were one.

Peace and joy were theirs.

"What really happened in town today?" Callie asked Tanner as they reached the line shack. She went inside ahead of him and lit the lamps. She'd been very aware that he'd avoided talking about the trip to town during the ride. Now that she could look him in the eye, she was sure she would get some answers from him.

Tanner had known this moment was coming. There could be no hiding the truth from her, so he figured he might as well tell her everything. It would be better if she heard it from him.

"Blackie Sherwood was in Sidewinder looking for me."

"He was?" she asked in a strained voice. "What happened?"

"If it hadn't been for Chase, I'd be dead right now."

Shock bolted through her. "What?"

He quickly told her about Blackie following him and Chase saving the day. He also told her of the sheriff's death. Callie threw herself into his arms. The thought of losing him was more than she could bear. He cradled her near as she cried out her terror of losing him.

"If anything had happened to you, I don't know what I would have done."

"I'm fine," he said, trying to calm her.

She just held on to him even more desperately. "I love you, Tanner."

Tanner bent and scooped her up into his arms. Cradling her to him, he strode to the bed and laid her there. He started to move away from her to undress, but she wouldn't let him go. With eager hands, she began to work at the buttons on his shirt. He surrendered to her mastery and enjoyed every minute. They made love with a fierce intensity that surprised them both.

In the aftermath of their passion, Callie said a silent prayer of thanks that her husband was safe and that Chase had been there to save him. She didn't know how she was ever going to thank Chase, but she would think of something.

Chase was in no hurry to leave the sanctity of their bedroom the next morning. He had cherished the long hours of loving he'd shared with Faith. If he had his way, they would never get out of bed again. He realized he might have had to leave her for a moment or two to forage for food, but otherwise, he would be perfectly happy to spend the rest of his natural life in her arms — and eternity, too, now that he thought about it.

"We should get up, you know," Faith said, her voice a purr of pure satisfaction as she lay nestled by his side. "Jeb is probably looking for you."

Chase only grunted in response as he gathered her in his arms for another kiss. He never tired of kissing her.

"Are you sure you want to get up?" he growled.

Faith gave a throaty laugh. "Actually, I'd be happy if we never had to leave this room again. I like it being just the two of us without anyone else around."

Chase was silent for a moment. His reason for being in Sidewinder was over. His job was done. As much as he'd tried to avoid thinking about it, he would have to send a wire to his captain today and let him know that Blackie Sherwood was dead. It was time for him to move on to his next assignment. The thought of heading out again bothered him. He didn't know what kind of a life he could have with Faith if he was constantly on the move. He had no place to leave her while he worked. He had no home.

Or did he?

He thought of Tanner and how they had bonded.

"Why are you frowning?" Faith asked, wondering what could be bothering him so much.

"I was just thinking that there's no reason for us to be here any longer. We can pack up and leave today, if you want."

"The thought of being away from Clare thrills me, but this decision isn't up to me, Chase," she said softly, emphasizing her words with a soft, quick kiss. "It's your choice. I know you're a Ranger, and you've got a job to do. I've known that from the start. I'll do whatever you want to do, and I'll go with you wherever you go."

Chase pulled her down for a heartfelt, cherishing kiss. He'd never had anyone but his mother care for him and love him this way before. He felt like a whole new world was opening up to him. A world of commitment and dedication, and he found that he liked that world very much.

"I'll wire my captain today and then we'll see what happens."

"So we're going to stay on here for at least a little while longer?"

"Yes."

"Oh, good."

And she showed him why she was glad they were staying.

Clare had gone pale. She looked stricken as she spoke with Hiram and Bill.

"I had no idea," she gasped. "They came home last night, but they never told me any of this."

"It was damned scary, I tell you," Hiram

said. "Chase is a fine lawman, though. He took care of everything. You should be proud of him."

"Of course." Clare hid her utter disgust at their high praise of Chase. She managed a tight, pained smile. "They both could have been killed by that outlaw. And to think, he almost shot Tanner down in cold blood!"

Clare didn't know what she'd do if anything ever happened to Tanner.

"It was Chase who saved him," Bill pointed out again.

"And that's why we're here," Hiram went on. "We need to talk to Chase. Is he around?"

Clare could not imagine what these two upstanding citizens of Sidewinder wanted with Chase. "Well, yes, but he hasn't come down yet this morning."

Hiram chuckled. "I'm not surprised. He and Tanner raised a few at the Roundup after all the excitement."

"Let me go get him for you. Why don't you two make yourselves comfortable there in the parlor?"

"Don't mind if we do."

Clare went upstairs, but she didn't have to knock on Chase's bedroom door. He was already on his way down with Faith by his side.

"You've got company," she said sharply. "Bill and Hiram are downstairs."

"I saw them ride in," Chase said. "What do they want?"

"They didn't say, other than to speak with you." Her tone was cold as she demanded, "Why didn't you and Tanner tell me the truth of what happened in town yesterday? Why did I have to find out from Bill and Hiram?"

"We wanted to tell Faith and Callie privately. We would have told you today."

"How kind of you!" She was sarcastic. "Surely your father had a right to know that his son was almost killed!"

"His *sons*," Faith emphasized.

Clare turned away. "I've got to tell Tom. Hiram and Bill are waiting for you in the parlor."

As she walked away she couldn't decide which was worse — listening to the two men talk about how wonderful Chase was or spending time with Tom.

Chase and Faith went downstairs to meet with the two men.

"Here's our hero," Hiram said with pride as he stood to shake hands with Chase.

"Good job," Bill added.

"What brings you out to the Circle M?" Chase asked once they'd all been seated.

Bill and Hiram exchanged glances, then Hiram spoke up.

"Chase, I'm here representing most of the businessmen in Sidewinder, so I'm speaking with authority."

"We've come here to offer you a job," Bill explained.

"I've got a job."

"We know you're a Ranger, but now that you've got family here in Sidewinder, we thought you might be considering settling down, and if you were — "

"We'd like you to take over for Sheriff Scott," Bill finished. "Sidewinder could use a good man like you."

"You want me to be sheriff?" Chase said aloud, surprised by the offer and not quite sure what to think about it.

"That's right. You've already proven yourself. We know you're good. We know you could handle it," Hiram insisted.

"I know Tom wanted you to live here at the Circle M, but I think if I talk to him, he could be convinced to let you take up residence in town," Bill added. "I can speak to him now, if you're interested in the offer."

Chase frowned as he tried to imagine quitting the Rangers and becoming the sheriff of Sidewinder. He'd been worried about the future and Faith. This seemed like the perfect opportunity for him.

Hiram thought Chase's hesitation meant he would refuse, and he quickly added, "I own a nice little house in town. You could live there rent free as part of your pay. What do you say? Sidewinder needs you, Chase."

Faith couldn't believe what she was hearing. It seemed the answer to their dilemma. Chase would still be a lawman and they would still be in Sidewinder, but they'd have a place of their own. They'd have a home and they would be together. She looked over at him to find him gazing down at her.

"Would you be happy as sheriff?" she asked.

"It might be tough at times," Chase warned her.

"But we'd be together."

That was what mattered to him. She was his love, his life. He didn't want to be apart from her.

Chase looked at Bill and Hiram. "It looks like you've got yourself a new sheriff."

Both men stood, and Chase rose, too. They shook hands all around.

"Let me talk to Tom. Once that's settled, everything will be just fine," Bill said.

Bill went upstairs to find Clare in the room with Tom. Tom looked about the same as usual, which wasn't good.

"I need to talk with you," Bill told him.
"It's important."

"I can leave you alone," Clare offered,
glad for a chance to get out of the sickroom.

"You might as well stay. This affects you,
too, indirectly," Bill said.

"What is it?" Tom demanded.

"Did Clare tell you what happened in
town yesterday?"

"She told me," he growled. "That Tanner
has always been a damned fool!"

"I'm not here to discuss Tanner. I want to
talk to you about Chase."

"What about him?"

"Hiram and I spoke with some of the
other merchants in town overnight, and we
want to hire Chase to be the new sheriff."

Tom was truly surprised by this. "They
want to hire a half-breed?"

"They want to hire a damned good lawman, Tom," Bill shot back, angered by his
remark. "He's your son. You should be
proud of him."

Tom said nothing.

"Chase has agreed to take the job. The
difficulty comes from your requirement that
he live here on the Circle M. He can't do the
job from here. We need him in town."

"That would be fine!" Clare put in excit-
edly. The thought of having the bastard out

of the house delighted her. It would give her far more opportunities to get Tanner alone.

Tom cast her a cold look, then turned back toward Bill. "You think he'll do a good job?"

"No doubt about it. Sidewinder needs the likes of Chase McBride."

Tom fell silent, glowering as he thought about it for a long minute. He knew if Chase took the job, he would stay on for a while. He finally answered, "All right."

"Good. I'll go tell him."

Chapter Thirty-one

Chase and Faith rode out to see Tanner and Callie as soon as Hiram and Bill left. Chase wanted to tell Tanner right away about his decision.

"What are you doing here?" Tanner asked, smiling as he came outside to greet them.

"I've got some news for you," Chase told him as he and Faith dismounted and tied up their mounts.

"The heck with your news, Chase McBride," Callie said, running off the porch and going straight to him.

With Faith looking on, Callie grabbed Chase by the arm and pulled him down to plant a big kiss on his cheek.

"I love you, Chase," Callie told him, her eyes filled with warm emotion.

He looked at her in surprise.

"Thank you for helping Tanner. You're the best brother a man could have."

Chase swallowed tightly at her words. "You're welcome, Callie." He looked up to where Tanner stood on the porch and asked with a grin, "Does your wife always run around and tell other men she loves them?"

"No, Chase." Tanner turned serious. "Only you."

Callie and Faith hugged each other, and they all went inside and sat down at the small table to talk.

"So what news have you got for me?"

"Bill and Hiram came out to the house," Chase began.

"Was something wrong in town?"

"No. They came out to make me a job offer. You're looking at the new sheriff of Sidewinder."

"What?" Callie was delighted and shocked.

"They offered me the job, and I decided to take it."

"You're willing to quit the Rangers?"

"Yes," Chase answered. "I won't be traveling so much this way, and Faith and I will have a home."

"What did Pa say? You'll have to move into town, won't you?"

"Bill talked to him. He said it was all right, but I would have taken the job whether he approved or not." At Tanner's surprised look, Chase went on, "There's something I never told you. I didn't come here for any inheritance or looking to develop any family ties. I was on assignment. I used Hanes's letter as my excuse, but I was in Sidewinder to get Blackie Sherwood."

"And you did," Tanner said.

"That's right. The Ranger he killed in the shoot-out was my friend Frank Anderson. I was going to find Blackie no matter how long it took."

"So why are you staying on? You could just leave, ride on out of here," Tanner said.

"Not anymore." He looked up at Tanner. "I may not have come here looking for family ties, but I've made them. We're staying."

"And we're glad," Callie said with a smile. "I don't care what brought you to us. I'm just glad you're here."

"We're going to be a lot happier once we've moved out of the main house away from Clare," Faith said, sharing a knowing look with Callie.

"We understand."

They talked for a little while longer, then Chase and Faith returned to the main house to pack up their things and get ready to leave. The hours couldn't pass quickly enough for Faith.

Clare sought Chase out late in the afternoon to tell him that Tom wanted to see him. He went to the bedroom, knocked and let himself in when Tom called out to him.

"So you're leaving the ranch," Tom said, his gaze sharp upon Chase as he stood at the foot of the bed. "Can't wait to get out of here, huh?"

"To tell you the truth, you're right. I can't. I have to thank you for all your hospitality, *Pa.*"

"That's the first time you've called me Pa. I been waiting for that."

"Don't get used to it."

"Watch your mouth! You're getting to be a lot like Tanner."

"I'll take that as a compliment."

"Well, take it and get out."

"My pleasure," Chase said with an indifferent shrug.

And he left.

As he walked down the hall, he couldn't help wondering why Tom had wanted him there. What was the point?

As he thought about it, though, Chase realized he was glad that he'd come. Now he had Tanner. He had a brother.

He sought out Faith and told her it was time to go. She was delighted to be leaving the ranch that night. She'd thought they

381

were staying until the morning.

They went downstairs to say good-bye to Tiny and to tell Jeb what was happening before they rode out.

Clare saw them coming out of the kitchen carrying their things, and she went to confront them.

"Where are you going? I thought you weren't leaving until tomorrow."

"We've decided to ride on into town tonight," Chase told her.

"I'm sorry to see you go." She kept her tone sweet, but it was a lie. She was delighted to be rid of them.

"And we're sorry to be going," Faith lied back. "We'd love to stay on, but we can't."

"I understand." She looked at Chase. "Good luck with your job. I'm so happy for you."

In her heart, Clare was hoping Chase would be shot soon by some crazy drunk — if the Lawsons didn't get him first. She hoped Manuelo would come back soon with good news for her.

"Thanks, Clare. Take care of the old man."

They went out on the porch. She didn't bother to follow.

"Don't worry. I will."

She shut the door on them.

Faith and Chase went down to the stable and sought out Jeb. They told him all that had happened, and he was sorry to see them go. He helped them saddle up their horses. Chase decided to ride Harm and leave his other mount at the ranch for now.

"You take care, Sheriff," Jeb told him with a smile.

"We'll see you in town," Chase said.

"Just make sure you don't go arresting me!"

"Stay out of trouble and you'll be fine. Be careful, though, I might need to hire you to be my deputy."

"There are days when that might sound like a good idea, but I can't leave the Circle M."

They shook hands, and Faith gave him a quick hug before they mounted up and rode for Sidewinder to start a new life together.

"This is the house," Hiram said as he opened the door and held it wide for them to enter.

Chase and Faith walked into the small frame house, smiling. This was going to be their home. They liked it immediately. It was not a large house, but it was big enough for them — and it was already furnished. There were two bedrooms, a parlor and a kitchen.

"It's perfect, Hiram. Thank you," Faith said.

"Well, we townsfolk thank you. We appreciate Chase taking the job. We've needed a strong lawman for a long time now. Sheriff Scott was a decent enough man, but he liked to avoid trouble."

"Sometimes there's no avoiding it," Chase said.

"And that's why we wanted you."

They had already discussed his salary and had come to an agreed-upon amount. Things were working out nicely.

"Here are the keys to the office and the house," Hiram said, handing them over. "If there's anything else you need, just let me or Bill know and we'll take care of it."

"Thank you."

"And here's your badge."

Chase took the tin star from him. He was now officially the law in Sidewinder.

Hiram left them then, wanting to give them their privacy.

Faith went from room to room checking over everything.

"I can't believe that we're actually alone in our own house!" she said in delight as she went to Chase and hugged him.

Chase had never had his own home before and he smiled down at her. "It is ours — and we are alone, aren't we?"

Faith's eyes glowed as she shared Chase's thought. "Clare is not going to come through that door."

"And neither is anyone else," he finished.

He bent and scooped her up into his arms. "I think we need to take a look in the bedroom and see how comfortable the bed is. What do you think?"

"I think you're right, Sheriff," she laughed, kissing him as he carried her away.

The next few hours passed quickly for them, and they enjoyed every minute.

It was late afternoon when Chase finally left the house to send the wire to Captain Hale. He was glad to be notifying him that Sherwood was dead, but also that he was tendering his resignation. He hoped his captain would understand, and he hoped he would be able to clean up Sidewinder. It was not going to be easy. The town had run wild for a long time. It might take him a while, but he would do it. This was going to be his home. He wanted to make it safe.

"I need to send this wire," Chase told the telegraph operator as he entered the office.

"Yes, sir." He took the handwritten message from Chase and read it over quickly. He looked up at Chase with new respect. "So you're the one everybody's been talking about. It's a pleasure to meet you, Sheriff. I'm Clark Hodges."

"Nice to meet you, Mr. Hodges."

"Clark, please. And it's good that you came in. This wire came for you this morning, but I wasn't quite sure where to deliver it." He handed Chase a folded sheet of paper.

"Appreciate it." Chase went on to tell the man where the house was in case he ever needed to get hold of him again. "If I'm not there, I'll be at the sheriff's office."

"That's good to know. If I hear anything back on your wire, I'll get word to you right away."

Chase left the office and paused on the sidewalk to read the telegram. He saw his captain's name at the bottom and wondered why he'd contacted him. Something important must have happened. A quick scan of the message proved him right.

Texas Ranger Chase McBride,
    Received word today from the Benton authorities that the Lawson gang broke out of jail and are on the loose again. Be careful and keep watch.
                            Captain Rod Hale

Chase swore silently to himself. He had thought he was done with the Lawson gang. He'd thought they'd go to trial and pay for the cold-blooded murders they'd committed, but they'd escaped justice again. He knew his captain was serious about the "be careful and keep watch." When he'd brought them in, the gang had vowed to get even with him one day. He'd hoped that day would never come, but now he wasn't so sure. He grew tense thinking about it. He not only had to worry about keeping watch for himself. Now he had to protect Faith, too, and that worried him more.

Chase knew what he had to do. He stopped at the gunsmith's on his way back to the house and bought a derringer. He already knew Faith could handle a gun; now he wanted to make sure she was able to defend herself when he wasn't around.

"What took you so long?" Faith asked when he finally returned to the house. "I missed you." She expected him to smile, but his expression remained serious. "What's wrong?"

"There was a telegram waiting for me from Captain Hale," Chase told her. "The Lawson gang escaped from jail."

"Oh, no."

"We're going to have to be careful. I don't know that they'll be coming after me, but they made a lot of threats when I brought them in."

"What kind of threats?" A chill of apprehension skittered up her spine.

He gave her a twisted grin. "The usual ones a Ranger hears when he's done his job."

"Oh, those." Faith went to him and slipped her arms around his waist to hug him. Since he wouldn't tell her, she could just imagine the danger this gang represented. "What are we going to do?"

Chase was struck by her use of "we." He'd never thought that way before now. "We're going to make sure you carry this with you all the time," he told her. He took the derringer out of his pocket and handed it to her.

She took it in a practiced grip and looked the small gun over.

"I know you know how to use a gun. We can practice with this one, if you want, just to be sure."

"It couldn't hurt."

"We'll start tomorrow."

Her gaze caught and held his. "Do you really think they might come after you?"

Chase did not look away. He wanted her to know how serious this threat was. "Yes, and if and when they do, I want to be ready for them."

"We will be."

The next morning Chase pinned on his sheriff's badge and went to the office early. He cleaned up a lot of the paperwork Sheriff Scott had left behind and then made his rounds. He introduced himself to the merchants around town and generally made his presence known. He wanted to be visible to the community. He wanted everyone to know he was there, keeping an eye on things, and that he would take action if action was needed.

The man from the telegraph office sought him out to bring him the answer to his wire. Rod Hale was glad to know that Sherwood was dead, but the Ranger captain was not pleased with Chase's resignation, although he did accept it reluctantly. Hale praised him for all his hard work and wished him luck in Sidewinder. He also informed him that there had been no news concerning the Lawson gang. He promised to let Chase know if they were recaptured or sighted anywhere. Chase had been hoping to hear that they'd been caught already, but they were still on the loose.

Chase settled into his new routine more easily than he'd thought he would. He walked the streets of Sidewinder, keeping a lookout for any sign that something wasn't right in town. There were the usual disturbances, but no indication that the Lawsons were hiding out in the area.

Chase found he was beginning to enjoy his new way of life. Having Faith to come home to every night was heavenly for him.

Chapter Thirty-two

"I've been worrying about you," Clare said in a low, desperate voice when Manuelo presented himself late one night as she sat alone in the parlor. "You've been gone so long. It's been more than two weeks! What happened? Did everything go all right?"

"Everything went as we'd hoped," Manuelo replied without going into detail. The less she knew about what was to happen, the better.

"It did?" Her eyes lit up at the thought. Soon now, very soon —

"Yes, Senora. They were most appreciative and will repay us as we expect, I'm sure."

"Good — good. You've done a fine job, Manuelo. How long do you think — ?"

"There is no way to know, and I did not want to know. It is better this way."

"There have been a few changes while you

were gone," she began. "I hope this doesn't cause any trouble."

"What is it, Senora?"

"Chase and Faith aren't living here on the ranch anymore." She quickly explained to him how the sheriff had been killed. "They've moved into town with Tom's blessing, and Chase has accepted the job as sheriff."

"I can only hope that our 'friends' will be smart enough to figure that out," he answered. He was troubled that things weren't as he'd explained them to the gang, but it couldn't be helped.

"You could always try to contact them," she suggested.

"Never, Senora! There must be no connection between us. I would not endanger you that way. No one can know!"

"All right," Clare replied, irritated, but realizing he was right. She couldn't endanger everything by being too anxious. She had to sit back. She had set a plan in action, and now she must let things take their course. "These next few weeks aren't going to be easy."

"No, Senora, they will not be, but we will manage."

"You're right, Manuelo. We will manage. We always have."

They shared a look of understanding.

★ ★ ★

Faith lay in Chase's arms, reveling in the peace and beauty she had found with him. They were perfect together.

Every now and then she realized they had only been together for a short period of time; but it didn't matter. He was her soul mate. She felt as one with him. She truly believed she'd been blessed when he'd saved her from the renegades.

Memories of that terrible time sent a shiver through her.

"Faith? Are you all right?" Chase felt her tremble and was immediately concerned.

"I was just thinking of how I came to find you that night."

"To this day, I am thankful I was there."

"So am I." She raised herself up and pressed her lips to his. "I don't know if I'll ever completely get over my parents' deaths. It was all so senseless. I will miss them forever."

"I know," he told her.

She believed that he did know, having lost his own mother. He understood what it was like to be alone in the world, and so did she. But they had found each other. They would never be apart again. They were a family.

And that was what brought her to the question she wanted to ask him.

It was important — very important.

"There's something I wanted — no, needed to ask you," she began hesitantly.

She sounded so serious that Chase was concerned all over again.

"What is it?" He waited.

"Chase . . ." She paused, trying to think of the best way to say this to him. "I know how you feel about Tom McBride, and I do understand. But I want to know, how do you feel about becoming a father? About having children?"

Chase went completely still as he stared at her. She was lying on her stomach, so he couldn't see if there had been any change in her figure, any roundness to her waist, but he thought it was much too soon for her to be expecting.

Or was it?

He was silent for a moment, not able to speak as he considered that she might be with child.

A father?

Him?

The possibility worried Chase. What did he know about being a father?

Even as he thought it, though, the question answered itself. He knew exactly what it took to be a good father, because he'd never had one. He knew what a child needed, what a child wanted, and he knew he could do it.

"I think it would be wonderful to have children," Chase answered.

"Then there's something I need to tell you," she said softly. "Especially since we have the extra bedroom — "

"What is it?" He waited.

"I want you to do something for me — and for yourself."

"What?" He didn't know why Faith was taking so long to tell him she was going to have a baby.

"I want us to be a real family, now that we have this home and you have a job where you're not traveling all the time. Let's send for Luke." She had been thinking of the orphaned boy and knew how much Chase cared about him. He'd reminded her of what Chase must have been like as a youth.

"Luke?" He was completely taken aback.

Her expression softened as she talked about the boy. "I want him to come live with us. He loves you, and I know you could make him happy. Padre Rodriguez would let us adopt him, wouldn't he?" she asked.

Chase didn't think he'd ever heard anything so wonderful in all his life. He loved Luke and was in awe of Faith's generosity and loving kindness. They hadn't been married long, and yet she wanted to bring the orphaned boy into their home and try to make his life better.

"I love you, Faith," he told her, drawing her to him for a kiss. It was a sweet kiss, an adoring kiss that spoke of love rather than passion — gentleness rather than desire.

She drew back when the kiss had ended, her eyes aglow with excitement. "It'll be wonderful having him with us, you'll see."

"I have no doubt about that. We'll send word to Padre Rodriguez in the morning."

It was late when Ben Lawson sidled up to the bar in the Golden Nugget Saloon and ordered a whiskey.

Roy, the bartender, served him and stood there waiting for him to pay up. He'd learned long ago not to trust strangers who came into his place of business this late at night.

Ben gave him a dirty look, but finally pushed the cash across the bar to him. "I heard Sidewinder was a wild place, but it's awful damned quiet around here tonight."

"It has its moments," Roy answered. "Hell, the sheriff was gunned down not long ago over by the Roundup."

"Couldn't have happened to a nicer man,"

Ben laughed, always enjoying the death of a lawman.

Roy glanced at him sharply. "You knew Sheriff Scott?"

"No. I just hate lawmen." He took a deep drink.

Roy was growing more and more uneasy talking to this man. "Blackie Sherwood was the one who did the shooting. He was a wanted man."

"He ran with Malone, didn't he?"

"Yep, but Malone's dead, too. McBride got him."

"Chase McBride?" Ben asked quickly, looking up at him.

"No, it was Tanner who got Malone. Chase's brother. You know Chase?"

"I heard of him. He's a Ranger, ain't he?"

"He was."

"Was?" Ben suddenly wondered if they were too late . . . if someone else had already taken care of McBride for them.

"He quit the Rangers. He's our new sheriff. He just took over the job last week."

"Ain't that something. It ain't often you hear of a Ranger quitting his job."

"I guess he wants to settle down and enjoy that pretty little wife of his. Who knows? All I know is that things will probably be a lot quieter around here now that he's taken over."

Ben smiled to himself as he finished off his drink. So McBride had a wife and he was settling down in Sidewinder, was he?

They'd just see about that.

Leaving the bar, Ben rode slowly through town. He located the sheriff's office and was glad to see that it was dark. If McBride had been in there, he would have been tempted to go after him right then and there.

Ben realized he'd been lucky tonight. If good old Sheriff McBride had been out making the rounds while he'd been in the saloon, there might have been trouble. He wanted the element of surprise to be on their side, not McBride's, when it came time for their final showdown — and that final showdown would be coming real soon.

He rode out of town, heading for where Jay and Carlos were camped out. He had a lot to tell them, and they had some plans to make.

"Thanks, Hiram," Faith told the shopkeeper as she gathered up her packages.

"My pleasure, Faith. It's good to see you. How's Chase doing?"

"He's doing fine."

"Good. You enjoying living in Sidewinder?"

"Oh, yes. It's such a pleasure to have our own home." She started for the door.

"You take care and tell Chase hello for me."

"I will."

Faith made her way home, her mood light. It was late afternoon, and Chase would be coming home soon. They had not heard from Padre Rodriguez about Luke yet, but hoped they would any day now. The only thing she regretted about living in town was not having the freedom to wear her pants. Being the wife of the sheriff, she had a standard to uphold. She'd been comporting herself like a lady ever since they'd moved to Sidewinder. It was confining, but she was adjusting.

Worry about the Lawson gang never left her, but it had faded a bit in the days since Chase had first told her about the criminals' escape from jail. He'd insisted she keep the derringer with her, so she did. It was in her pocket even now as she let herself into the house. She just hoped she'd never have to use it. She'd had enough terror in her life. Now she only wanted to spend her days with Chase, loving him and showing him what it was like to be part of a real family.

The thought of her husband made Faith smile. He'd be home soon. She couldn't wait. She felt in dire need of a kiss right now.

Faith made her way to the back of the

house. It was time to start thinking about what to feed her sheriff for dinner. Unless there was trouble in town, Chase would be home in less than an hour. She walked into the kitchen, her thoughts centered on what they were going to do after dinner.

The surprise attack was powerful and overwhelming. The man grabbed her from behind as she entered the kitchen and clamped a stifling hand over her mouth before she could scream.

"Keep it quiet, girlie, or we might just have to shut you up real good," a nasty voice snarled in her ear as two other men quickly came out of hiding to help subdue her.

Her captor was handling her just fine, though. Faith was slammed back against his chest and held in an unrelenting, bruising grip. She wanted to go for her gun. She wanted to free herself, but pinned as she was, she could barely move.

Fury filled her. She was angry with herself for letting her guard down. She should have been ready. She should have been more aware of the possibility of danger, but in her own home, she had thought she was safe. Now she knew different. She glanced toward the back door and saw how they'd broken the window to get inside.

Terror threatened as memories of the raiding party haunted her. She remembered how she had felt being a helpless victim, and she swore that it would never happen again. Faith put the terror from her. They might have her right now, but she had outsmarted the renegades and she could outsmart these fools.

Faith stopped fighting them and started playing the helpless captive. The knowledge that the derringer was in her pocket gave her confidence. She wanted them to think she was just a weak little woman.

"That's better, sweetheart," another man said as he came to stand before her. "Now, there's no reason for you to get all upset with us. We'll treat you real nice if you're nice to us, right, Ben? Carlos?" He smiled at her leeringly as the other two laughed. "We're just here to pay a little visit to your husband."

"Yeah, your 'husband.' How come a pretty little white girl like you lets a breed touch her?" asked the man who was holding her, tightening his grip even more.

Faith couldn't answer with his hand over her mouth. It didn't matter anyway. She knew they weren't making conversation. These had to be the Lawsons, and they had come for only one thing — to kill Chase.

She wasn't going to let that happen. She still had an hour to figure out a way to save him. Somehow, some way, she would alert Chase that they were here.

Chapter Thirty-three

Chase had been uneasy all day. Something was bothering him, but he couldn't quite figure out what. Things had been relatively quiet in town. He'd found Bud Sanders drunk on the street and brought him in to sleep it off, and he had helped Hiram catch a would-be thief. Other than that, it had been quiet. Even so, he had found himself worrying. He'd even taken an extra walk around town just to make sure he hadn't missed anything, but there was nothing unusual about the evening. It was a peaceful night in Sidewinder.

Chase supposed that was what was bothering him. He wasn't used to things being this calm. Probably, he decided, it was just the lull before the storm. With any luck, he might get a few hours to relax before something went wrong.

"Come on, Bud," Chase said as he

opened the cell door to turn him loose. He'd found the older, heavyset man passed out in an alley on his first day on the job and had been keeping an eye on him ever since. Chase didn't know much about him, but he wanted to help him if he could.

"You making me leave, Sheriff?"

"That's right. It's closing time. Why don't you go on home tonight and stay away from the liquor for a while?"

A strange look passed over Bud's face. "Yeah, sure."

Chase had a fondness for the man, although he wasn't sure just why. Maybe because he seemed to be a basically gentle man.

"You fighting with your wife?" Chase asked with a grin.

"My wife's dead," he muttered, starting for the door.

"Well, I tell you what, why don't you come home with me tonight?"

Bud looked at him, puzzled. There was hardly anybody in town who talked to him these days. This was the first gesture of friendship he'd had in a long time. "You sure?"

"Yes. We haven't had any company since we moved in, so you'll be our first guest."

Bud suddenly stood a bit taller and he

managed a smile. "Thanks."

Chase locked up the office and the two men started off toward the house.

"You got her all tied up?" Jay asked Carlos.

"She ain't going anywhere," the other outlaw replied. He'd bound the woman hand and foot, and gagged her, too, before leaving her in the bedroom. "She didn't put up much of a fight."

"Good. I like women who are easy to control."

"I like dead lawmen better."

Ben had been keeping watch out back, but he came into the parlor to speak with them. "It's starting to get dark. He should be here any minute. This was about the time he left the office yesterday."

The three of them had kept watch to see what Chase's schedule was so they could plan this confrontation tonight. They were ready for him.

"So we let him come inside and then take care of him." Jay repeated what they'd planned.

"Yeah. If we start shooting too soon, the whole town will come down on us. We need to keep it as quiet as we can. That will give us the time we need to get out of here."

"What about the woman?"

He shrugged. "I say we just leave her be. She's useless to us and she's so scared, she's not going to cause any trouble. We'll just take care of our business with McBride and then disappear."

"Looks like Sidewinder is going to need another sheriff real soon. That's two in less than a month."

The three of them laughed.

"This is our kind of town."

Faith was close to hysteria, but she controlled it. She could hear the gang's conversation even with the door to the bedroom closed, and she was determined to find a way to save Chase. She'd been working on the rope binding her wrists ever since they'd left her. It was tight, and time was running out. She still had her derringer, though. If she could just slip one hand free, she could get herself untied and climb out the window. Once she was out of the house, she was certain she could catch Chase in time. Again and again, she twisted her hands, her fingers working at the knot, trying to loosen the rope. Her wrists were almost raw as she struggled to free just one hand.

Faith looked around the room, frantic for something sharp to use. She was tempted to knock the lamp over and use a piece of glass, but she was certain the Lawsons would hear the crash and come running. It was then that she saw it on the washstand — Chase's razor. If only she could get to it, she knew she could cut the rope enough to break free.

As quietly as she could, Faith slipped from the bed and hobbled toward the washstand. She turned backward and managed to grab the blade. The razor was sharp and she cut herself several times as she tried to slice the rope, but she didn't care. It was her only hope. Over and over she worked the razor, straining to pull her wrists apart, to force the rope to fray. And finally, at last, it gave way.

Faith bit back a choked sob of relief as she stripped off the ropes at her wrists and quickly untied her ankles. Silently she rushed to the window and opened it.

"There he is."

The outlaw's voice came to her and she knew Chase was getting close. Drawing the derringer, she slipped out the window and dropped the few feet to the ground. She took off at a dead run, desperate to stop Chase before he went inside. She could only thank God that they hadn't decided to shoot him down on sight in the street.

Faith charged around the side of the house with her gun in hand. She raced forward, catching sight of Chase walking with another man near the front walk. She knew she could wait no longer.

"Chase! *No!*" Faith shouted, running toward him.

"What the hell?" Jay shouted in frustration and fury.

She'd gotten away!

Carlos was furious that she'd managed to escape.

At the sound of Faith's cry, Chase had started to draw his gun. He turned toward her as she came at him, and they fell together to the ground, partially hidden by a watering trough. As Chase hit the ground, his gun was jarred from his grip and flew from his hand.

The outlaws started to shoot the instant they realized their plan had failed. They wanted Chase dead, no matter what.

When the shooting started, Bud dove for cover, too. He found himself pinned down a short distance from Chase. He could see Chase's gun close by him, and he scrambled to grab it.

"Sheriff!"

Chase had been watching Bud's heroic actions, amazed by his bravery.

"Here!" Bud tossed the gun over to him.

Chase caught the gun and was ready to

take down the Lawson gang one more time.

"You're all right?" he asked Faith quickly.

"Yes — and I've got my gun, too!"

"Stay down." It was an order as he crouched low and made a dash away from her, shooting as he went.

Faith saw one of the Lawsons in the window trying to get a shot at Chase as he ran across the yard, and she took careful aim. She got off her one and only shot, and was rewarded when the man let out a scream of agony and collapsed.

Shots were flying as Chase made his way closer. He got off a round that took down another of the outlaws. He heard crashes inside and the sound of someone running for the back of the house. Staying low, he circled to the back and got there in time to see Jay run out of the house toward his horse, which was tied up out back.

Chase fired at the outlaw, hitting him. Jay shot back and somehow, though he was bleeding heavily, managed to mount his horse. He tried to take another shot at Chase, but found that he was out of bullets. He threw the empty gun down in disgust and spurred his horse to a run. He thought he was getting away.

But Bud was ready for him.

As the outlaw came racing out from behind the house, Bud dared to jump out, frightening the horse. He grabbed the wounded outlaw and yanked him down from the horse's back just as Chase came running up, gun in hand.

Some townspeople had come running to help, and they were gathering now, looking on in shock.

"Chase! Faith! Are you all right?" Hiram asked. He had his shotgun with him and was breathing heavily from the run from the store.

Chase looked at Faith. He could see the blood on her wrists. "You're sure you're all right?"

"I'll be fine. They tied me up, so I had to use your razor to cut the ropes and get free," she explained quickly as she went to his side.

Chase put an arm around her and drew her near. He looked over at Bud.

"Good work. Thanks."

Bud just nodded as he stood over the fallen outlaw, who was lying in the street, bloody and barely conscious.

"Hiram, come with us," Bud said, "while I help Sheriff McBride get this fellow over to jail."

Hiram was ready and willing to stand guard.

"I'm going to check in the house first,"

Chase said. "I want to make sure all the Lawson gang is accounted for."

"So these were the Lawsons?" Hiram asked nervously. He'd heard of them and knew how deadly and dangerous they had been.

"That's right. I don't think they're going to be hurting anybody else ever again."

Several men from town went in the house with Chase. As they suspected, the two inside were dead.

One man went for the undertaker, while another went after Doc Rogers. Chase and Bud managed to carry the wounded outlaw to the jail. Faith went along, not wanting to be alone in the house until Chase was with her.

Doc Rogers arrived at the office right away. He quickly checked Faith's cuts. Then he went to see to the outlaw. They all waited in the outer office while the doctor worked to save him. It was a long time before he finally came out, his expression grim.

"I'm sorry, Chase. I couldn't stop the bleeding. He's dead. I'll tell the undertaker he's got another one here to take care of."

"Thanks, Doc."

Faith looked at her husband. Unmindful that Hiram and Bud were still there, she went straight into his arms. "I was so worried about you. They were going to kill you as soon as you walked in the door."

"You saved me," he told her, looking down at her. "What happened? How did they get in the house?"

Faith quickly explained how they'd broken in and taken her by surprise. "I'm just thankful I got away from them in time to warn you."

"So am I." He didn't care what anybody thought. He gave her a soft kiss.

Chase looked at Bud. "That was a brave move you made out there, Bud."

"Thanks."

"After today, I'm more convinced than ever that I could use a deputy around here. What do you think, Hiram? Can Sidewinder afford to hire a deputy?"

"I think so," the shopkeeper answered in complete agreement.

"If you want the job, it's yours, Bud. There's only one condition. No drinking — ever. Not on the job or off. I need to know you're sober all the time. If you give me your word, we'll consider it settled." Chase met the other man's gaze.

Bud blinked, surprised by the offer. His life had been empty and without meaning for a long time. Chase's friendship and this job were just what he needed. "I'm ready to go to work, Sheriff."

"You're hired, Deputy Sanders."

Bud smiled.

"I'll expect you on the job first thing in the morning."

"I'll be here."

Hiram looked at Chase. "You're a good lawman, Chase McBride. We're proud to have you here."

"I'm glad to be here," he answered.

And he found he truly meant it.

With Faith by his side, he belonged here. He was happy. Sidewinder was his home.

Epilogue

"So this is your father's ranch?" Luke asked Chase in awe as they rode up to the main house.

"Yes. My brother Tanner and his wife Callie live here on the Circle M, too. You'll get to meet them today," Chase told him.

"Do you think they'll like me?" the boy worried.

"Of course they will," Faith put in quickly, wanting to reassure him. Then she teased, trying to lighten his fears, "But are you going to like them?"

Luke nodded, his eyes aglow. "I've never had an uncle or aunt or grandma or grandpa before."

"You do now," Chase assured him.

The boy smiled up at him, his excitement obvious. "Are you sure they'll all be here?"

"I'm sure. I sent word that we had a surprise for them."

"Me?"

"You." Chase returned his smile, his heart touched by Luke's happiness.

Luke had arrived in Sidewinder two days before and was settling in nicely. Chase hadn't brought him out to the Circle M before now because he wanted Luke to get used to living with him and Faith first. He'd been delighted at how quickly Luke had adapted. The memory of the hug Luke had given him when he'd gotten off the stage was burned into his heart and would remain there forever.

Chase cast a sidelong glance at Faith as she rode beside him. He'd have to remember to tell her later just how much he loved her. Her idea of adopting Luke was just one of the reasons why. He planned to spend the rest of his life proving to both of them just what a wonderful husband and father he could be.

Chase turned his gaze back up to the ranch house. His mood darkened a little at the thought of seeing Tom again. He still had trouble thinking of him as "Pa." He intended to see to it that Luke would never have that problem with him.

As they reined in before the house, Callie came hurrying outside to greet them, with Tanner close behind her. Callie and Tanner looked from Luke to Chase and Faith with open curiosity.

"We're glad you're here. I've brought someone along we'd like you to meet," Chase said as they dismounted and tied up their horses. He'd borrowed a horse from the stable in town for Luke to make the ride out to the ranch. He planned to take his other mount back with them so the boy would have his very own horse.

Luke hung back a little, letting Chase and Faith go up the steps first. Chase turned to put an arm around his shoulders and draw him along with them.

"Luke, this is my brother Tanner and his wife Callie. Tanner, Callie, this is Luke. Our son."

"Your son?" they both repeated, surprised.

"We didn't you know you had a child!" Callie declared.

"We just adopted him. Luke's been living with Padre Rodriguez at the mission where Chase grew up. He came to join us a few days ago," Faith explained.

"It's wonderful to meet you, Luke!" Tanner held his hand out to the boy, and Luke shyly took it. "Just call me Uncle Tanner."

"Yes, sir."

"And I'm Aunt Callie."

"Come on in," Tanner said, smiling in warm invitation as they all started inside.

When they made their way into the parlor, Clare emerged from the back of the house.

"Who do we have here?" Clare asked, eyeing the dark-haired boy with disdain. She didn't like children.

Chase spoke up. "Luke, I'd like you to meet your grandmother. This is Grandma Clare. Clare, this is our son, Luke."

"What?" Complete and utter shock flashed in Clare's eyes at the announcement. She hadn't thought she could have any more surprises as ugly as discovering that Chase existed, but this — this was outrageous. She was no one's grandmother! She wasn't even anyone's mother! Anger took over.

"Luke is our son, Clare," Faith repeated. "Your grandson."

Clare wanted to rage and scream at them, but drawing deeply on her acting ability, she gave the boy a tight, cold smile. "How nice, but you could have told me sooner. I didn't even know you had a son."

"We've adopted Luke. He just joined us here in Sidewinder."

"Oh," was all she could respond. "I think you should take him upstairs to meet his grandfather." She wanted to get this visit over with and get them away from her as quickly as possible. *A grandmother!*

"Let's do that right now," Chase said, leading the way upstairs. "Come on, son."

Luke and Faith followed him while Tanner and Callie seated themselves in the parlor. Clare went upstairs, too, wanting to see Tom's reaction to the news.

Chase knocked once at Tom's bedroom door. At Tom's answering call to enter, he opened the door and they went in.

Tom looked no better than the last time Chase had seen him, but his eyes were sharp, missing nothing as they entered the room.

"Who's he?" Tom demanded when he saw the boy.

"This is my son Luke," Chase told him proudly. "We wanted him to meet his grandpa."

Tom glanced at Chase sharply at the news and frowned.

"Come here, boy," he ordered gruffly.

Luke looked up at Chase, and at Chase's nod, he approached the bedside. He was a little frightened of the old man lying there.

"Luke," Tom said thoughtfully as his gaze went over him. Even though the boy's coloring was dark, Tom noticed immediately that his eyes weren't blue. Tom looked away from the boy up to Chase. "He doesn't look a damned thing like you," he said harshly. "Are you sure he's your son? He doesn't even have the McBride blue eyes. He could be a bastard."

Luke was startled by the man's cruel words, and he took an instinctive step back toward Chase. Chase immediately put a supportive hand on Luke's shoulder.

"Luke's my son," he declared. "There's no doubt about it."

"So I'm your grandpa, am I?" Tom said, slowly considering the thought as he glanced back at Luke. "Well, if you're a McBride, act like it. Come here." It was an order.

Luke responded to the challenge. He straightened his shoulders a bit as he stepped away from Chase's protection and went to the bedside. "Yes, sir."

Tom gave him a curt nod. "You're learning. That means you're smart, and that's good." His tone wasn't warm, but those words from Tom were high praise. "Now, get your ma and pa and get the hell out of here. I need some rest." He dismissed them all.

Only Clare lingered behind when Faith, Chase and Luke had gone.

"Can you believe that? Trying to pass him off as your grandchild — "

"*Our* grandchild," Tom corrected her.

She stiffened at his reminder. "But he's not even your flesh and blood!"

"What are you talking about, woman?" he demanded.

"The boy's adopted!" she said scathingly.

Tom shrugged. "If Chase claims him, that's enough for me."

"So you're going to claim the child, too?"

"What's wrong, Clare? Don't you like being a grandma?" He pinned her with a knowing look. "You may be Luke's grandma, but you're the youngest-looking grandma I've ever seen. And you're still my woman. Come here —"

She gritted her teeth, wondering if her life could get any more miserable. As she moved a step closer to his side, Tom's hand snaked out and snared her wrist, pulling her down to him. She was amazed at how strong he was when he looked so weak and pale.

Tom kissed Clare and reached up to fondle her. He might be sick, but he wasn't dead — yet.

"Are you going to stay for a while?" Tanner asked.

"No, we're heading back to town. I've hired a deputy, but I can't afford to be away too long," Chase told him.

"Did Pa tell you the news?" Tanner asked

as they walked outside to the horses.

"What news?" Chase stopped to face him.

"Bill Hanes rode out yesterday. Word came — Lauren's on her way home."

"Who's Lauren?" Luke asked.

"Lauren's our sister," Tanner answered for them both. "She'll be here real soon."

"You'll let me know?" Chase asked.

"As soon as she gets here," Tanner promised. Then he looked down at Luke. "You be good for your ma and pa."

"I will, Uncle Tanner," Luke promised.

They finished saying their good-byes and headed for home.

Chase lay awake long into the night. He needed sleep, but sleep would not come. He carefully left the bed, not wanting to disturb Faith, who was slumbering beside him. He wandered silently through the house.

All was quiet. All was peaceful.

Chase opened Luke's bedroom door to look in on him and make sure he was safe. It relieved him to know the boy was sound asleep. He'd been proud of the way Luke had conducted himself out at the Circle M today. They'd warned him ahead of time about his grandpa being sick, and Luke had handled himself well. Chase was still surprised by the way Tom had treated the boy.

Chase closed the door and made his way back to his own bedroom. Pausing in the doorway, he watched Faith as she slept. A sense of awe filled him as he realized how much his life had changed since that first night when Faith swept into his life like a whirlwind. In the last few months he'd gone from being a loner to being a family man. He had a beautiful wife, a wonderful son and his own home. Looking back, Chase understood now how empty his bachelor days had been, and he felt very blessed.

"Chase — " Faith said his name in a sleepy voice as she stirred and awoke, realizing he wasn't beside her.

"I'm here."

He returned to the bed, and she opened her arms to him, wanting him near.

Chase held her to his heart as his lips sought hers.

"I love you, Faith."

"How much?" she asked, all thoughts of sleep suddenly gone.

And Chase spent the rest of the night showing her just how much.